Readers everywhere are in lov

by

The Secret Li

Jones
Jones, Lisa Renee
Forsaken

$15.00
ocn894747047
First Gallery B   10/08/2015

"Intoxicating, intense,

—RT Book

"Suspenseful and packed with questions."   —*Fiction Vixen*

"The slaps to the face, the sucker punches, and the too-good-to-be-true moments will have you audibly gasping and wondering if you're going to get your HEA and still be in one piece."   —*The Book Vamps*

"Suspense, suspense, suspense . . . all over the place and within every page."   —*Cristina Loves Writing*

"It has everything anyone could want. Mystery, intrigue, suspense, enough heat to melt an iceberg, and characters with depth. Do yourself a favor and start this one now!"

—*The Book Hookers*

"A great story that's wrought with tension and fear of kidnapping and murder."   —*Diary of an Eager Reader*

"An amazing storyline with twists and turns; a roller coaster of highs and lows; and at no point could you sit back and relax. Lisa Renee Jones has stepped forward and claimed her place in the new adult category, and *Infinite Possibilities* will leave you breathless and wondering where it will all end."

—*The Reading Café*

"Lisa Renee Jones will have you gripping the edge of your seat and biting your nails, and will leave you with a book hangover." —*Lisa's Book Reviews*

Praise for the "passionate, all-consuming" (*PopSugar*)

Inside Out Series

"If you haven't started this series yet, run to grab the first book and dive in! This easy-reading series is compelling—sucking the reader into a dark and seductively dangerous world of art, BDSM, and murder." —*Fresh Fiction*

"Lots of dark, suspenseful twists."

—*USA Today* (A Must-Read Romance)

"Great characters, angsty and real, that draw me in to their worlds, and storylines that hook me every single time."

—*Smut Book Junkie Book Reviews*

"Darkly intense and deeply erotic. . . ." —*RT Book Reviews*

"Intimately erotic . . . Jones did not hold back on the steam factor." —*Under the Covers Book Blog*

"A series that will completely captivate you—heart, mind, and soul." —*Romancing the Book*

"Powerfully written. . . . A tumultuous journey." —*Guilty Pleasures Book Reviews*

"A crazy, emotional roller-coaster ride. . . ." —*Fiction Vixen*

"Brilliantly beautiful in its complexity. . . . This book had my heart racing." —*Scandalicious Book Reviews*

"Breathtaking in its suspense and intrigue." —*Heroes and Heartbreakers*

"Leaves you begging for more!" —*Tough Critic Book Reviews*

"Dark and edgy erotica that hit all my buttons just right." —*Romantic Book Affairs*

"If you haven't read Lisa Renee Jones's Inside Out series then you are seriously missing out on something fierce! It's a great blend of sexy, suspense, and kink." —*Talk Supe*

"These stories just keep getting better and better. . . . Every single one of them leaves you wanting more!" —*Ramblings From This Chick*

ALSO BY LISA RENEE JONES

Forsaken

Lisa Renee Jones

G

Gallery Books

New York London Toronto Sydney New Delhi

G

Gallery Books
An Imprint of Simon & Schuster, Inc.
1230 Avenue of the Americas
New York, NY 10020

This book is a work of fiction. Any references to historical events, real people, or real places are used fictitiously. Other names, characters, places, and events are products of the author's imagination, and any resemblance to actual events or places or persons, living or dead, is entirely coincidental.

Copyright © 2015 by Julie Patra Publishing, Inc.

All rights reserved, including the right to reproduce this book or portions thereof in any form whatsoever. For information address Gallery Books Subsidiary Rights Department, 1230 Avenue of the Americas, New York, NY 10020.

First Gallery Books trade paperback edition August 2015

GALLERY BOOKS and colophon are registered trademarks of Simon & Schuster, Inc.

For information about special discounts for bulk purchases, please contact Simon & Schuster Special Sales at 1-866-506-1949 or business@simonandschuster.com.

The Simon & Schuster Speakers Bureau can bring authors to your live event. For more information or to book an event, contact the Simon & Schuster Speakers Bureau at 1-866-248-3049 or visit our website at www.simonspeakers.com.

Designed by Davina Mock-Maniscalco

Manufactured in the United States of America

10 9 8 7 6 5 4 3 2 1

Library of Congress Cataloging-in-Publication Data

Jones, Lisa Renee.
Forsaken / Lisa Renee Jones.—First Gallery Books trade paperback edition.
    pages cm. (The secret life of Amy Bensen ; 3)
  I. Title.
PS3610.O627F67   2015
813'.6—dc23
                                              2015010299

ISBN 978-1-4767-9379-5
ISBN 978-1-4767-9380-1 (ebook)

Six years ago . . .

HOT. STICKY. PISSED OFF. That's how I feel as I skid my motorcycle to a halt on a country road just outside of New Braunfels, Texas, a limo idling to my right, the sun starting to set on my left. Removing my helmet and brushing away wisps of the long blond hair that clings to my face, I dismount. After setting my helmet on the seat, my hands settle on the waistline of my faded Levi's and T-shirt as I watch the limo doors open. Two beefy dudes in suits exit the front doors. One of them opens the back door of the vehicle, and my jaw clenches as Rollin Scott, the thirty-two-year-old son of oil mogul Sheridan Scott, steps out of the car. He straightens his posture, his suit expensive, his black hair neatly styled, as always—unless my mother's fingers had been running through it. The idea that she slept with the bastard, trying to get him to forgive a debt owed by my father is still hard to fathom. She had no idea what we were into—what that debt truly entailed, how big it was, or what I agreed to do to make it go away.

The dickhead gives me an arrogant smirk, and I console myself by visualizing a short, pleasant fantasy in which I slam his fucking head against the window of the limo. Over and over. And over. Near euphoria washes over me as I promise myself I'm going to kill him before this all ends.

"I hope that smile means you have good news for me," he comments as he and his Doublemint duo of security guards stop in front of me, crowding me. He has no idea how brave he is to step into my personal space. He's close enough for me to wrap my fingers around his throat and smell the same sickening scent of his expensive cologne I've had the displeasure of smelling on my mother on more than one occasion.

"Was I smiling?" I ask. "I guess I'm just glad to see you. Where's your father?"

"I told him that you and I needed to have a chat. Have you found the cylinder?"

"Not yet," I lie, having done more than found what he

wanted. I now know what it is, and why Sheridan can never have it.

"Really? Because I heard from a reliable source that you do indeed have it. In fact, I understand that you've had it for weeks, while we've been patiently waiting for months for you to locate it and turn it over."

My blood runs cold at his announcement, which, if true, can mean only one thing. Someone inside the elite group of treasure hunters I work with has betrayed me, but I don't miss a beat. "A source is not reliable just because you pay them—not unless they have proof. And since I don't have it, looks like you got taken for a payday."

"You told us yourself you had a solid lead. Some man who was supposed to have what we're after."

"He was a solid lead, until someone killed him. He died over some fucking cylinder the size of a pencil eraser. I won't. I'm out."

I expect cursing. I expect anger. I don't get it, and it feels off. Really damn off. He stares at me, seconds ticking by. "If you're playing games with us for more money—"

"This isn't a negotiation. I'm *out*."

He glares at me, time stretching painfully. "I have to call the consortium members for more money."

"Call Donald fucking Duck and quack for all I care. I told you, it's not about money."

"And yet your father owes us money."

"Not anymore." I walk to the back of the bike, untie a duffel bag filled with half of my savings, and toss it onto the ground, wishing I'd just paid these bastards off in the first place.

Rollin motions and his guard grabs the bag, handing it to him. "Ten million?"

"That's right. Treasure hunting has been good to me. So, like I said, I'm out. My family is out. And stay the fuck away from my mother or I'll kill you."

Contempt slides over his face. "We've told you, we don't want your money. You aren't walking away that easily. The word on the street is that you have the cylinder. Let me be very clear, every member of our eleven-person consortium would kill for what you have, as would many others. In other words, it's in your best interest, and your family's, for it to be known that we have it."

My blood turns to ice, but I stick to the only plan I have that might work. *Denial.* "Fuck you. I don't have it. All the threats in the world aren't going to change that."

"Five hundred million."

And there it is: the offer that confirms that a dying man with a knife in his chest had been telling the truth when he begged for my help. That tiny cylinder somehow generates enough clean energy to power the world and destroy the oil industry, and Sheridan Scott with it.

"I guess that number rendered you speechless?" he presses.

"I don't know what language you need me to speak. I don't have it." I repeat it in Spanish, French, and German. "*No lo tengo. Je ne l'ai pas. Ich habe es nicht.* Should I continue?"

Apparently not entertained by my smartass reply, Rollin ignores it altogether and demands, "Forty-eight hours. Right here in this spot. Have it here, or pay the price." He turns and walks toward the limo, getting in without another word or even a look.

I stand there staring at him, feeling like Satan just crawled out of the ground and fucked me over. If that old man was telling the truth, handing over that cylinder is like handing Sheridan a key to ruling the world. He could single-handedly destroy industries, and create a new one to make the world dependent upon him. Or he could destroy a clean energy source that might save the world one day.

A bastard like him cannot have that kind of power. But with all the money trails connected to oil and coal, many of them running through our own government, can anyone? I put on my helmet and climb onto the bike. I knew a day might come when I'd have to decide to put protecting the cylinder above money, and I'd come up with a plan. There has to be someone in my circle of resources who can create a fake prototype to hand over to Rollin and at least buy some time. And then I'll take care of whoever betrayed me inside The Underground, and they will pay for their sins. I never thought I was a man who'd look to spill blood, but the day I met Sheridan, everything changed. *I* changed, and there's no turning back.

FOUR HOURS LATER, I'm on the other side of Austin, Texas, back at my family home in Jasmine Heights for the night. Sitting at the small, square kitchen table, I sip the cup of coffee I settled for after my mother protested the beer I'd favored. Seems twenty-four is still a baby to her. I scrub my day-old stubble, trying to remember back to five years ago, to a time before The Underground, when I was that person she wants me to be now. Lara appears in the doorway looking younger than her eighteen years, her long blond hair touching her shoulders, her blue eyes as wide and innocent as ever. I give the familiar brown T-shirt she's paired with sweatpants a once-over and laugh as she approaches. "Aww, little sis, you still wearing my old shirt?"

"It was lucky when we were in Egypt," she says, slipping into the seat across from me. "I wore it when we hit that tomb, remember?"

"How could I forget? You screamed like you were being attacked."

"It was exciting," she says through a laugh as she reaches for my coffee, takes a sip, and crinkles her cute little nose. "Don't you have hair on your chest yet? That's strong enough to burn a hole in my belly."

"Then don't drink it. We don't want *you* getting hair on *your* chest."

She laughs, but quickly turns somber. "I'm glad you came home for my graduation."

"You know I wouldn't miss it."

"Dad's going to Mexico right after it's over."

"I know," I confirm, having secretly arranged the offer for my father to take over a dig site that will keep him away from here or Egypt, and away from Sheridan in the process.

"Are you leaving again, too?"

"Actually, I talked to Dad about all of us going together."

Her big blue eyes go wide. "What? Are you serious? You mean me, you, Mom and Dad?"

"That's right."

"What happened to you pushing me to stay in school?"

"Once you start school, you're committed for four years, and Dad's not getting any younger."

"Chad! You didn't tell him he was getting old, did you?"

"He knows he's old, sis. Believe me. He knows."

"So this is real? He agreed?"

"He's leaning toward yes."

She squees and stands up and rushes me, giving me a hug that I return a bit too tightly, but regrets and fears are eating me alive. I need my family close and safe. "Chad," she whispers, leaning back to look at me. "That man who visits Mom. He was here last week right before Daddy got back from his last trip."

"Don't talk about this," I warn her, wanting to beat his ass all the more for letting my sister see him with my mother. "I told you that."

"But Dad knows. Or I think he knows. I heard them fighting."

"Leave it alone. Understand?"

"How? How can I?"

"Because I damn well said you can."

She reddens with anger, but my cell phone rings on the table before she can reply. I glance down to find a call I've been waiting on is coming in. "I need to take this," I say. "And you need to stay out of things I tell you to stay out of."

"You're such an ass sometimes."

"An ass who loves you. Go to bed."

"I love you, too, asshole," she says, rushing out of the kitchen.

Scrubbing my jaw, I answer the call. "Jared, man, I need you to put your hacking skills to use."

"I told you. I did one job for The Underground, and now I'm my own man."

"Right. You 'went legit.' We both know that's a farce."

"I work for myself. The end. You have hackers working for The Underground."

"No one is as good as you. I need you, not them."

"Look, Chad, don't get me wrong. That one job I did made me enough money to pay for my sister's chemo. Without it I might have lost her, and I will never forget what you did for me. But the bottom line here is that working alone is safer. No one can run their mouth and screw you."

"I couldn't agree more."

He snorts. "You started a chapter for those people."

"And I'm walking away. I'm in something deep, man. Really deep. I've started taking steps to protect my family, but I'm not sure it's enough."

There's a beat of silence. "Give me the details."

"Sheridan Scott has a consortium of eleven powerful people he does business with. I've been gathering dirt on them all."

"Sheridan Scott as in the oil man? *That* Sheridan Scott?"

"That's him."

He whistles. "Just what the hell are you into?"

"I can't tell you without putting you in danger."

"But you want me to help you."

"That's right."

"Blind faith. What the hell, I'm in. How fast do you need me?"

"Yesterday."

"Tell me what to do."

"Not on the phone."

"You know where to find me. Don't go getting yourself killed before you get to me."

"I'm not planning on it."

We end the call and I push myself to my feet, walking to the back of the house, not bothering with the light as I step onto the porch and lean against the wall, using darkness as a cloak. *Think, Chad. Think your way out of this. You found the cylinder when no one else could. You can find a way out of this.* I push myself off the wall to pace for a minute and a flicker of something to my left catches my eye—a flashlight, maybe? Every nerve in my body screams in warning, but I tell myself I'm being ridiculous. Sheridan wants the cylinder. He won't kill me. My next thought is hurl-worthy, the obvious danger I should have considered: He could try to make me talk through my family.

The idea has me inching down the steps and squatting,

pulling the leg of my jeans up and removing the Glock holstered at my ankle that my father had insisted Lara and I learn to shoot back in Egypt. Intending to seek the shelter of the wall, I inch a step forward, but freeze when I hear a sort of crackle and snap. A second later the house explodes, and I am thrown into the air. Time seems to stand still—no sound, no reality—until I hit the ground with a hard thump that rattles me to the bone, pain radiating through my body.

For a moment I'm dazed, unsure of what has happened, but then I lift my head to take in the sight of the house, burning at every corner. Emotions erupt inside me. "No! No!" Terror, pain, and grief overtake me and I am on my feet running, numb to my own injuries but bleeding fear. This isn't happening. It can't happen. I will not lose my family. I will not. I can't. I won't! I charge up the stairs and enter the burning house.

ONE

Present day . . .

DRIP. DRIP. DRIP.

"Fuck! Fuck. Fuck. Fuck."

I lift my aching head that feels like it weighs a hundred pounds on my stiff neck and stare at the concrete walls of what has become my cage. Where is that fucking noise coming from?

Drip. Drip.

Feeling like I'm losing my mind, I tug at my hands, which are tied behind my back, the rope biting into my flesh. The chair at my back biting into my shoulders. "Fuuuuuuuck!"

My head drops between my shoulders and I stare at the ground.

Drip. Drip.

Red dots clutter my gaze, and I focus on the red puddle beneath me. Blood. Oh, yeah. I'm bleeding. That's why the strand of my hair hanging in my eyes is red instead of blond.

The door opens with a loud grinding of metal and I squeeze my eyes shut, ready to die, hoping it's time. If Jared did what he was supposed to do and saved Amy, it will be. She deserves to live. I do not. But I will not go out a coward. Defiantly, I lift my head, and I think I blink. My eyelids are too swollen to be sure. Considering there's a gorgeous brunette in a slim-cut black skirt that hugs her curves in all the right places standing in front of me, maybe I'm dead already. Her creamy ivory skin and pale blue eyes are pretty angelic, so, yeah, I think I'm dead. Fuck, though—I still hurt all over, so I must have gotten what I deserve. I'm in hell, and the devil is a hot bitch playing games with me. But I could think of worse nightmares. Like my life.

Drip. Drip.

Or not. The dead don't bleed, and since I sure the fuck am, I guess that means she's not here to be my new personal assistant in hell. My happy bubble bursts, and I give my new bitch a smirk, eyeing her with a nice long inspection meant to make her feel uncomfortable, and to send me to my hell with at least a little pleasure.

"Sweetheart, you're going to need a whole lot more than stilettos and great legs to get me to talk, though I'm pretty sure I have some moans left in me. I'll let you have a few, too."

She pulls a knife out from behind her back. "Ah," I murmur. "You like it kinky, do ya? I guess this is where things get interesting."

"Yes, Chad," she murmurs, her voice as sexy as her legs. "It is." And then she and her knife move just where I want them—nice and close, the steel pressed to my jawline, my five-day stubble providing a layer of protection I doubt she's counting on. Her eyes meet mine, and they are cold, blue, and unreadable, the kind of eyes that make a man want to fuck a woman until she begs for more, just to prove he can do it. I wait for the blade to cut me. I hope for it, but it doesn't come.

"Get naked, sweetheart," I order roughly, intending to rattle her, to get under her skin, and to ensure I win this hand of poker, not her. "At least then you'll have my attention. It'll give whoever's watching through that camera in the corner the thrill of a lifetime, too."

Apparently unintimidated, she settles her hands on my shoulders, the blade still in one of them, and I'm just about to make a smartassed comment about her breasts when she brings her knee between mine, giving my groin a calculated nudge. "Now do I have your attention?" she hisses.

"Good try," I reply glibly, pretending I didn't just have an *oh shit* moment, "but I prefer your hand, or other body parts. I'm certain you would mine as well."

A frustrated purring sounds in her throat, sexy enough to get me hard if she hadn't just caused my balls to retract damn near to my nipples. "This isn't a game," she bites out, thankfully dropping her knee rather than planting it—but her fingers, and the handle of the knife, remain on my shoulders. "Sheridan might need you alive to get what he wants," she continues, "but you underestimate him if you think he won't start chopping off body parts."

At the mention of my bastard captor, all fun and games are over. My jaw clamps down, shoulders hunching beneath her touch. "Your boss knows the rules of my organization. If I show up anywhere near the people who can get him what he wants, and I'm less than a hundred percent, I'll be considered compromised. It'll be snatched out of my reach faster than I could make you scream my name, and that's fast, baby."

"There are ways to hurt you that won't be seen. You know it. He knows it. He'll make you talk." She leans forward and presses her cheek to mine. A sweet, floral scent teases my nostrils as her long brown hair slips over my face and she whispers, "I can't let you tell him where it is."

She shoves herself off me, standing with the blade at her side, blood, *my blood*, staining her pale cheek, tension blasting off her and punching me in the chest. She looks determined, pissed off even, and for survival's sake, I have to assume she means to act on her proclamation that she must ensure that I not talk. Which leaves me with only one question: What will she do to keep my mouth shut? The thought has me suddenly giving new respect to the knife in her hand.

"He can't make me talk," I promise her. "He's tried."

"You're good," she counters, using my words against me. "But I promise you, you're not *that* good." She doesn't wait for a response, walking around me, disappearing out of sight for a moment before one of her hands comes back down on my shoulder. I don't fight. It's a worthless effort, and I don't believe in wasting energy. Instead, I steel myself for the blade that's sure to pierce my flesh at any moment, and I'm calm—at peace, even. I've done a lot of shit in my life. Somehow, this feels profoundly like the right way to go, dying to protect a secret I should never have unearthed in the first place. A secret that could either destroy, or save, the world. I don't want to be the one who makes that decision.

No. Not me.

I'm fine with dying to protect this secret, I think, but as soon as I have that thought, an image of Amy's face fills the empty space of my mind, and the innocence in her eyes shreds me. I left Jared a message asking him to protect her. I don't know for sure that he got to her in time, and even if she is okay, who knows for how long? I fucked up, and now Sheridan knows she's alive. He'll go after her. He'll think she has the secret only I hold. And others will go after her, too. I'm the only one she has to protect her, even if she doesn't know I'm alive.

My fight returning, I try to look over my shoulder. "Don't be a coward, woman. Face me if you mean to use that knife." The instant I make the demand, a loud blast shakes the ceiling above us, confirming what I suspected: I'm in some sort of basement. Another flash of a second and smoke starts forming by my feet, fast filling the room.

The woman shakes my shoulders, shouting, "What did you do? What did you do?" when we both know a smoke grenade just went off. Since my hands are tied, she's responsible. But I give her credit, and an A for acting skills. She appears in front of me and grabs chunks of my longish blond hair in her hands, jerking my head to the side. "What did you do?"

My eyes narrow on hers. "Payback is Rosemary's baby, bitch," I promise, a moment before the smoke consumes her and me.

She releases my hair, her hands coming down on my knees, and it's clear she's squatting in front of me. "What the—?" I begin, swallowing my words as she cuts free one of my legs and then the other.

She leans into me, pushing herself to her feet, and as much as my instinct tells me to stand up with her, I'm not doing anything to spook her before she cuts my arms free. Her hand goes to my shoulder, as if she's afraid of losing me in the smoke, and freedom is so close I can taste it; adrenaline is pouring through me like liquid fire. She grabs my forearm, and every muscle in my body is tense as I wait for my bindings to be cut. Instead, there's a new plastic cuff attached to my wrist that I instinctively know is about to be connected to her arm as well.

"Don't even think about it," I growl, using all of my energy to jerk the chair which barely moves. The original binding between my arms goes slack and I'm on my feet in an instant, the weight of another arm connected to mine evident. I can't see my new ball and chain, but I damn sure can grab her. Yanking her hard against me and cursing, I reach for the knife, only to hear the clanging of steel on the concrete somewhere in the smoke cloud.

"Bitch," I murmur. I've lost the only means I had to cut us free. I cup the back of her head, pulling her ear to my lips. "You just made a mistake you're going to regret."

Her fingers curl around my shirt. "I couldn't let you leave me," she hisses fiercely. "He'll kill me if you leave me."

"Don't be so sure *I* won't kill you," I counter, releasing her and dragging her to the door, which I don't hesitate to pull open. Sheridan doesn't want me dead. My guess is he wants me to escape with this woman, whom he intends to have seduce me into taking him to his treasure. Obviously he, too, thinks I'm stupid.

I stop inside the door frame, inching around it just enough to see what my blindfold hadn't allowed me to see upon my arrival. We're inside some sort of unfinished office space on what appears to be a windowless basement level. "This way," the woman says, moving in front of me and taking a step.

Given that my feet are firmly planted, she is promptly jerked back to me, at which point I demand, "What happened to pretending I was forcing you to help me?"

She swipes the long brown strands of hair from her eyes. "There's no camera past the doorway, and whatever you think I'm up to, I'm not. I'm just trying to stay alive."

"And keep me from talking," I add flatly, my belief in her story right up there with my belief in Santa Claus. "How many men up top?"

"Ten in the warehouse and another ten in the lab, but the explosion should have blocked the door between them and us. I can't be sure. I winged it."

I arch a brow. "Winged it? You did this on your own?"

"Yes. And I didn't make any plans. I didn't have time when I found out what they were planning." She doesn't wait for me to ask the question I wasn't going to be baited into asking anyway, continuing with, "We should be able to take the emergency stairs and exit into the back alley, but we have to hurry. They'll call for help that will enter the same way we're exiting."

"What city are we in?"

Ignoring my questions, she insists, "We have to go," while looking exceedingly uncomfortable.

"What city are we in?" I demand again, no give in my voice.

"Austin. This is where—"

"Sheridan runs his oil empire. I know." Close to home, but a long way from Denver, where I was captured. "What part of Austin?"

"Downtown," she replies as we cross the unfinished concrete floor. "When we go out into the hallway, we'll take the stairs and then it's a left to the exit. Right is the door that should be blocked. That's the main warehouse."

"What's outside the exit?"

"An alleyway, but we're right off Seventh Street. And since that exit is the only way in or out now, I'm really scared that there will be trouble waiting for us. Someone has to have called for help by now."

"I'm good at handling trouble—something you'd do well to remember, since I consider you to fit that description." I stop at the exit door and turn to look her in the eyes. "I can think of twenty different ways the next five minutes can go, and in nineteen of them, you die. In eighteen, I'm the one who kills you."

"Then you'd have to drag my body with you."

"Good exercise, sweetheart. As Clint says, 'Make my day.'"

She doesn't see the humor in my Eastwood impression, and while her glare suggests anger there's a flicker of fear deep in those blue eyes. The kind of fear I have nightmares about seeing in Lara's eyes. Maybe Sheridan isn't so stupid after all, considering it was a woman's betrayal that got me here in the first place. And this one is smart. "Fool me once," I murmur, "and I'm a fool. I'll kick you in the teeth before you fool me again."

"I'm not trying to fool you—"

"Save it. I don't want to hear it." Frustrated, ready to get this woman disconnected from my arm sooner rather than later, I yank open the door at the top of the stairs, inching forward to study the hallway. Sure enough, smoke pours from a steel door to the right. But it's contained, which tells me either Sheridan's men hit it with an extinguisher before it could draw attention, or . . . this is all a setup.

Irritated all over again, I drag my ball and chain with me, heading for the exit, already planning how to get rid of her in the next fifteen minutes. We're at the door and in the empty alleyway in a matter of seconds. It's dead out here, like we're in a shopping mall parking lot after closing at Christmastime and we're the only ones who have nowhere to be.

"My car is parked on the street down there," my former captor says, pointing to the right. I go left. "My car," she insists, stumbling in her high heels as she tries to keep up.

"Will be tracked."

"No. I told you. I'm not with Sheridan."

"Do you work for him?"

"Yes."

I don't look at her. "And you know about what he's looking for?"

"Yes, but—"

"Then your car's being tracked," I say as we round a corner and I scan the street, finding it nighttime-empty, all the businesses closed, the streets deserted.

"We'll be spotted here." She lifts our wrists. "Look at us."

"Take off your shoes," I order.

"What? I need—"

"I don't have time to argue with you." My fingers span her tiny waist as I lift her, peel off her high heels with my foot, and then bend down to scoop them up. "We need to get to the other side of the highway quickly," I say, handing them to her.

"That's East Austin. It's dangerous, and—"

I start moving, giving her no choice but to keep up, while I battle limited vision in my left eye from the swelling—even more reason that we can't be across the I-35 fast enough for me. I can handle a rough neighborhood to escape Sheridan.

We reach the highway and I make sure we dart through traffic against the light, putting distance and the major thoroughfare between us and Sheridan's warehouse, and quickly trek up a hill toward the neighborhood beyond it.

"This is gang turf," she warns again. "It's dangerous. And can you even see? Your eye—"

"I'm fucking dangerous," I growl at her, "and your boss is equivalent to the kingpin of these so-called gangs."

"He's not my boss. Or, he is. It's complicated. But I'm serious about this neighborhood. We shouldn't just walk around in this area of town even if it were daylight."

"You're right. It's not safe, but it's the right place to get lost with a woman cuffed to your arm and not have the cops called on you." I cut her a hard look. "So I suggest you keep quiet, so we won't draw attention we don't want." We top the hill and I spot the piñata shop that's been around since before I was old enough to come to Austin to party, and is the marker for gang town. Everything beyond it is a bitch-fight waiting to happen. As we approach the shop, a forty-something Mexican man is closing up the gated area that displays all kinds of colorful hanging objects.

He pauses there, cautiously tracking our approach, and when we stop on the opposite side of the gate his intelligent eyes meet mine, no doubt taking in my beaten face, and then shift to the woman next to me, who is still sporting my blood all over her cheek. He glances at the cuffs, then at me again, and no doubt back to my blood on her face. He gives a snort and returns his attention to me.

"*Qué chingados paso?*" he demands, in what I translate to mean "What the *fuck* happened?"

Already having formulated an idea in my head, I answer in Spanish, giving him my quick and outrageous explanation and plea for help. He listens intently, his eyes going wide with sympathy before he murmurs an introduction and a fast invite inside, opening the gate as he does. My ball and chain looks up at me, the streetlight illuminating her expressive eyes. "What did you say to him?"

"Do you really want to know?"

"Yes," she insists, making it clear that either she doesn't know Spanish, or, again, she's a damn good actress.

"Too bad," I say, motioning her forward, and when she

doesn't move, I pull harder on the restraint locking us to-gether and drag her along with me, murmuring an apology to Hugo, as he claims to be called, and explaining to him that she's "embarrassed." I pause to face Hugo, who barely contains a smirk as he shuts the gate and steps ahead of us.

"This is dangerous," she murmurs as Hugo stops at the entryway of a broken-down house.

"He's not as dangerous as I am," I promise. We follow Hugo directly into a room that's been converted into a storefront with a counter and a cash register, and pass through to a very seventies puke-green kitchen. My shadow and I linger in the hallway as Hugo walks to a drawer and removes a pair of scissors. He hands them to me, with in-structions to use the spare bedroom and bathroom down the hallway to clean up.

"Telephone?" he asks in English.

"No," I say quickly, half expecting my companion to argue, but she wisely does not.

A knowing look settles in Hugo's eyes and he gives me a nod. Thanking him, I accept a first aid kit and urge the woman to lead the way to the single door to our right. She opens it and I follow her inside a small bedroom that is sim-ple but clean, with a door to what Hugo has told me is a bathroom. I shut us inside and toss her high heels, along with the first aid kit, onto the rainbow-colored Mexican blanket that's spread over the top of a twin bed. She grabs the plastic between our arms, as if trying to stop me from cutting us apart.

"Move your hand or I'll cut it," I warn, blood trickling irritatingly down my cheek. "We don't have much time, and we can't leave with these cuffs on."

"You can't leave me."

"Says who? Besides Sheridan."

"Me." Her voice quakes. "I say."

I narrow my eyes at her, or I think I do. I can't feel one of my eyelids, and—damn it to hell—blood drips down onto my arm. "What's in this for you?"

"I told you. I don't want him to get what he's after. And how do you know that man isn't just buying time to call the police or some gang?"

I ignore her question, and my desire to ask her a few of my own. "Move your hand."

"You're bleeding again, badly."

"*Move* your hand."

"Please," she whispers. "Don't leave me behind. I gambled on you helping me when I chose your silence over Sheridan's demands. He doesn't forgive or forget, and I don't know how to hide from him. I don't know what to do."

The desperation in her voice does nothing but irritate me. It reminds me of that lying bitch, Meg. I'd fallen for her desperate damsel-in-distress routine, and she'd been nothing but Sheridan's puppet. The thought spurs me to anger and action, and I reach under her arm and grab her elbow, twisting our arms and forcing her to let go of the cuff. Wasting no time, I cut the plastic tying us together and then make fast work of the bracelet remaining on her arm and then the three on mine. Unwilling to let her get her hands on the scissors, and not ready to let go of my only weapon, I shove them in my pocket.

My hands come down on the wall on either side of her head and I find myself staring down into her sky-blue eyes, a fear in their depths that she seems to try to hide with a defiant lift of her chin. Her attempt at bravado is my undoing, a reminder of my sister's youthful, spirited replies. Amy is nothing like this woman, who is maybe five years younger than my thirty years old, with experience and secrets in her eyes where Amy is innocence and truth, but it doesn't seem to matter. This woman, this stranger and enemy, keeps making me think of her anyway. And that's a dangerous path I'm not letting myself travel.

"You're in the forest with wolves, woman, and even if you think you're one of us, you're not. We'll *all* eat you alive. Get out of my forest before I'm the one who has you for dinner."

Shoving myself off the wall and away from her, I swipe

some blood from my face and grab the first aid kit from the bed. I've only taken a step toward the bathroom when it hits me that she could be wearing a wire, or a tracking device. "Scared, my ass," I mumble, angry at myself for being even somewhat gullible.

Rotating to face her again, I shackle her wrist with my hand and haul her with me to the door. It amounts to a toilet and a sink, which suits my needs just fine. Pulling the woman in front of me, I place her in front of the sink and mirror, stepping behind her, my hands framing the dip at her waist, and I am far from oblivious of the curvy but slender hips and the round, rather perfect backside. No doubt, both assets are reasons Sheridan would pick her for this job.

Fuming with the thought, my eyes meet hers in the mirror and I see a panic in hers that no one can fake. Good. She should be panicked right about now. "What are you going to do?" she demands.

"Dinner came early."

She tries to turn but I counter her move, stepping into her, using my thighs to pin her legs. Shifting to hold her more snugly in place, I fit her backside to my front, her soft round rear fitting against my groin. My cock reacts like it's just been given a reward, thickening instantly, apparently not giving a flying fuck that she's Sheridan's bitch, even if I do.

"Let me go," she demands.

"You just ordered me to do the opposite in the other room."

"I told you not to leave me behind, not to pin me against a bathroom sink."

She tries to shift again, and my zipper stretches to painful limits. "Enough," I grind out shortly through clenched teeth. "I need to be sure you aren't wired, or wearing a tracker."

She stills, her eyes meeting mine in the mirror again, her dark brown hair lying haphazardly over her brow. "Wire? Tracking device? No. No, I don't have either."

"Forgive me if I don't take you at your word."

"What you are going to do?" she asks again, the panic in her eyes from before now radiating in the quiver of her voice.

"I'm going to find out for myself, and we can do that one of two ways." I turn her around to face me, my legs clamping around hers again instantly, my hands returning to her waist, where I intentionally allow my fingers to flex. "I can search you, and do so intimately and completely"—I pause for effect, the air between us thickening a bit too readily to suit me—"or you can strip down for me and prove you're clean."

Her lips part in a silent gasp. "You can't be serious."

"As serious as a wolf about to rip out a deer's throat, sweetheart, and this needs to happen now. Decide. Which will it be?"

"Sheridan wouldn't have me wear a wire. He'd know you'd do this."

"Of course he would. The whole idea here is for me to get you naked. He wants you in my bed. And if you're offering, I won't decline, but it'll be me fucking you, not you fucking me."

"I'm not offering anything." Her hands press hard against my chest. "Let me out of here."

"Not a problem," I say, doing what's no doubt the opposite of what she expects, releasing her and moving the few inches away the space allows. But we're still close, a few inches separating us at best, and I can smell the damnable floral scent of her skin. She grips the sink behind her, her chest rising and falling in steady, heavy movements, but she doesn't leave. Of course not. She works for Sheridan. Even if she wants to go, she can't.

She says nothing. Does nothing. I give her a grand gesture toward the door. "Feel free. You're on your own."

Indecision flickers over her face, that streak of my blood a drastic contrast to her beautiful porcelain skin. Damn it to hell, why am I noticing her skin? Irritated at myself and at her, my hands go to her waist and I literally lift her and set

31

her aside. Stepping to the sink, I grab the towel on the rack and turn on the water.

"What are you doing?" she asks.

I glance up at her. "That question is getting old, but if you must know, I'm cleaning up to get the hell out of here—and so we're clear, I'm leaving without you."

"If you think I'm being tracked, why aren't you leaving now?"

"Because you being wired means Sheridan set up this escape, and he simply wants to keep an eye on us. In which case, I actually have more time, not less."

"Then you need to know you have less. I'm not bugged. I'm not wearing a tracking device." She grabs my arm and I face her as she promises, "I'm also not the whore you seem to think I am. But I can't get naked to prove it."

The conviction in her voice is pretty damn believable, and so is the desperation in her eyes, but then, why wouldn't it be? Failing Sheridan isn't a mistake that comes without a price. And she sure didn't seem anything but tough in that interrogation room. "Suit yourself," I say, removing her hand from my arm to face the sink again and bending over to splash water on my face. She doesn't move or speak, and while I am as aware of her standing there as I am of each breath I take, I ignore her. Using the bar of soap by the sink, I clean up my arms and then my face, my efforts only serving to irritate the gash on my cheek, which starts oozing blood all over again. "Fuck," I murmur, turning off the water and reaching for the first aid kit, aware that I need stitches I won't be getting.

"Why are you still here?" I demand, grabbing two Band-Aids out of the kit.

"I don't know where to go."

"Away from me," I say, tearing open a wrapper to bandage up my wound.

"I told you, I don't know where to go."

"And yet you acted really damn confident when you were working me over for the camera."

"My hands were shaking. I was terrified."

"Well, you put on a good show, sweetheart."

"I was running on adrenaline. Now reality has hit me."

"Stop fretting. You made it seem like I kidnapped you."

"In case I was captured—but Sheridan's not easily fooled. Please. I need help. I just . . . do what you have to do to believe me. Pat me down. It's better than getting naked. I think. I hope. Just get it over with."

It's all the invitation I need. Shackling her wrist, I pull her back to the sink and in front of me again, my legs once again pinning hers. She twists her fingers in my shirt, her lashes lowered, dark stains on her pale cheeks.

"Look at me," I order, trying to figure out why I can't quite turn on the ice in my veins with this woman.

Her eyes open, her chin lifting, and I study her, reminding myself that I have every reason to make this hard on her—except one: the vulnerable, shaken look in her eyes. The woman who betrayed me had convinced me she was Sheridan's victim, and yet never once had I seen such a look on her face.

I squat down in front of her, wrapping my hands around her slender ankles, where I linger, reminding myself that I need to treat her like a hostile. This needs to make her uncomfortable—but I can't help but think of my sister, whose life was ripped out from underneath her by no choice or action of her own. The idea that this woman could be the same kind of victim as Amy does not sit well with me.

Letting out a heavy breath, my hands begin to explore her body, running up her legs to the top of her thigh-highs, where I search the elastic for a hidden device. Next, I move up her hips, and she sucks in the same breath I'm now holding as I run my fingers between her thighs. She's wearing a thong, so as tempting as her ass might be, this isn't about sex, or taking advantage of her. If I knew she was Sheridan's bitch, the story would be different.

Trying not to give either of us time to think about the invasion this is for her if she is truly an innocent in all of this, I stand up and turn her to face the mirror again. She drops her head forward, her long, silky brown hair draping her face. I tug her black silk blouse from her skirt and my fingers tunnel underneath, deftly searching her slender waist, her ribs, and the sides of her breasts. I hesitate only a minute and then do what has to be done. I search the most obvious of potential hiding places for a tracking or recording device, cupping her breasts, and when I feel nothing but curves and woman, I shove down the lace cups, ensuring there's nothing inside. She pants. Hell, I think I do, too, and I remove my hands, tangling my fingers in her hair and parting it, searching her neckline.

Finally, I turn her to face me all over again, planting my hands on either side of her. She stares down, as far from playing seductress as you can get, but then, she's probably doing just that—playing me. Still, she's not wearing a device, and I find myself saying, "I had to do that."

Her gaze jerks to mine, her cheeks flushed. "I know," she whispers, delicately clearing her throat. "I get it. I . . . appreciate that you didn't— "

"Don't. Don't appreciate anything, because I will turn on you in a minute flat if you give me even a flicker of a reason to do it. I don't trust you."

"I don't trust you."

"You shouldn't. What's your name?"

"Gia Hudson."

"Is that your real name?"

I don't miss the two beats of hesitation or the lowering of her lashes before she says, "Of course it's my real name." Her gaze finds mine. "Is Chad yours?"

I ignore the question, which hits a nerve I don't examine right now. "What were you doing with Sheridan in the first place?"

A knock sounds on the door of the bedroom, and I shove myself off the counter. "Clean the blood off your face," I order, not waiting for a reply as I head through the small room to greet our visitor, my nerve endings buzzing, and my damn cock hard. Cautiously, I crack the door open to find a teenage boy who resembles Hugo standing in the hallway.

"Trouble, señor," he says in English. "There are men searching the neighborhood. My father turned down the lights and bolted the door, but he says you should leave out the back."

I curse under my breath and scrub the whiskers I can't wait to shave. "We're going." I turn to get Gia but she's already here, her shoes in hand.

"I heard," she says. "And 'we' better mean you and me together, because you aren't leaving me. Not after I just let you search me."

The smart thing to do would be to do just that—leave her. The odds of her being part of a setup are a good 90 percent, which leaves only a 10 percent chance she's a victim and/or an ally. And it's not like I'm a saint here. In fact, I'm a pretty damn accomplished sinner, but I choose the targets of said sins with care. I didn't choose this woman, and I know how dangerous Sheridan is. If she really crossed him, he'll kill her.

I grab her wrist and pull her to me. "You do exactly what I say, when I say it. Understand?"

She swallows hard. "Yes. I understand. I will."

I grab her hair, twining my fingers in the long, silky strands, and force her gaze to mine. "Fuck me over and I'll fuck you ten times harder and faster. And not in the way that feels good." My warning issued, I release her. Still holding onto her wrist, I enter the hallway, Gia—or whatever her real name is—in tow, and I swear I can almost see Sheridan's laughing face and hear him calling me a fool all over again. But it doesn't seem to matter. I've made up my mind. This woman is coming with me, at least until I decide what to do with her.

TWO

I'M STILL HOLDING Gia's wrist as I lead her out the back door of Hugo's house into the dark, muggy Texas night—so unlike the New York winters I've become accustomed to now. Stepping onto some kind of concrete patio, I can barely see my own hand in the inky black of the space around us. A few more steps and Gia hits a piece of furniture, and I grab her, pulling her against me to keep her from falling and covering her mouth with my hand. She is tiny, easily injured, as is my sister. It doesn't make her innocent, but handing her over to Sheridan, if she truly betrayed him, would assure her death.

I'm a lot of things, but a murderer, even indirectly, is not one of them.

She grabs my arm as if she's panicked, her hair catching on my whiskers as I whisper a warning: "One little peep and we could end up dead." I wait for her to nod and release her, shackling her wrist again to lead her across the yard. It's so damn dark; I silently curse as I nearly stumble myself. The inky blackness surrounding us might offer a cloak, but it also renders us blind, on top of being unarmed in a rough neighborhood riddled with gangs and now, with Sheridan's men.

Reaching the chain-link fence, I release Gia and hurdle it with only a quick, short shake of metal. "Come on," I order when she doesn't immediately follow, and I watch her shadowy outline as she seems to struggle to lift her skirt and stick a foot in the fence. I grab her free hand, her shoes dangling from the other, balancing her as she crosses over the top. Her sudden intake of breath, followed by a few short pants, tells me she's hurt and, afraid she'll fall, I wrap my arm around her and lift her the rest of the way down to the ground. In the process she ends up flat against me, my hand on her mostly bare backside. Grinding my teeth, irritated at the tightening in my groin for too many reasons to count, I intend to set her away from me but she pushes out of my arms before I can, yanking down her skirt.

I give her two beats to pull herself together, but when

she starts fiddling with her shoes, I wrap her tiny wrist with my hand again and start running, which means she has to run as well. Blinking rapidly into the darkness, I head down a narrow alley that runs behind a row of small houses, unhappy when our passing sets several dogs barking, but I've committed to this direction and we're charging forward. The path runs out and I stop, Gia running into my back, but I am unfazed. I squat down, and she follows as I look left and right, spotting the flicker of flashlights to the left only.

Leaning in close to Gia, I whisper, "We're crawling to the right, along the edge of the building."

She gives me an impressively calm, decisive nod that I manage to see now that my eyes have adjusted. Holding up a hand, I silently warn her to wait, then wave it a moment before I take off in a crawl toward what looks like one of the giant warehouses that are planted smack-dab in the middle of residential territory here.

We travel the length of a steel-sided building and enter the parking lot of another. The instant we're at the next building, I shift into a squat, leaning against the wall. The streetlight above us is burned out, offering us the shelter of darkness. Gia slides in beside me, and I'm pretty sure her knees are feeling the pain of our hasty escape, but I can't save her skin *and* her life. I listen for any activity around us, picking up the sound of muffled voices to both our left and right, and the realization that we are sandwiched in between them is not a good one. The only way out is forward or backward, and I'm not sure either is clear, but then, the gambler in me is genetic.

"We're going forward," I instruct Gia softly, "back where we came from, exactly where they won't expect us to go, and we're going now."

I don't give her time to think, or our enemies time to catch up with us, pulling her to her feet and running across a road. We quickly travel down the side of one warehouse, and then another—both illuminated by streetlights I don't welcome right now, but fortunately the street is deserted. The voices of Sheridan's bastard lackeys fade behind us and it gives me hope of escape, driving me to run harder and faster. Minutes become a blur of adrenaline that pumps harder and faster at the sight of the highway and the two blocks of open space we have to cover to get to it, but I don't miss a step. I grab Gia's hand and charge forward with determined steps that continue right up to the edge of the highway, and still I don't stop.

Determined to put distance between us and Sheridan's men, I tighten my hold on Gia and enter traffic, cars speeding toward us too rapidly for comfort. Our destination is a huge parking area favored by downtown partiers. Once there, I squat, taking Gia with me, and begin checking for unlocked doors. All the while, cars zoom past us on either side of the parking lot and above us on the ramp, and there are people around us—lots of people, considering it's Friday night and the nearby Sixth Street is the city's weekend hot spot. But then, getting lost in a crowd is exactly what I'm after.

Two people pass right by Gia, and her expression is pure terror but it works in my favor, setting her in motion as she starts checking doors with me. "Bingo," I say, opening the door to an F-150 pickup. "Get in," I order her.

Whatever her motivation for sticking with me right now, she doesn't have to be told twice, quickly scrambling inside the vehicle. I follow her and order, "Stay low," but apparently she's smart enough to set a bomb and knows to get down on the floorboard, because she's already there.

Crouching in the driver's seat, I yank the plastic panel from under the steering column. "You're stealing the truck?" she asks anxiously.

"If you wanted to grow morals, you should have done it before involving yourself with Sheridan."

"Says the man looking in the mirror."

"I never claimed to have morals," I assure her. "In fact, I don't have many. You should remember that the next time you want my help."

"Won't a stolen vehicle get more attention, not less?" she

asks, leaving my smartass comment alone. "What if it's called in to the police? Can't Sheridan track us on a scanner?"

I ignore her, yanking out the wires and going to work, all the while wondering if that was a question or a warning from someone far too close to Sheridan to earn my trust. She had better not hold her breath on that one. It takes me sixty seconds to get the engine started, and I stay as low as possible as I put us into gear. "Don't get up," I warn. I notice the blood-stained tissues in her hand and wonder if that's from the fence—but I plan to save her life, not take her for a manicure.

Backing out of the parking space, I spot a couple of men at the edge of the highway, both waiting a lot more patiently than I did for traffic, and I take the opportunity to leave via the farthest exit from the parking lot, out of their sight. "I don't have my purse," Gia says. "Or my credit cards—not that I think I can use them, but I have nothing, is my point. I have to go to the bank, maybe in another city so I don't draw attention. I'll grab cash and then we'll be gone before he can get to us."

"There is no 'we,' sweetheart, and I have a plan that includes untraceable resources." I turn into traffic and take the ramp to I-35. "Why don't you?"

"I told you before. I acted spontaneously. They were about to give you truth serum. You would have talked."

I give a bark of humorless laughter. "Sheridan should know that I'm ready for that. It wouldn't have worked."

"It's a drug. It's not torture and mind over matter."

"I have a plan for everything," I assure her, which is a lie, considering truth serum had never crossed my mind.

"If you're pointing out my lack of a plan," she replies, climbing off the floor and onto the seat as we change lanes onto and take the exit for Ben White Boulevard, "you're right. And I'm going to pay the price. I know you know that you don't betray Sheridan and get away with it."

My fingers flex on the steering wheel at her statement, which hits close to home, and the loss of my parents. "Who are you to him?"

"I'm the secretary to the head of the chemistry department," she declares, and despite the quickness of the reply, it rolls off her lips awkwardly, the way most lies do.

"A secretary," I repeat flatly.

"Yes. A secretary, and my boss is very close to Sheridan, so I do work for them both. The bottom line here is that I was in a position of trust. That means my betrayal will be unforgivable."

Yanking the wheel sharply, I pull in at the storage facility I'd rented when I was here doing surveillance on Sheridan, putting the vehicle in Park and turning to face Gia. "I hate lies." My voice is low, rough, vibrating with the six-year-old anger she's managed to stir. "I hate the people who tell them even more." I don't wait for her reply, opening the door and storming toward the security system panel to punch in my code.

The gates start to open and I head back to the truck, my mind running in circles as I try to decide exactly what to do with Gia. Obviously she's been close to Sheridan, deep inside his operation, which makes her a resource, but also dangerous as hell. With what I know is nuclear-level agitation, I yank open the door and climb inside without even looking at Gia. When I look at her, she stirs the protector in me, and makes me want to believe every damn lie she tells me.

I drive inside the facility, and Gia twists around to watch the gates shut. I have no doubt she's on edge, afraid I might turn on her. I'm no murderer, but if I find out she had anything to do with Sheridan killing my family, I'm not responsible for my actions. No one works closely with Sheridan Scott and remains innocent for long. We halt in front of one of the many storage units in a row, a streetlight illuminating the cab of the truck. She reaches for the door. I grab her arm, cursing the rush of male awareness she stirs in me. "Stay here," I order. "I'll only be a moment."

It's her who avoids eye contact this time, giving me a choppy nod. Yep. She's nervous all right—unsure if I'm here to do her harm. Good. Bad.

Fuck.

If she's innocent, I don't want her to feel fear. I shove open the door again and exit the truck, scrubbing my itching jaw, and retracing in my mind how Meg fooled me. I've been too busy taking my beatings to even think about it.

I use my code again to unlock the steel door of the unit and open it, walking inside toward a pile of newspapers, a kid's mini swimming pool, and six bean bag chairs, all meant to make anyone who looks inside think this unit is full of nothing but crap. I walk to the extra-large red bean bag chair and turn it over, ripping open the hole I'd sewn shut after I removed the stuffing, and pull out three duffel bags, one at a time. Despite the fact that everything that matters to me is in these bags, I lock the door again as I leave, fully intending to keep the unit for future use if needed.

Returning to the truck, I find Gia still there. Of course she is. Either she's setting me up or she really doesn't have anywhere to go. Throwing the bags on the seat between me and her, I climb into the cab, still without a damn clue what I'm going to do with her. I flip on the overhead light and unzip a bag that I know has a weapon inside.

"I guess you know Austin," she observes.

"Am I supposed to believe you don't know I grew up an hour from here?"

"How would I know? I told you. I'm just a secretary

46

who clearly got in over her head—but with good intentions, I swear."

She's no secretary, I think, but I let her enjoy the false comfort of her lies. Propping my foot on the dash, I raise the leg of my jeans to wrap a gun holster around my ankle before I level her with a hard look. "Know your enemies and their territory better than they know you and yours." I reach back inside the bag and remove a handgun. "Isn't that why you're here?" I challenge. "Because Sheridan thinks a pretty woman in trouble is my weakness?"

She turns and leans her back against the door, a defensive posture that tells me I've succeeded in making her uncomfortable, and I'm pretty sure her hand behind her back goes to the door. "I'm not a setup. I swear."

I pop an ammunition clip into place. "Then give me a solid reason why you're involved."

"Will you believe me?"

"Just answer the question."

"If you have what I think you have, it can't end up in the wrong hands. And Sheridan *is* the wrong hands."

"What is it that you think I have?"

"A cylinder that generates enough clean, safe energy to replace all other sources and make the nuclear, oil, and coal industries obsolete. And since Sheridan is an oil man, it would make *him* obsolete."

It would make a lot of very wealthy and incredibly vicious people across the world obsolete, I think, but I don't say that, or confirm or deny her words. "And you know this how? Wait. No. You know what? Don't tell me. I'm not going to believe you, anyway."

"Last night, I was working late and I overheard Sheridan and Sergio, the head of the chemistry department, talking about the cylinder. It's a miracle I couldn't believe, but the more they talked, the more certain I was they didn't intend to let the world know—at least, not until it served their agenda. I didn't know what to do. Fast forward twenty-four hours: I intentionally left my wallet in my desk, and came back to the office to get it and nose around. That's when I heard Sheridan going off on Sergio, demanding he make the 'treasure hunter' talk. Sergio said he could make a truth serum, and Sheridan wanted it tonight. Sergio is gifted. He could do it; I know he could. I didn't have time to weigh my actions. You were going to talk, and maybe end up dead." She takes a deep breath. "So there you have it. That's my story."

"So you want me to believe you overheard this and just charged over to the warehouse to free me."

"Yes. I told the staff that Sergio sent me to see if a woman could make you talk. They didn't believe me, and to make a long story short, it didn't go well. I just winged it, and here we are."

"Why Sergio and not Sheridan?"

"To buy time. They'd call Sergio first, and he'd be confused and investigate."

I study her long and hard, and to her credit, she doesn't blink or look away. That gets points with me. Liars look away. I hold up the gun, the barrel facing the ceiling. "Do you know how to handle one of these?"

"I know how to shoot a gun," she replies, her voice taking on a hint of desperation as she changes the subject. "Do you have the cylinder?"

"You know how to handle a gun," I say, ignoring her plea for information I don't plan to give her. "Why does that not surprise me?"

"I'm a single woman in a big city. I've made it a point to be able to protect myself. Chad, please—"

"You're just a single girl who needs to protect herself. I believe that about as much as I do the one about you being Sheridan's secretary trying to save the world from his greed." I shove my gun into the ankle holster. "Secretaries don't know how to set bombs." She opens her mouth to give me some perfectly formed explanation, and I cut her off. "Don't. A lie is just going to piss me off all over again."

"If you believe nothing I say, then why am I here?" she demands, actually sounding indignant and angry. "Why haven't you just dumped me or killed me?"

I face her, making sure she gets the full force of my one open blue eye that's probably more red right now as I reply. "Because I haven't decided if you're useful or not." And it's true. Until her boss, murder wasn't on my list of skills, but he's changed that. *Oh yeah, he has,* I think, adding aloud, "I'm leaning toward no, you're not."

Her bravado, which I'd seen in the bedroom earlier, flares into a full-blown glower now as she taunts me. "They say you'll do anything for money."

The words send a slicing blade of hard, brutal guilt right through my heart. "Who exactly is 'they'?"

"Does it matter who? Is it true?"

"I find what no one else can, for a cash price, yes." I move without thinking, grabbing her and pulling her to me, driven to escape the truth in her claim, to find the reality behind her lies. My fingers tunnel into her hair, tugging none too gently, bringing her mouth to mine, where I linger long enough to murmur my own accusation. "But money isn't what you're offering, now is it? And like I told you: If you offer, I won't decline."

She presses weakly against my chest, her hand flat over my heart, which has been bleeding for six years straight. "I offered you nothing," she hisses. "I'm not his whore, or yours."

"Prove it." My mouth comes down on hers, punishing,

hard and full of demand, my tongue stroking against hers, and she tastes like bittersweet temptation, like she is Eve and I am Adam, desperate for the poison apple. I don't trust her. I still want her. I taste her again and again and she doesn't respond, but I expect her to hesitate, to make this look good. And then it comes. Her moan and a soft swipe of her tongue against mine. It ignites passion in me, but it infuriates me just as much. I tear my mouth from hers and set her aside, having the answer I sought: She's Sheridan's bitch. And I tell myself knowledge is power. Taking by choice, not seduction, is power.

"That meant nothing," she whispers, hugging herself, her breath coming in fast, hard pants.

If only that were true, I think bitterly. "We both know that's the biggest lie of the night." I reach inside one of the duffel bags and she cringes, as if she expects another gun, when actually I'm removing the cell phone inside instead, along with a battery I slide into place.

"It proves nothing," she whispers again. "It *means* nothing."

She sounds like she's trying to convince herself, but we both know that she's trying, and failing, to convince me. I shift the truck into Drive and pull a fast U-turn. She reaches for the door. I hit the brakes and grab her arm. "Don't make me tie you up."

"Do you have the cylinder?" she demands. "Tell me I'm going through this for a reason."

"If I did, I'd make sure it wasn't found by anyone I didn't want to find it, and no one could fuck me good enough, or hard enough, to get it. Ask Meg, Sheridan's last bitch. She tried and failed. That's how I ended up there with you tonight. As for Sheridan, that bastard can go fuck himself—he'll never get that cylinder." I pause, my teeth grinding together. "*If* I had it."

"I don't know Meg. I'm not trying to seduce you. And I know you don't fully believe I am, either, or I'd already be tied up."

My jaw clenches and unclenches, several beats passing as I stare at her, wishing like hell she wasn't right. But she is. I have doubts about her guilt that I can't afford to entertain. Releasing her, I put the truck in motion and accelerate again, feeling more of that nuclear-quality energy radiating off me—and apparently she does, too, because she zips her lips. She starts to move toward the door, and I grab her arm again, shoving the bags to the ground and then dragging her to me.

My hand clamps down on her inner thigh and her left hand that seems to still be wrapped around a tissue. "Just let me go," she pleads. "I'm resourceful. I'll figure it out without you."

"That's not what you said an hour ago."

"We were in East Austin and I'm in heels and a skirt with no phone and no resources. Of course I needed help. I'll figure it out from here."

"You're right. You will."

"What does that mean?"

"You'll find out." I accelerate again, a plan in my mind. It's then that I realize her knee is bleeding, along with her hand. I don't comment, and I tell myself I don't give a damn. *I don't give a damn.* There is only one thing on my mind right now, and that's my sister's safety. I'm not losing my sister.

THREE

FAR TOO AWARE of my hand still on Gia's leg, I navigate the truck onto I-35, and it takes all of my willpower to resist the urge to call Jared, one of the few people I've trusted in the last six years, to check on my sister. Instead I slide the cell phone into the pocket of the door, not about to give Gia ammunition to use against me or risk putting Amy on the radar any more than I did by trusting Meg in the first place.

"Ouch," Gia hisses, punching my hand with her fist. "You're cutting off the circulation in my leg."

I blink as I realize that I'm squeezing her leg hard, and

now I'm back to thinking about the blood on my palm. "Go back to your side of the truck," I order, releasing her. "But don't even think about going for the door."

"The last thing I want is to greet the pavement with my face," she assures me, scooting to the side. "I thought you wanted to get rid of me."

I don't reply. I have no intention of explaining myself and giving her time to adjust to my plan. I'm done talking. It opens the door to mistakes I can't afford to make. Not with Sheridan and every oil tycoon across the world after what I have in my possession. Probably a few from the coal industry, too. And then there's the CIA, the worst fuckers of them all outside of Sheridan.

Exiting the highway, I cross over to a service road, cutting behind the adjacent strip mall and turning down a side street to enter the parking lot of the bus station, where I pull into a space. I reach to the floorboard and set the bags between us again. I stuff money in a small, as of yet unused bag and hand it to her.

"That's for you. Fifty thousand dollars." I grab a pen from inside the duffel and scribble a name on a piece of paper before stuffing it in her bag. "Go to New Mexico and see the guy on that card. He'll get you a new identity, but that alone won't protect you. Don't do anything Sheridan would expect you to do—not the same work, not the same lifestyle. Don't touch your bank account or call anyone you know, or he will find you."

Her lips part in shock, and I really hate that I remember kissing them as vividly as I do.

"That's it?" she says, disbelief wrenched into her voice. "Just 'get out'? You're done with me?"

"That about sizes it up."

I can almost see the arguments running around in her head, but to my surprise, she clamps her lips shut and puts on her shoes, slipping the bag over one shoulder. She reaches for the door, and for some godforsaken reason, I grab her arm and she turns to me, her brown hair waving around her heart-shaped face. Her blue eyes, illuminated in the overhead light, hold a hope I'm not going to give her as I say, "You're a risk I can't take. Too many lives are on the line."

A hint of anger replaces the hope in her gaze. "And here I thought you cared about money, not lives."

"If that were the case, sweetheart, I would have taken the five hundred million dollars your boss offered me for his prize. This isn't about money anymore. It hasn't been for a long time. Sheridan made sure of that."

"Or it's about you not having what he wants at all. Maybe that's why you were so confident you wouldn't talk."

"If you're baiting me, it won't work."

Her far-too-kissable lips tighten; her voice with them. "I was just trying to figure out if I lost everything to save a man who didn't even have the secret I was protecting."

"This conversation is over."

"I can't just leave town."

"Stay, then, and die. My conscience will be clear knowing it was your foolish mistake, not me, that got you killed."

She inhales, telling me that she feels the cold bite I know is in my words, looking like she just dug herself six feet under. "Right. You're welcome. Happy to save your life by screwing mine up," she says.

"He wasn't going to kill me."

"I stand corrected," she snips, bravely managing to bristle despite clearly feeling the intended heat of my actions. "You were just going to be injected with truth serum and who knows what else, until they got the information they wanted from you. *Then* they would have killed you."

"I told you. I plan for everything. What they would have gotten from me would not have led to my death."

She looks conflicted and then blurts out suddenly, "Let me help you protect the cylinder. Please. Let me feel this was all for something."

"If I had it," I bite out, irritated that I'm presently thinking that she's convincing *and* beautiful, which only makes Sheridan more of a bastard for choosing her, "I wouldn't need any help protecting it, and you're a fool if you don't get as far away from this as you can. Get on the bus. Go to New Mexico and get a new identity. If you're telling me the truth, and you were smart enough to pull off what you did tonight, then be smart enough to do what I'm telling you now."

"I'm not whoever that woman was who screwed you over. I'm not her, and I'm not like her. I promise."

I can almost feel my face harden, my voice lashing out like a whip. "Go, get on a bus, and get out of town."

She glares at me for several long seconds, her bottom lip quivering perhaps from anger, perhaps from some other emotion, before she says, "Sheridan didn't think about the betterment of the world. He thought about the betterment of himself. I gave up everything to protect you, and it."

"The bus," I repeat, not willing to be swayed by the passion in her voice that could be truth or fiction.

"If you—"

"*Get out*, Gia, or I swear to you, I'll put you out."

She inhales, clearly shaken by my threat, and it works. She shoves open the door, exiting quickly and sealing me inside, alone. I rev the engine, backing out of the parking space before she can return, eyeing her in my rearview mirror, the bag clutched to her chest. She looks defeated, when she's already proven she's a small package that packs a big punch. I refuse to feel guilt. I simply want the answers I'm about to get.

Exiting from the driveway, I turn into the hotel parking lot across the street and pull into a spot that is obvious—out of sight but also right in front of Gia's nose—and park. And now I wait. She's too smart not to figure out the bus station is dangerous, a place that Sheridan will look for her. That means she's either going to go inside and call someone who will come and get her, or she's going to start walking, looking for safety. What it won't tell me is if she's looking for escape from Sheridan's anger at her failure, or Sheridan's anger at her betrayal. But either way, I'll know she's no longer loyal to Sheridan.

Grabbing the phone from the door pocket, I dial Jared, and curse when I get his voice mail. "I'm alive," I say after the beep. "So break out the confetti, but not until you call me back. And my sister better be alive and well, too, or soon you won't be." I end the call and dial again, thinking a woman *is* my weakness: my sister. Jared's voice mail picks up again and I'm about to redial when Gia comes walking out of the parking lot on the opposite side of the road.

I set the phone to vibrate, stuff it in my pocket, and watch as she scans the area, passing right over me as she does the rest of the parked vehicles. Seeming to make a decision, she crosses the road between us and begins walking down the one to my right, toward the mall. I crisscross the two remaining duffel bags over my shoulders and exit the truck, intending to follow her, then ducking when she appears to consider going into the hotel itself. I curse at the idea of it, certain she's either foolish, or planning to wait on Sheridan's people there. She hesitates, though, and then starts walking again, headed toward the dark, deserted strip mall parking lot. On any other occasion, I'd say a woman alone headed toward a dark, empty parking lot was foolish. But when hiding from Sheridan it's smart.

The minute she fades into the black hole of the night— her target obviously the shelter of the mall, though I'm fairly certain she's ultimately going to the front of the building and the highway—I start my own wheels into motion. Trekking through the hotel parking lot I find another unlocked truck, toss the bags inside, and hot-wire it, certain whoever it belongs to won't miss it until morning, by which time I'll be long gone.

By the time I'm driving along the access road by the mall, I see Gia's outline moving toward a twenty-four-hour breakfast joint. I hang back, making sure she enters before I turn into the parking lot and grab a spot at the curb just beyond the restaurant's private lot. I climb out of the truck, shoving the bags into the back seat of the four-door vehicle, wishing like hell I could lock the door.

Tracking forward, I jump the curb and take long strides toward the side door of the restaurant. Inside, I find the hostess is not at the stand, and I scan the dining area to find Gia nowhere in sight. I cut to my left and follow the signs toward the bathroom, specifically the ladies' room, and I don't stop, shoving my way inside. I find her standing at the sink of the two-stall room, the bag open, her stockings missing as she doctors the many cuts on her knees.

I stalk toward her, crowding her against the sink, hands shackling her waist.

Her hands press to my chest. "Let me go."

"Did you call Sheridan?" I demand, gripping her knee where it rests against my leg.

"What? Why would I call Sheridan?"

"Did you call Sheridan?"

"No. I don't have a phone, nor do I plan to call and invite him to torture me like he did you. Did *you* call Sheridan?"

"Why the *fuck* would I call Sheridan?"

"Isn't that why you left me at that bus station? So he'd find me? Why'd you bother to give me real money?"

"I left you there to see what you would do, and you damn sure didn't go to New Mexico like I told you to. What was your plan?"

"I'm not getting on a bus, where Sheridan is sure to find

me. Thanks for that death sentence of a suggestion, but no thanks."

"I repeat: What was your plan?"

"Walking to a twenty-four-hour Walmart to buy supplies."

"Walking? Do you know how far that is?"

"Yes, but a cab is like a bus, a direct link to radios and records I don't want any part of tonight. Or, I guess, for pretty much the rest of my life."

"After Walmart, then what?"

"Then I walk to a used car lot to sleep in a car and buy one with cash in the morning, with a big tip for the paperwork getting lost."

Her answers are perfect. I wonder if they aren't even a little too perfect. I study her, looking for a blink, a flinch, anything I missed in Meg that I might find in her now. She's cleaned up the melting mascara from under her eyes and tamed her hair, clearly trying not to draw attention to herself, but she still has a tissue in one obviously injured hand.

My jaw flexes, my lips setting in a thin line. I believe she's running, and I can't know her motivation. But I know what's important at this point: Whatever their relationship may be, she was close to Sheridan Scott. She can help me take him down. I snatch her bag, interlace her arm with mine, and start for the door. She grabs the wall. "No. Stop.

I'm not leaving with you without an explanation. Where are we going?"

"Wherever I say we're going." The door opens and a woman enters. "Get out," I bark at her. Looking startled, she backs out of the room, and I turn to Gia. "Don't make me carry you out of here, because I will."

"That'll get attention we don't need."

"I'll do whatever I have to do. You don't seem to get that. If Sheridan is the devil, then I'm his redheaded step-brother who has been locked away in hell for six years. I'm very cranky and very pissed off."

"You're not worse than Sheridan, so if you think that scares me, it doesn't."

I turn her back against the wall, flattening her against the hard surface. "You should be scared. Because if I find out you had anything to do with what happened six years ago, I'll kill you."

She swallows hard. "I didn't even know Sheridan six years ago, I swear. If you hate me this much, why would you want me to come with you?"

"Because it's not you I hate. It's him, and you're going to help me take him down."

"You left me at the bus station to die."

"I needed to know if you'd contact him. Now, are you walking, or am I carrying you?"

"I want him to go down, too. You don't have to threaten me to do it, but I'm not his whore, or yours either. Don't treat me like I am, or I swear to you I'll fight you like no one ever has. And the answer to your question is I'm walking."

I give her a look that has to be cynical. It's all I can be anymore, besides pissed off. "Then let's walk." I grab her wrist and waste no time leading her out of the bathroom and down the hallway to the hostess stand, where the woman who'd tried to join us in the bathroom is talking to a man in a suit who I assume to be a manager. "Bathroom's all yours," I say, continuing to the front door and shoving it open.

I pull Gia forward, in front of me, and she glances over her shoulder at them and calls out, "Have a good night."

I snort as we fall into step together on the sidewalk, her strides keeping remarkable pace with mine as we travel to the back of the restaurant. "'Have a good night'?" I ask. "Really?"

"I didn't want them to call the police and risk Sheridan monitoring the police frequency, which is why you should hold my hand or let me go. Right now, I look like your prisoner."

I stop walking, dragging her in front of me, towering over her by nearly a foot. "You *are* my prisoner, and you'll stay that way until I'm done with you." I start walking again.

She double-steps to keep pace, and instead of fear in her

voice, there is disbelief. "'Done with me'? Then what? You'll kill me? Or hand me over to Sheridan so he can do it?"

I step over the curb leading to the mall parking lot and she stumbles, forcing me to wrap my arm around her waist and catch her. She is tiny against me, soft and womanly, and I feel a warmth deep in my gut that I do not want to feel. I set her away from me and lead her to the truck, then quickly release her wrist, and it's like ice on fire, a swift, welcome relief.

I yank open the door and motion her forward. She steps toward the cab but then whirls on me, the moon peeking from behind clouds, casting her in a warm glow. "You didn't answer my question," she whispers. "What are you going to do with me whenever you're done with him?"

My hand comes down on the top of the window and I step closer, crowding her. "The same thing I was going to do for you with that fifty thousand dollars, but better."

"You set me up to fail back there."

"I told you. It was a test. Don't stand in the way of me and Sheridan and we won't have any problems."

"Why doesn't that answer make me feel any better?"

"It's the only one you're going to get right now." I motion to the truck cab. "Get in."

"If I say no?"

"You won't."

"I was doing just fine in that bathroom. I had a plan."

"A fifty-thousand-dollar plan won't help you escape Sheridan long term, and we both know you have one of two reasons to hide: Either you really betrayed him, or you let him down when you couldn't fuck me into stupidity. Either way, you need me. If the latter's true, you'll still try to fuck me into stupidity."

"I'm not—"

"Save it."

"I'm not his whore, or yours," she hisses. "Maybe if I keep repeating that, you'll get it. You want information from me, and I want a real escape that doesn't get me killed. The end. There's nothing more to this story." She climbs inside the truck, but her words linger in the air. *Nothing more to this story.* Suddenly, I'm transported back a year in time to the New York subway station where I'd met Meg.

I step off the car, trying to get to Amy's job before she gets off work, keeping her close even if she doesn't know I am. It kills me not to be able to talk to her, but I don't dare. I am poison. I'm the reason she's going through this hell in the first place. And she's doing fine. She doesn't seem to need me, but if she ever does, I will not fail her again, the way I did so long ago. The way I did our parents. Sometimes I just need to see her alive and well.

I push through the busy Grand Central crowd, about to

exit to the street when a woman tries to go up the stairs at the same time as me. Our shoulders collide and I grab her arm and it's thin, and she is petite and blond, like my sister, and I have to see her face, but she won't look at me. She murmurs an apology and tries to move away. I hold onto her. "Are you okay?"

"Yes. I—" She seems to look at me despite trying not to, the mascara smudged on her cheeks, one eye black. She is small, fragile. Lost. I can't leave her without helping her.

I jerk myself back to the present and blink Gia into view. She won't look at me. But Meg did. She looked me straight in the eyes and lied without a blink, and I never guessed the "more" of her story. After five years of staying off Sheridan's radar, I didn't make mistakes, *she* became my one and only mistake, and I didn't even love the bitch.

Angry, I slam the door shut and round the truck. I won't be played by another devil in high heels. Once is enough. And I won't start thinking Gia deserves a hero for what she did tonight. Even if she does, there's a reason I've stayed away from my sister. I'm nobody's hero.

Inhaling, I climb inside the truck and shut the door, the powerful crackle of Gia's anger a brutal contrast to the soft scent of woman that teases my nostrils with punishing precision. I don't remember Meg ever working me over like this.

I glance in Gia's direction and she stares forward, refusing to look at me, further proving she is not planning to play the wilting flower. Nope. She is not playing the victim like Meg at all. The question remains though, is she a lying bitch like Meg?

Flipping on the overhead light, I lean down to reconnect the wires in the dash when Gia makes a soft sound and says, "You know what's pathetic?" I still, waiting for an answer, not sure what to expect as she adds, "I don't know you or trust you any more than you do me, but I trust you more than anyone else I know right now."

That statement reaches inside me and burns me in places I keep telling myself can't be burned anymore. No one understands what "trust no one" means more than I do. *No one.* If Gia is telling the truth, if she's ultimately the innocent victim that she's trying not to be in a world she doesn't belong inside of, then maybe, just maybe, I do have a chance to be her hero. The truth shall set me free. And her, too. "Then you're a fool," I tell her, "because even I don't trust me."

FOUR

"HOW LONG ARE WE GOING to be on the road?" Gia asks about thirty minutes after we hit the highway, the first thing she's said since my warning about trust. But then, I get the feeling she chooses her battles cautiously, which tells me her decisions tonight, no matter what their motivation, weren't made lightly. She knew the magnitude of every choice she made, including getting in this truck with me instead of screaming for help.

I glance at the dash that reads midnight, calculating the drive to our Lubbock destination. "Five hours."

"I can take a shift driving."

I snort. "Not a chance in hell."

"There's no way you've had any sleep," she argues, clearly not intimidated by her role as captive.

"Staring at the walls of the interrogation room wasn't exactly exciting."

"Bleeding while tied to a chair doesn't count as sleep."

"I'll sleep when I can actually close my eyes."

"It's not like I'm going to stab you to death with my finger while you sleep and I'm trying to drive this monster of a truck."

I give her an incredulous look. "Are you daring me to kill you?"

"If I was, I'd just let you drive without complaint."

"You do remember me saying you're my prisoner, right?"

"I also remember you saying you need my help. That makes me pretty safe until you don't need me anymore."

"You have big balls for a woman, but then, I guess that's what it takes to set off a bomb like you did."

"They're called brains, not balls, as my mother used to love to tell my father."

"No one likes a smartass," I comment dryly, not missing the past-tense reference, and reluctantly admiring her fearless determination, even if it is irritating as hell.

"Then you, Chad, must not have any friends."

"You think I'm a smartass? Well, fuck me. I was shooting for asshole, not smartass. I'll try harder. And I don't keep friends around to stab me in the back. Or prisoners, for that matter."

"Oh, you're an asshole, but from what I overheard when I walked into that warehouse tonight, Sheridan's crew seemed to think you'd taken smartass to epic proportions while they questioned you. They hated you; they were plotting to cut one of your toes off so the injury wouldn't show. It was the head of the chemistry department who chose the truth serum option. He has a weak stomach."

"I guess I should thank him the next time I see him—right before I kill him."

"Don't bother. He's a bigger asshole than you. And what you said about friends—friends don't stab you in the back. Real friends are family, and you can count on family. They don't let you down."

Until they do, I think, her declaration like acid burning through an open wound, leaving me ready to end this conversation. Reaching behind the seat, I snag the bag I'd given her earlier and set it between us. "Your fifty thousand dollar pillow. Never let it be said I don't know how to treat a lady. Lie down and rest."

"You told me not to trust you," she argues, curling her feet onto the seat toward the door and staring out of the

71

windshield. "So I don't. That means I'll have to make sure you stay awake. We'll just have to talk for four hours. Or five, right?"

"Forget it. We are not talking for five hours."

"Not about anything important, of course," she says, as if I haven't spoken, "since we don't trust each other. How about football? I personally think the Cowboys will never win again until Jerry Jones retires and hands over the leadership to someone else."

I don't do random conversation. It's dangerous. It makes you give away little details, like Gia's past-tense reference to her family—but I have to give it to her. Every male born and raised in Texas has an opinion about the Cowboys, and I fight the ridiculous urge to give her mine now by turning up the radio. A Garth Brooks song, "Friends in Low Places," instantly transports me to Jasmine Heights. To home and family. To a white-painted wooden house, green grass, and family barbecues. A few lines play in my head and then those images go up in flames, the house on fire, and I am living the part of my history I don't want to relive. The part I'm *always* reliving.

Shoving away the bitter memories, I force my mind to travel to Egypt, to the archaeological dig site where Lara, because she had been Lara to me then, and I had spent a chunk of our pre-teen and teen years with our parents, learning far more from our explorations with them than our homeschooling. Those had been good times, filled with sibling arguments, lots of laughter, and plenty of shared excitement over historical discoveries. But as easily as I embrace the good times, they always shift into darkness, and soon the images of those days transform into memories of Sheridan meeting my father at that same dig site, before my business with the bastard overtook my father's.

The music shifts, the station's wild mix delivering every genre under the moon that's nowhere in sight on what has become a cloudy, eternal night. Gia caves to the drugging effect of the road and lies down. Sleep rarely consumes me. Guilt keeps me up and pacing, often running the streets of New York that somehow take me to Amy's apartment—before I had to move her to Denver.

The song "Breakdown" by Seether begins to play, the words seeping deep into my soul, burning. *And I'm the one you can never trust/ 'cause wounds are ways to reveal us.* The words speak to me on every level. Glancing at Gia, not for the first time since she fell asleep, I stare at her long dark hair draped over the makeshift pillow, trying to figure out why I keep doing it. I didn't stare at Meg. I just fucked her. And filled the void of six years alone I'd thought she'd needed filling in her own way as well. Somehow, I'd let a crack in the wall I'd built around me open up and she'd crawled in, like a true wolf in sheep's clothing.

Dialing Jared, I get the same voice mail I'm coming to expect with growing concern. He's the only one left I completely trust, no matter how much I might lead Sheridan and even my fellow treasure hunters at The Underground to believe otherwise. If he's not answering my calls, I have to consider that he might be dead. And if he's dead . . . I can't even think about where this is leading me. I can't lose Amy. I can't. I *won't*.

Instantly ready to come out of my own skin, I start tapping my left foot up and down, needing out of this truck and out now. Bypassing a rest stop, I force myself to endure another ten miles, and finally we hit Abilene, Texas, where I get off the highway in hopes of finding a less conventional place to grab supplies and a bathroom, scoring that twenty-four-hour Walmart Gia wanted after all.

At two a.m., there are only a half-dozen other vehicles in the lot, and I pull into a spot to the left of the doors, allowing us a fast departure should it become necessary. I kill the engine and Gia seems to jolt awake, sitting up and blinking, looking stunned and confused. It pisses me off. "What happened to not sleeping?" I snap, and before she can possibly process my irritation, I'm out of the truck and opening her door.

"Get out," I order.

"Why are you so angry?" she asks, slipping on her shoes,

her hair wild, sexy like she is, and it only serves to add an extra level to my anger. "Did something happen I don't know about?"

"You went to sleep."

"Yes," she agrees, scooting to the edge of the seat to face me, her skirt riding high on her killer legs. "I went to sleep. Oh, God—did you almost fall asleep? Did you want me to stay awake and talk to you?"

I shackle her arm and physically slide her out of the truck, my arm wrapping around her waist, her soft curves melding to my now very hard, very tense, body. "Your trust does not equal my trust."

Her hand presses to my chest. "Let go. Stop being a bastard."

"Stop trusting people you shouldn't trust."

"I don't trust you. You need me. That keeps me safe for now. I told you that frankly and honestly. And why do you care? You think I'm out to get you anyway."

"Because it doesn't matter if I'm right or wrong about your intentions. You're two steps away from death, and I'm one of those steps. That means your fate is in the hands of someone who can't afford to see you as anything but the enemy, which means you are the enemy. And I'm yours. I could have no choice but to kill you. Don't forget that."

"Why? So you don't have to feel guilty if you do? Well,

forget it. If you kill me, I'll haunt your ass. You can count on it."

"Ditto, sweetheart. I'll come fuck you in your sleep." I reach around her to shut the door, when my gaze lands on her hand and the blood trickling down her fingers. Cursing, I grab her wrist.

She tries to tug herself free. "Hands bleed easily. It's nothing."

"I'll be the judge of that," I tell her, hanging onto her as I lean inside the truck, opening the glove box, and scoring a handful of fast-food napkins. "Open your hand," I order, and when she reluctantly complies, I wipe away blood and inspect the deep wound in her hand. "You need stitches that we can't get you right now." I close my hand over hers, forcing her to apply pressure on the napkins and the wound. "Hold it tightly until we get inside and get it cleaned and wrapped."

I shove the door closed and release her hand. "I'm okay," she assures me. "I'm tough. I won't get an infection and die on you without helping you take down Sheridan. I hate him, too."

I arch a brow at her fiercely spoken proclamation. "Hate him, do you? Good to know. *If* it's true." I grab her arm and pull her to me. "I'll want details later." Our gazes lock, that spark of attraction that's been with us from the moment we laid eyes on each other ever present.

"He's a greedy monster."

"We both know it's more than that, and you're going to tell me the what, when, where, all of it. But right now, I want in and out of here in fifteen minutes."

"You keep threatening me. What if I try to escape?"

"Run if you want to. Die by Sheridan's hand. Feel free." I turn us to the building and head for the automatic doors, stopping just inside the entryway to scan the store, counting not more than two handfuls of shoppers and staff combined.

"Are you at least going to tell me where we're going?" she asks as I take her uninjured hand in mine and direct us toward the pharmacy.

"You can't repeat what you don't know."

"Kind of like you not being afraid of the lie detector test?" she asks.

"Bait is for stupid fish, sweetheart," I say, stopping at the aisle of first aid supplies. "I'm not one of them." I release her and grab a basket from the end of the aisle, filling it with items she needs to doctor her hand that I hope like hell doesn't become an issue.

"I need to know this is all for something," she argues. "I need to know I'm protecting something."

"You proclaimed your hatred of Sheridan," I say, sticking the basket in her uninjured hand. "Destroying him will have to be enough." I glance at her feet and back up. "What size shoe do you wear?"

"Seven."

"And pants?"

"Six. Wait. Are you shopping for me?"

My answer is to point to the bathroom sign in the corner. "Go clean up. We'll pay for your supplies when we leave."

"What if they think we're stealing them?"

"We'll risk it." I turn her in the direction she needs to go, my hands on her shoulders as I lean in close, wishing like hell she didn't still smell so damn good. "Five of the fifteen minutes I'm willing to spend in here are gone. Go now. I'll be right here waiting on you."

Fortunately, she doesn't argue, and I watch her until she disappears into the small hallway beneath the sign. Scanning the store, I flag down a store employee, a redheaded kid not more than seventeen who quickly joins me.

"Yes, sir, can I help you?"

"Long story short, my wife and I missed a flight and the airline lost our luggage. I have to make it to Austin in two hours or they're giving away our tickets on another flight. Can I give you a hundred bucks to gather some supplies for me while we freshen up and use the bathrooms?"

The kid's eyes light up and he pulls a small pad and pen

out of his pocket, and I write down a list for him. "Have it all at a register in ten minutes and there's an extra fifty in it for you."

"Yes, sir. Absolutely."

He rushes away and I do another quick scan of the visible areas of the store before following Gia's trail and entering the women's bathroom. Rounding the corner of a short hallway, I find her alone at one of two sinks, washing her hand, with three open stalls to her left.

She whirls around to face me, her hand dripping water and blood to the floor. "You scared the crap out of me. What are you doing in here?" She grabs paper towels to dry her hand. "Is something wrong?"

"Just making sure you're safe," I say, moving to inspect the rest of the room.

"You can't keep coming into the ladies' room," she insists, following me into the last of the three stalls, this one the larger, wheelchair-ready handicapped space, where I give her my back and unzip my pants.

"Are you—Chad!"

I glance at her over my shoulder. "It's called seizing the moment, sweetheart. Go finish playing doctor so I don't have to."

She makes a sound of frustration, her heels clicking as she departs, my lips curving with the silent admission that I enjoy the hell out of aggravating this woman. Finishing my business, I join her at the sink, where she's struggling to get the bandage wrapped around her palm. I wash my hands, then grab her hand and take over and our eyes lock and collide, the air instantly thick with a huge dose of lust-filled distrust.

"You're going to get caught in here," she warns softly, as if she can't quite find her voice.

"It's a Walmart in Texas," I tell her. "They're happy if you manage to show up with pants on."

She laughs despite an effort to stop herself. "I suppose so. I'm just nervous about getting attention we don't need."

"We're fine." I fit some tape over the bandage on her hand and dump the supplies back inside the basket sitting on the counter.

"Right," she agrees. "I know we are."

She doesn't sound convinced, and I can't seem to quell my need to convince her otherwise. "Don't let my getting captured fool you. It took him years to find me. I'm good at what I do. He won't find me again. That means he won't find you."

"Until you're done with me," she murmurs, cutting her gaze away from me, and for the first time since that bedroom in East Austin, fear radiates off her. I tell myself to let it go, that she could be working me over, but I can't seem to care.

I slip a finger under her chin and force her gaze to mine. "No matter what your intentions were when this started tonight, if you help me, *really* help me, I'll make sure you stay protected."

"I don't work for him, and I don't know why I'm even saying that again. I know I can't convince you."

"I told you. *Help me.* I'll help you. Okay?"

"Yes. Okay." She's not convinced, and the truth is, neither am I. I stayed away from people until Meg, Amy included, for a reason. People die when they're near me, but I'm not telling Gia that, and I let my hand fall away, settling both on my hips.

She hugs herself and for several beats we simply stare at each other, until she wets her lips, and I try not to look at her mouth, or think about kissing her, but I fail. I think about it. In vivid, I-want-to-fuck-her detail.

"This is what you do?" she asks. "How you live? Always looking over your shoulder? Is that how I have to live?"

"What I do is exactly what you said earlier. I, like others in the organization I work for, find what no one else can find."

"For a price."

"Yes. For a price. We also hide things so no one else can find them."

"Sheridan hired you to find the cylinder for him."

"Yes."

"And did you?"

"Whether I did or didn't isn't what's relevant. Clearly I didn't give it to him."

"But he thinks you found it."

"Yes. And that's exactly why we need to get moving. He'll have a reward out for finding us. A big one." I motion to the bathroom stalls. "You'd better go 'seize the moment' yourself. We aren't stopping again anytime soon."

"Okay. But you have to leave."

"I'm staying. Shut the door."

"No." She shakes her head. "No. I'm not doing that. You have to go. Please. I'll hurry."

It's the pink flush of embarrassment in her cheeks that makes me concede. "Two minutes or I'm coming back inside." I don't waste any of the precious time ticking on the clock hanging around, quickly rounding the corner and exiting the bathroom and the hallway beyond it. Doing another quick scan of my surroundings, I'm satisfied we are not in imminent danger. I lean against the wall, and check my phone for any missed calls I might not have heard, frustrated to find no record of Jared responding to my attempts to contact him.

My mind replays the short message I'd left him when I hadn't thought that I'd survive another hour, let alone the

two weeks I'd managed to stay in hiding before I'd been captured. I'd been attacked before I could mention Meg, and
that could have been a lethal mistake for him and my sister.
Gia appears in front of me and I need answers. I take the
basket from her and drop it to the ground, my hands closing
on her shoulders. "What do you know about my sister?"

"What? Nothing. I know nothing."

"You know nothing about Amy?" I press. "Nothing at all."

"Amy?" She looks stunned, her voice taking on a rasp.
"Her name is Amy?"

"What do you know about my sister?" I demand, tension
coiling in every part of my body.

"Nothing. I mean, I heard something. Maybe."

My fingers flex into her arms. "What? What did you
hear?"

"He was talking to someone."

"*He* who?" I demand.

"Sheridan. He told them to find Amy."

"Who was he talking to?"

"I don't know. It was a phone call he was on, and I didn't
answer his calls."

"Are you sure it was on the business line, or was it a cell
phone?"

"I don't know that, either. I walked to his door and it
was open a crack."

"How long ago?"

"Last week."

"Last week," I repeat. "You're sure it was last week?"

"Yes." Her fingers curl around my shirt. "Chad. If he had her, he would have used her against you. That's the kind of man he is. You know that."

"If he didn't have her, he would have used her against me, too. So why didn't he?"

"I don't know. I didn't know you had a sister. It makes no sense that he didn't."

"If I find out you know more—"

"You won't. I don't."

There was a time in my life when her answer would have been enough, but that was before I made a deal with the devil that got my parents killed. I search her face, and deep in those blue eyes I see what someone else wouldn't see. What I breathe for breakfast, lunch, and dinner: the lies, the secrets, the guilt. I reach up and drag my finger over her cheek. "Meg didn't fuck me into submission as I know Sheridan believed she could. I felt sorry for her. I don't feel sorry for you."

"Am I supposed to be upset or say thank you?"

"I don't care what you are. Just know this. It's only a matter of time before we're alone."

"I'm not sure what that means, but I'm guessing it's a threat."

"It's a promise." I grab her hand, and leaving the basket behind, head for the front register where all the supplies we need should be waiting. Why didn't Sheridan use Amy against me? And why did Gia just assume he didn't? Getting Gia alone and to myself is sounding better every minute.

IT'S TWENTY MINUTES from the time we enter the store until the time I'm pulling out of the driveway of Walmart and back onto the highway. Beside me, Gia eagerly trades her high heels for the flat sandals the clerk picked out for her. "My feet thank you," she says, slipping them on. "I thank you."

"Dig out that screwdriver I bought, will you?" I ask, focused on more important matters.

She leans over the seat, digging around and producing it as I cut left onto a residential street where I park next to a dark house. "What are we doing?"

"Covering our tracks," I say, taking the screwdriver from her. "Stay put." I climb out and make fast work of removing both license plates, returning to set them on the seat between us.

"Won't we get more attention without plates?" she asks as I start driving again.

"Yes," I agree. Cutting to the left and back to the access road, I turn into the parking lot of a twenty-four-hour Denny's with rear parking. Quickly claiming a spot between two pick-up trucks, both with Texas plates, I put us in idle.

"Stay put," I instruct again, grabbing our plates and squatting low as I exit the truck, and then making quick work again of removing the plates from the truck next to us and replacing them with ours. Once I've attached the new plates to our stolen vehicle, I return to Gia and put us in Drive.

One problem solved. Next up: the one sitting next to me.

FIVE

ABOUT AN HOUR into the ride, my eyes are heavy and the gas tank is empty. I make a quick stop for gas at a deserted twenty-four-hour store, careful not to be spotted by the attendant. Despite a need for caffeine and food, I skip a trip inside the store and opt for a drive-thru not far down the road, parking in a dark corner at a closed retail store as Gia and I all but inhale our burgers and fries.

"That was so bad for my waistline," she murmurs, finishing her food and stuffing the wrappers into the bag. "But I can't seem to care. I might die soon. I'm not doing it without one last order of French fries."

"I don't give a damn about my waistline," I say, stuffing my wrapper in the bag. "And if you're telling the truth, you aren't going to die. I won't let you." I pull onto the road again. "Unless I fall asleep at the wheel. In which case, we both just had our final meal."

"Well, thank you for wiping out my momentary comfort. Good thing you aren't a doctor. You'd have a horrible bedside manner." She drapes her new Walmart hoodie over her lower body and turns toward me, folding her legs in front of her on the seat between us. "I'd offer to drive again, but I know you're not going to let me. Sooo, back to Plan B: How about them Cowboys?"

Desperate for anything to stop my mind's continuous instant replay of the fact of Jared's damning silence, I decide 'what the hell' and reply with, "They never should have fired Jimmy Johnson."

"Isn't that the truth? You know Jimmy has to be secretly gloating at Jerry's failure to run the team himself."

Impressed with her reply, I test her knowledge with a number of questions and find myself in a worthy debate over the merits of certain players, and eventually shift topics from the Cowboys to the Longhorns. Miraculously, I blink and an hour has passed and we aren't far from Lubbock. I've avoided both sleep and all the demons running around in my head, causing havoc. "How'd you get so into sports?"

"Texans love our football. My father certainly did."

"Did?" I ask, seizing the first opportunity I have to find out more about her. "Why past tense?"

"He's gone. Car accident years ago."

I don't miss the choked sound of her voice that she tries to cover by clearing her throat, nor do I offer her an awkward expression of sympathy that solves nothing. "And your mother?"

"Died of an aneurysm while giving birth."

"I've never heard of that."

"It was an underlying condition triggered by the stress of labor."

"That's rough."

"I didn't know her, so I don't feel the impact the way I do with losing my father. It's more like this empty hole in my life that is ever present."

I give her a quick glance. "Any siblings to help fill that void?"

"I was the first for my parents, and my father never remarried."

"That's a long time to never remarry."

"He was terrified of losing me. I don't think he had the capacity to fear losing someone else. And he was passionate about his work. It consumed him."

"Which was what?"

"Both of my parents were researchers for the University of Texas in Houston. That's where I grew up."

"Impressive. I come from a family of archeologists. I suspect we both had some interesting dinner-table conversations." I pause a moment and shake my head, the realization hitting me. "Wait. Research? Is that how you learned to make a bomb?"

She laughs a bit sadly. "Yes and no. My father said I had a knack for making things that weren't supposed to blow up quite explosive. It terrified him. Needless to say, my lab time was quite stressful to my father."

I inhale, her explanation jolting me with a realization: She set a bomb. A bomb blew up my family home. It's a close connection I do *not* like. "How is it that your father was a researcher and you ended up a secretary in Austin?"

"I finished college at Berkeley, but California didn't suit me. The university offered me a job, but the program was cut before I got home. I tried to stay, but without the university, all I had was missing him."

"You're a chemist?"

"Yes."

"Working as a secretary," I press again.

"I was with Sheridan as a chemist for almost a year, then there were layoffs, and I was kept on as a secretary."

It's a ridiculous story. Completely fucking ridiculous. "You know I can check all of this, right?"

"It's the truth."

"How old are you?" I ask, trying to find truth of my own.

"Twenty-six."

Four years younger than me, which would have made her only twenty when my parents were burned alive. But that means nothing. I did a lot of shit at twenty I'm not proud of. I reach down and turn up the radio, needing out of this conversation and back into my own head. Trying to put the pieces together again, with Gia as a possible part of the puzzle. Could she have been there that nightmare of a night six years ago? Or maybe her father? My gut says no, but something doesn't add up with her. In the absence of Jared's aid, I'm going to have to use one of my familiar private for-hire contractors to check her out.

Gia seems to get that we're done talking, and lies down across the seat again, but she isn't sleeping. I sense her unease, her alertness. I wonder if she regrets the story she just told me, or simply everything about tonight, the way I regret so many of my decisions. It's a thought that shifts me back in time, and I am twenty-two again and of the opinion that I am invisible, refusing to listen to my father's always sound advice. I can almost smell the smoke and wood from the crackling fire my father and I sat around that night, years ago, almost taste the strong-ass coffee we were drinking.

"You don't have to run around the globe with this 'treasure hunting' operation chasing God-knows-what for rich old farts."

"Isn't that what we do, anyway?" I argue. *"Treasure hunt?"*

"You're chasing money, not history, and history is often the key to the future."

"Sheridan wants me to locate a piece of art for him, Father. It's not that big a deal, and he's offered to wipe away your debt to him."

"He's the wrong person to get into bed with."

"You borrowed money from him to fund this dig site."

"Which is how I know he's the wrong person to get in bed with."

I drift into more of those moments, revisiting my mistakes, promising myself that Gia won't be one of them, until near dawn, when we finally enter Lubbock, Texas. After surveying my options, I pull in to one of the many cheap motels in the city, this one with not a big rig in sight, which is the idea. We don't need CBs radioing us in to Sheridan for cash, and we don't need lobby cameras or extra eyes.

Beside me, Gia stirs and I flatten my hand on her shoulder. "Stay down. We're at a motel, and Sheridan will have a reward out for a man and a woman fitting our description."

She slides onto the floorboard and sits, the hoodie over her legs again. "Where are we?"

"A motel," I repeat, irritated at the way the soft, sexy whisper of her voice radiates through me. I let down my guard while we were driving, the way I let down my guard with Meg, and it can't happen again.

"Which city?" she presses.

"The one we're spending the night in." I grab a baseball cap from a bag behind the seat and tuck my way-too-long blond hair underneath it to hide the color. Climbing out of the truck, I say, "I'll be right back, and don't even think about getting out and finding a phone. The motel has an outdoor check-in and the window is right in front of the truck."

"Darn. I really wanted to call Sheridan and ask him to go ahead and kill me and get it over with."

"You're brave for a prisoner."

"And you're tolerant for a killer."

"I told you. I'm not planning to kill you."

"I hate that word, *planning.*"

I think of the bomb she set, and my temper flares as hard and fast as the fire that killed my parents. "Let me make this real damn clear," I bite out. "No reading between the lines. If you were in any way responsible for my parents being burned alive, then you're dead. If anything happened to Amy, and you were a part of it, you're dead. Stand between me and Sheridan, and good luck—we'll see where that takes you. Otherwise, you're safe." I slam the door, every muscle in my body burning with the fierceness of my anger that isn't even about Gia. It's about Sheridan. It's about me.

Walking away, I lower the bill of my cap, feeling zero regret over my bluntness with Gia. We're living on the edge, and I can't afford to operate with anything but the facts. Reaching the hotel office, I hit a buzzer, and the attendant, a white kid not more than eighteen with dreadlocks and a baseball cap, enters the glass-enclosed check-in kiosk from a back room. Barely looking at me, he takes my cash payment for a room. Considering it's five in the morning, I pay for two nights, certain we can't sleep and take care of business in the six hours left until checkout. I keep an uneasy eye on the truck while I wait, replaying those moments on the back porch just before the explosion: the flash of light, the crackle of sound. A shiver of unease runs up my spine. Who was behind that damn explosion? I've tried to find out without any success, and I damn well need to know.

Finally, I'm given a key, and I return to the Ford, finding Gia still huddled on the floorboard. "At least you didn't steal the truck."

"I didn't know about your family," she says, her voice

raspy, affected. As if she really gives a damn. "God, Chad, I *didn't* know. I promise you, I wasn't involved. I'll help you. Tell me what to do and I'll help."

I want to believe her. *Fuck. Fuck. Fuck.* I climb into the truck and shut the door. "Don't talk. It's only going to rub salt in wounds neither of us need irritated right now."

"I understand."

I don't look at her. I can't look at her. My fingers tighten on the steering wheel. "No," I say sharply. "You *do not* understand." I drive around back to a twelve-unit building, the lot deserted except for us, which is good and bad: We're alone, but we can't exactly get lost in a crowd, either. Killing the engine in a spot in front of our door, I grab the bags from behind the seat. "Stay here and watch for my sign. I don't want us lingering in the open together." I don't wait for her reply, exiting quickly and unlocking our room before motioning her forward.

She doesn't miss a beat, hurrying out of the vehicle with another bag in tow and the hoodie in her hand, darting past me and inside. I follow her, kicking the door shut.

"Lock it," I order, tossing the bags on the full-sized bed with a sunken mattress and some sort of blue blanket on top. Eyeing the window beyond a wobbly-looking wooden table, I cross the cracker box–sized room, with its scuffed walls and ugly, worn gray carpet and attempt to seal the gap in the curtains that refuse to stay shut. Grabbing one of the two chairs by the table, I force the material together, using the wooden chair back to hold it in place, and then turn on the air conditioner, which roars to life like a hundred-year-old Chevy.

Hands on my hips, I stand there a moment with my back to Gia, dreading the next few hours alone with her in this room. Wondering what it is about her that makes me want to believe her. Questioning why I never doubted Meg. Why I believed she was helpless and alone, when she was a conniving bitch.

Determined to control the here and now, I grab the unused tie hanging by the curtains and turn to find Gia sitting on the edge of the bed. She gives the tie, and my expression, one look and stands up. "What's that for?"

"I need a shower."

"I think there are much larger towels in the bathroom."

My lips quirk at the silly remark. "Always a smartass."

She inhales and lets it out, folding her arms in front of her chest. "Sorry. It's a nervous thing. My dad said my mother did it too, and, well, you're really making me nervous."

Her admission feels intense and sincere in a way I don't question as authentic, real in a way I find few people I've known ever are real about anything, let alone their insecurities. And yet she just made it to a man calling himself her captor. It's a level of trust I won't give her, and that I don't deserve to be given. I advance on her. She backs up, hitting the mattress after one step and tumbling onto it with a yelp. I'm there before she can get up, clamping my legs around her knees. She pulls herself to a sitting position, shoving against my stomach. "You're *not* tying me up."

"It's a necessary evil. You aren't calling Sheridan."

"I hate that man," she says vehemently. "I told you that."

"Even if I believe you—"

"Stop calling me a liar."

"Truth or fiction, it changes nothing. Safe is better than sorry." I reach for her hands, but she keeps squirming, desperately trying to get away. "That's it," I murmur roughly, shackling her wrists and laying her flat on the mattress. I follow her down, straddling her hips and pressing her hands over her head.

"No!" she yells, still trying to shift or twist with zero success before giving up and glaring at me. "Get off of me. Get off!"

"Calm down, Gia."

"*Calm down?* Have those two words *ever* been spoken to a woman successfully? You're on top of me! I'm not going to calm down."

"I'm not going to hurt you."

"I don't think you're going to rape or murder me. I think

someone could come through that door while I'm tied up, and I'll be helpless."

"I'll handle whoever comes through that door."

"Not if you're in the shower. And you told me not to trust you."

I stare at her. She stares back at me, and a battle of wills ensues, crackling with challenge that slowly shifts to something darker, hotter, and I reply with a low, rough tone. "Maybe I've changed my mind," I murmur, and suddenly I'm staring at her lips, her full, kissable, tempting lips. A mix of adrenaline and lust rushes through me, barely contained. My mouth lowers, my need to lose myself in this moment, in this woman a fierce beast that does not want to be ignored.

"Don't," she whispers urgently.

"Don't what?" I ask, lingering a breath away from touching her face, so close I can almost taste her.

"Kiss me again. Because I'll kiss you back, and we'll both hate me for it."

She's right. But I still want to kiss her.

"Please," she whispers.

"Please kiss you? Please tie you up and fuck you like you've never been fucked? Please make you come so many times you'll never forget who you fucked if you fuck me over?"

"Please don't do any of those things."

"Because you don't want me to?"

"I already told you why. You'll hate me later. And I'll hate me for giving you the chance."

"And what about me? Will you hate me?"

"I don't have a reason to hate you, Chad. I don't know you."

"But you want me."

"I don't know the right answer to that."

"The truth will set you free."

"The truth can't set you free if no one believes you."

Something about those words rips through me and cuts deeply. It's some long-buried memory that I can't seem to call to the surface, but it shakes me to my senses. Am I really about to bed a woman I was ready to believe helped kill my parents less than an hour ago? What the *hell* am I doing? I pull her arms forward and quickly wrap them.

"You're still tying me up?" she demands, sounding desperate. "Why? Please."

"I told you not to say please."

"You didn't say—"

"I am now." I stand and pull her to her feet.

"This isn't necessary. I don't have anywhere to go. I don't even know how to hot-wire the truck. You can take the phone cord."

"You knew how to make a bomb."

"I explained that."

"You're just full of answers. And I'm full of questions. Come with me." I start leading her toward the bathroom.

"I can't go in there with you. What are you doing?"

Stopping, I face her. "I told you. I always have a plan. I'm keeping you close and safe."

"No. You need privacy."

"Sweetheart, I don't give a fuck about privacy. Don't make this harder than it has to be." I start walking again and she tugs against me. Grinding my teeth, I give her a hard look. "My need for a shower and sleep is making me real damn cranky. Don't make me carry you."

She glowers, but she's smart enough to follow this time as I lead her into the canister-sized shithole of a bathroom and seat her on the toilet. "Make yourself comfortable." Anticipating her compliance, I return to the bedroom and snag the second tie dangling from the curtains. Returning to the bathroom, I kneel at Gia's feet, grabbing her ankles and wrapping them just tight enough to be sure she can't escape.

My hands settle on her knees, and when our eyes meet, hers burn with defiance, anger—but there is more there as well. There is the kind of simmering heat a man sees in a woman's eyes when she wants him. She knows it, too, lowering her lashes. Trying to hide it. Enemy. Ally. It doesn't seem to matter. Right now, we're alone, us against the devil himself.

"Seems the tide has turned and we're in reversed positions," I taunt softly.

Her lashes lift instantly. "I was helping you escape," she argues.

"And now I'm helping you escape."

"That's not what this feels like."

"What then, Gia, does it feel like?" My voice is a low growl of heat and desire, my fingers flexing into her skin.

"I'm tied up."

"Do you feel in danger?"

"No," she admits reluctantly. "I don't."

"Then what do you feel?"

Her beautiful blue eyes search my face, as if she's trying to figure out whatever mystery I am to her. "Confused," she finally confesses. "You are very confusing."

"Sweetheart, I'm a puzzle with so many missing pieces, even I can't find them. Don't try. You'll fail." I lean back on my haunches and lift my pant leg, grabbing my gun and placing it in between her hands. "If anyone comes in, remember your Texas roots: Shoot first and ask questions later."

"What? Wait. You've tied me up, but you'll give me a gun?"

"I can't help you if you shoot me. You can't call Sheridan to tell him our location if you're tied up. Pretty damn clear to me why this works." Standing, I tear my shirt off over my head and toss it away. Her eyes go wide and she gives me a fast but thorough inspection before her cheeks flush and she glances away.

"Don't look at me like that again," I warn, tearing off my ankle holster and setting it in the sink, "or I might stop caring who hates who until after we fuck." It's crass. I'm crass and suddenly pissed off, and I don't try to pretend I know why. I walk past her, so close in the small space our knees bump, and damn it, I jolt with the impact, and that pisses me off, too. I turn on the shower and adjust the water.

"Me," she supplies as I turn to tower over her. "Just in case you've forgotten how mad the kiss in the truck made you. *You'll* hate *me*."

"If I end up hating you, Gia, it won't have anything to do with how good you fuck or don't fuck. I promise you that." I step away from her, giving her my back and unzipping my pants. I shove them down my body and kick them away. Turning, I find her head on her knees, her long brown hair draped over her face.

"Tell me when you're in the shower."

This is not a seductress, or even an actress. No one is this good, and I have no idea why, but seeing her hiding her face is like a hammer cracking the ice I erect around me. I laugh, a low, deep, genuine sound I barely remember as belonging to me. I never laugh; I don't even smile all that much. I'm really not sure what to make of it. I was just pissed off. I *am* pissed off. And aroused, my cock thickening uncomfortably, in a way that would scandalize this woman, and oh yeah, I *want* to scandalize her, and a whole lot more. I want this woman like I don't remember wanting anything in a very long time. But I step past her, resisting the urge to touch her, because now is not the time for this. It may never be the right time.

When I climb into the shower the hot water pours over me, erasing the odd combination of laughter and lust of moments before and soothing the ache of my many beatings. I sigh with relief as heat seeps into my weary body. I needed this. Oh yes. I really needed this.

"Please don't make noises, unless you're going to sing something really silly that makes me forget you're naked."

My lips quirk. "What kind of noises am I making?"

"Pleasure sounds."

A full smile manages to find my lips. "I like getting dirty, sweetheart, but I enjoy cleaning up now and then, too."

"You're just trying to embarrass me now."

"If I can't fuck you right, I might as well fuck you wrong."

"You like the word *fuck*."

Lisa Renee Jones

I laugh again, working shampoo into my hair. "I suppose I do."

"My father liked it, too. It surprised people."

"A fancy university doesn't seem like a *fuck* kind of place," I comment, rinsing the soap off.

"Oh, don't let the prestige fool you. It's Texas, after all, and there were some redneck boys who held nothing back. And the thing is, my father was one of them, but he dressed and presented himself as very refined and proper, so it shocked people to see the other side of him."

I turn off the water and rip open the shower curtain, grabbing a towel and wrapping it around my waist. "And what the *fuck* does that make me?"

She laughs, keeping her eyes on my face, not my partially naked body as she says, "Very fucking different. And my father would be appalled that I used that word."

I grab another towel and dry my hair, struck by how fondly she talks about her father, and how difficult it's going to be to get her to let go of her past life. Either Gia isn't afraid of what the future holds or she's in denial. Tossing the towel over the edge of the tub, I face her, closing my hand around hers where it holds the gun. "Do you want to survive this?"

The light in her eyes fades. "I *am* going to survive."

"Good. Then the old you doesn't exist. I'm your safe

zone, the only person from this point forward who can know who you were or where you came from. Gia doesn't exist anymore. Nothing you've done before now can ever be a part of your life again, or Sheridan will find you."

"But you said you were going to destroy him."

"Destroying Sheridan isn't enough. He's aligned with other very powerful, very rich people who want that cylinder. Assuming you've told me the truth, you denied them their prize by helping me escape."

Her eyes glaze over, but she doesn't cry. "Tell me," she says, her voice quavering, "that I did all of this for a reason. I need to know. Or maybe you understand better like this. Tell me that I did this for a *fucking* reason."

"The more you know, the more danger you're in."

"That's bullshit. My life is ruined. I'm on the run. I deserve to know."

In this moment, I believe there is more to Gia than meets the eye, but I do not believe she's working for Sheridan. Or if she is, or was, it either wasn't by choice, or it's with the kind of gut-wrenching regret I feel over having made the same mistake. And I won't make it worse by putting her in more danger.

"If there's one thing I've learned," I reply, "it's that life is rarely fair. And death is the biggest bitch of all." I reach down and untie her hands. "Stay here." I walk out of the bathroom, setting the gun on the nightstand before grabbing all the bags with her things in them and returning to set them all on the floor in front of her.

"Chad—"

"There's no window in the shower. The bathroom's all yours. Make it quick, and be ready to leave suddenly if we have to." I back out of the room and shut the door. Needing space. Needing to think and figure out what to do about her and with her.

Leaning against the wall, I close my eyes, one clear certainty in my mind: Gia's the newest addition to the list of people I fucked over when I made a deal with the devil and found that cylinder. I shut my eyes against the sound of a soft, muffled sob from inside the bathroom, as if Gia's covered her mouth to try to hide any sign of weakness. But she's not weak. She's strong. The tears are a part of the process of acceptance she has to go through to survive, but they come with pain, and her pain cuts me. God, how it cuts me, carving out what's left of my soul and leaving me to bleed the only thing I have left: *vengeance.* Sheridan knows I'm alive. He knows Amy's alive. I'm not starting another hide-and-seek session with this man. This is war, and it's going to be nasty—bloody too, if that's what it takes to end this. After six years, I know there's no other option with Sheridan.

The shower comes on and it hits me that I am standing

around in a towel, a dangerous way to be when we need to be ready to leave at any moment. I quickly dress in faded jeans and a black Coca-Cola T-shirt the kid at Walmart picked out for me. Tomorrow we'll be able to tap into my many resources. Gia will have a proper fake ID, and we'll be staying in a much nicer hotel room that includes two beds, not one to share—tonight is going to be interesting.

The shower turns off and I sit down on the bed, setting the alarm on my phone for five hours from now. As much as I want to get to Denver and Amy, my body is going to force me to sleep, and I can't risk making stupid mistakes out of exhaustion. The wall-mounted blow dryer in the bathroom turns on and I grab the phone book, looking for the closest car dealer and typing the address into my phone. By the time I'm done and leaning against the headboard, my booted ankles crossed on the mattress, the bathroom door opens and Gia appears.

She's dressed in a simple black sleeveless dress, and her dark brown hair has been dried straight and sleek, falling around her slender shoulders. Her face is clean of blood and mascara, her skin pale and beautiful, a hint of pink on her lips that she must have found in the Walmart stock, but her eyes are bloodshot, the look in them tentative, perhaps tormented.

Fidgeting, she runs her hands down her hips. "The bags

actually had some makeup and a few hair products. I was shocked."

"Nothing I'm sure you'd pick on your own."

"Beggars can't be choosers," she says, clearly meaning to fill the awkward space, but still I get the impression she isn't cowering from our obviously difficult sleeping arrangements. She's tough, and yet somehow still feminine.

"Twenty-four hours from now you can shop for yourself, and we won't be sharing a lumpy bed."

"Where will we be in twenty-four hours?"

"You know I'm not going to tell you that." I scoot over and pat the bed. "Come here."

Her brows lift. "Right there. To that spot."

"That's right. To this spot."

"Will it do me any good to argue?"

"You either get me up close and personal, or you get tied up again. I don't want to do that to you."

She inhales and walks toward me, tentatively sitting down on the bed. Before she even fully settles, I grab her and lay us both down, curling around her, one of my legs wrapped around hers. My arm comes down over the top of her and I scoot in closer, molding our bodies together so well that if she moves a muscle, I'll know.

"Go to sleep," I order near her ear, her freshly washed hair a silky tease against my cheek.

"The light is on."

"The sun is coming up anyway."

She's silent a beat. "Most men would have—"

"Don't fool yourself, Gia. I'm not a good guy. I never was, and I never will be. Now. Do as I say. Go to sleep."

SIX

ONE MINUTE I'M LISTENING to Gia's soft, steady breathing, and the next I'm fading into sleep and with it, the memory of six years ago, in vivid, damning detail, the scent of smoke teasing my nostrils.

I burst through the door of the house, screaming, "Mom! Dad! Lara!" and immediately I'm consumed by smoke, my lungs convulsing in protest. Coughing, eyes burning, I use my shirt to cover my face, fear for my family sending adrenaline shooting through me, making me shake. Sprinting forward, I cross through the kitchen—no fire in sight, and I know that means it's all on the upper level. Rounding the corner, I reach the bottom of the stairs and see that flames cover the second floor landing. I launch myself up the stairs. "Mom! Dad!"

"Chad! Chad!"

The sound of my mother's voice is a relief, but the flames that greet me as I turn right toward her voice in the hallway blast me with heat. Panic overwhelms me. I can't get to her. There are too many flames. "Mom! Mom, you have to go out the window!"

"I can't! It's covered in flames. Save Lara! Get Lara out of here."

"Get something to cover yourself and go through the flames."

"I can't leave your father."

My gut knots at her words. "What's wrong with Dad?"

"He hit his head. Just get Lara out of here! I'll figure this out."

Tears burn my eyes, and not just from the smoke—I'm not sure my parents are making it out of this. Coughing, I cover my face and turn to the left, racing forward and around the corner, praying I can rescue my sister, but it's impossible. Flames cover her doorway, eating a path toward me.

"Lara!" I shout, my voice raspy with smoke and desperation. "Lara!"

My mother's bloodcurdling scream pierces the air and it's like a sword slicing me in two. "Mom! Mom!" I turn back toward my mother, rounding the corner and scanning for something, anything, to get me through the flames. There is nothing.

I'm shaking and coughing, and tears streak my cheeks because I know it's too late.

Lara's voice is a hard jolt as she screams, "Mom! Mom!"

Lara's alive. She's alive, and I'm keeping her that way. I turn back toward her room, rushing forward. "Jump out the window, Lara!" I shout, stopping at the very edge of the flames. Could I run through them to get to her? "Jump now."

"Not without you and Mom and Dad!" she shouts back, sounding desperate.

"You see the flames, damn it!" I answer. "I can't get to you." Behind me, fire consumes the hallway I've just traveled, leaving me only one escape: the spare bedroom directly in front of me. "I'm going out another window. I'll meet you outside."

"Mom's okay?" Lara shouts. "Did Dad get to her? Did he get her out?"

"Goddamnit, Lara. How many times do I have to tell you to jump out the fucking window? I'm running out of time. Get out, so I can get out."

She screams and my heart stops beating a moment; the helplessness of not being able to get to her is gutting me. "Lara!"

"I'm okay. Just get them out, Chad. Please. All of you get out."

"Jump!" I shout, heat licking at my back. "Jump, damn it!"

"What about Mom and Dad?" she stubbornly shouts back.

"Do what I say, Lara," I yell fiercely. "Jump!"

The sound of my mother's scream rips through the air again and I ball my fists at the agony in the high, pained sound, knowing that she's dying. Knowing that I can't get to her.

"Mom!" Lara screams. "Mom!"

Flames encroach on me and I'm out of time. "Jump now, Lara!" I shout, my voice guttural and fierce as I shove open the bedroom door and go for the window, hoping I can get to her and my parents from the roof.

"Chad. Chad! Wake up."

My eyes open and the motel room comes back to me. I'm squeezing Gia so tightly that I don't know how she's breathing. I'm barely breathing. I ease my hold on her. "Shit. Did I hurt you?"

"No, you just scared me. I was worried about you."

I release her and sit up, grabbing my head and willing away the scent of smoke that I can't seem to escape and the echoes of my mother's screams—those damn gut-wrenching screams. Made worse by that bitch named Guilt who lives in my head and laughs like a wicked madwoman at the effort I make to shut her out.

Beside me, the bed shifts, and Gia scoots closer to me, her leg pressed to mine, her hand coming down on my back. "Are you okay?"

"No," I growl roughly, irritated at the way she gets under

my skin, the way she seems to magnify every sensation in my body. "I *am not* fucking okay."

"I have nightmares. I understand."

I snap, turning on her, pressing her to the mattress, holding her hands by her head like I'd done before. "That wasn't just a nightmare. It was a memory. I was in my burning house, listening to my mother scream as she burned alive and I couldn't do anything about it. I couldn't get to her."

"Your sister was in the house?"

"Yes. Amy was there. But she was Lara then. She thankfully survived the fire and I had someone help me hide her. Then I left her alone, or thinking she was alone. She doesn't know I'm alive." More guilt burns through me and I release her and stand to pace the room, cursing the beam of sunlight coming through a tiny gap in the curtains that irritates me for no logical reason, wishing for the darkness that an adrenaline rush gives me. But all I have is this tiny room and the memory of my mother screaming. At least my father didn't know what happened to him, or her. I press my fists into the wall, letting my head fall forward and fighting the urge to punch a hole in the damn thing.

"Chad."

Gia's voice, directly behind me, radiates through me, and with it unwelcomed white-hot need. Desire. *Lust.* I tell myself that it's wrong. She's wrong for me, and yet for some damnable reason I can't begin to understand, this woman feels right in a way that nothing else has in a long time. Every muscle in my body tenses in anticipation of her touch, and the moment her hand comes down on my back, that blast of adrenaline I desperately need burns through me.

I grab her and pull her in front of me, stepping into her, my legs framing hers, my hands on her waist, fingers flexing into the soft flesh there. And when she looks up at me, I see none of the blame I feel toward myself. The understanding that I didn't think she could have is there.

And she's here.

Not offering words of sympathy that do me no good— offering herself. I see it in her eyes, her desire matching mine, and even if I believed she was still loyal to Sheridan, which I don't, I'm not sure I would care.

Wrapping my hand around her neck, I pull her to me, flattening her body against mine, bringing her mouth a breath away from the next kiss I've denied myself too long. "I don't care who's going to hate who later. I just want to fuck you."

She curls her fingers around my shirt. "Then stop talking and do it."

"You can't handle this part of me."

Her chin lifts defiantly. "Try me."

"Be careful what you ask for. You might get it."

"If you're trying to scare me, it won't work. In fact, it might make me want it more. Just like you want to escape your memories, I have a few of my own I'd like to forget right now."

That's all the encouragement I need. My mouth slants over hers, tongue pressing past her lips, and the heady taste of her, all sweet honey and temptation, fills my senses. I deepen the kiss, drinking her in like a drug I cannot get enough of. But she is more than a drug. She is now in my care, and I cannot, will not, let her die because later she might be looking for a rush or a high that I'm not around to give her. But I'm here now, and I have this oddly possessive, entirely selfish need to be the person who gives her that escape, who shows her what I sense she's never known: complete, utter sexual overload that leaves no room for anything else. The very idea has me deepening the kiss, licking into her mouth and demanding more. And when that soft, sweet tongue of hers, so innocent in its response, tries to match my command, it drives me wild.

A low, raw growl escapes my throat and I turn her to face the wall, forcing her to hold herself up with her hands. For a moment I feel the pain of that nightmare, and I wonder why I never used Meg as an escape, why I always contained who, and what, I am . . . but this woman is different. Reaching for her dress, I yank it up her hips to find her backside bare but for a thong with a happy face on it. She glances over her shoulder, offering a breathless, embarrassed explanation. "I didn't pick it."

"Good. I don't like it." I rip it away, leaving her gasping as I pull the dress over her head and toss it aside to find her braless, before stepping toward her. My hands cover her breasts, fingers teasing her nipples. Leaning into her, my lips near her ear, I say, "I'm going to own you before this is over."

"You can try," she says, the rebellious reply defying the inexperience and innocence I sense in her, an innocence that I now realize I never truly sensed in Meg.

That she has this courage speaks of strength, of being a survivor, and it heats my blood and makes me want her all the more. It drives me to show her just how wrong she is, how easily I *can* own her. I tell myself it's a lesson she needs to learn for her own good—but who am I fooling?

I want to fuck her. Right here and now, I *want* to own her. I need the rush of it, the control, the high I've denied myself during the entire Meg façade of reforming my ways.

Covering her hands with mine, I slide them upward, pressing them together over her head. Again, I lean in close to her, my lips grazing her neck, her ear. "I'll do more than try," I promise. "As long as we're in this room, I'm in control. I'm your Master." I tighten my grip on her hands. "I'm going to let go of you, but you will not move."

"If I do?" she asks, and I know she's pushing me, driving me to take her someplace that can be dangerous in other places, at other times, with someone else.

"There's a price."

"I don't understand. What price?"

My hands travel down her arms, and curve around her body to cup her breasts again, my fingers tugging roughly on her nipples and then twisting. A sound of one part pain, one part pleasure, escapes her lips. "Now do you understand?"

"Yes," she pants.

But she doesn't, and I suddenly realize how very dangerous that is. My sister damn sure didn't understand, or she never would have gone to work for a museum and put herself back on Sheridan's map. Gia needs to learn about keeping her guard up, and she needs to learn now.

Tangling my fingers in her hair, rough by intention, I pull her head back, dragging her mouth to mine. "I keep telling you that you don't understand, but you will." I kiss her, hard, deep, fast, before punishing her with a nip of my teeth on her lip that makes her yelp. "That's for trusting me when you shouldn't," I add vehemently. "If I were someone else—"

"But you aren't."

I grit my teeth, conflicted by how much I want her trust, how much I want to deserve it, and how much I fear that

I'm setting her up to give it when she should not. "Don't move your hands," I order gruffly, deciding that actions speak louder than words. "Understood?"

"Yes," she whispers.

Releasing her, I undress, my cock thick, hard, and throbbing with my need to be inside her, but she isn't one of the many fuck buddies that came before Meg, and my initial need to bury myself inside her is shifting rapidly to anger. I know I won't hurt her, but she doesn't. She can't. I'm a stranger, and she needs to learn the price of trusting anyone, especially when Sheridan is involved. I grab the one condom I have on me out of my wallet, roll it over my shaft, and then put my pants back on, the zipper down.

Returning to Gia, I squat at her feet, my fingers wrapping around her slender ankles, lingering there. And lingering some more. Waiting, waiting, and as I expect, she looks over her shoulder. "Face forward," I command and she tenses, but obeys. Intentionally, I stay just as I am, letting seconds tick by, ensuring that she feels my eyes once again raking over her naked body. Lingering, letting her feel vulnerable when she is safe, fighting a need to give her one last memory in her life that is without fear. We don't have that luxury. She doesn't have that luxury.

When I am certain she has waited long enough to feel every touch magnified, I allow my thumbs to lazily stroke her ankles. She stiffens but almost instantly softens, my cue to inch my way upward, caressing her calves. Moving onward I find the back of her knees, where my thumbs linger again, and finally I use my knee to urge her legs to part. "Open," I order. She starts to turn and I warn, "Don't."

She sucks in a heavy breath and sets her legs in a *V*. I cup her thighs just above her knees, still using my thumb as a seductive tool. Finally, I explore the lines between her inner thighs, using a teasing touch that doesn't stop until I almost reach the sweet spots in the *V* of her body. But I don't go there.

I want to. Hell yeah, I want to go there, but it's not time. Instead, I trail both index fingers over the curve of her gorgeous, heart-shaped ass. And the instant I travel upward, traveling the crevice of her cheeks, she gasps, shifting slightly, her hands starting to drop. I'm on my feet before she's fully moved, leaning into her, covering her hands with mine.

"Now you pay the price," I promise, and with the tie to the curtain still in the bathroom, I improvise, reaching down to pull my belt free from its loops. Still anchoring her body with mine, one hand holding her hands in place, I quickly wrap it around her wrists.

"What are you doing?" she demands, sounding panicked, uncertain, exactly what I'd expected, planning to make this lesson short and exact, moving on to the adrenaline rush, the pleasure.

"Consequences," I reply, tightening the belt and buckling it. "Making sure you remember that every decision you make has them." Still shackling her wrists, my free hand flattens on her bare belly, my fingers splaying wide, my lips brushing her ear as I add, "And now I can do whatever I want to you, and you can't stop me. Are you scared?"

"Do you want me to be?"

"Answer the question. Are you scared?"

She inhales and lets it out. "Nervous."

Nervous isn't scared. That isn't good enough. For just a few minutes, I need her to feel panic, to see what poison trust can deliver. I cup her backside with both hands, tightening my thighs around her thighs. "I'm going to spank you."

"What? No. No, I—"

"Then I'll fuck you."

"No, Chad."

"Yes, Gia. I'm going to step back and fully undress. If you move, I'll spank you the second you do."

"I'm going to move," she assures me.

"Then I'm going to spank you. It's your choice. I told you not to trust me."

"So you're going to prove I shouldn't. Is that it?"

I ignore the question. "Have you ever been spanked?"

"No, I haven't, and I don't want to change that."

"You might be surprised by how damn sexy and thrilling it is."

"Say that when someone spanks *you*."

Once again, I find myself smiling, which is pretty fucking amazing. I squeeze her cheeks. "I'm going to undress now, Gia. Remember my warning."

I step away and shove my pants down, and the instant I do, she turns. I'm back on her before she escapes, turning her back to the wall, locking my legs around hers. "Chad—" she hisses, but I cut her off.

"Don't object, or fight it," I say, cupping her backside and massaging it, warming her skin for what's to come. "It'll only make it worse."

"Chad," she pleads.

"What are you thinking right now?"

"That you're an asshole."

"What else?"

"That you're naked, and I don't know why I'm aroused and still want you, when you're such an asshole."

My lips quirk. "What else?"

"I can't think. I can't think!"

"That's what this is all about. It's the escape. There's

nothing else but you and me and here and now. And you know what I'm thinking? About fucking you. About being inside you and feeling how hot and wet and tight you are. Nothing else. But first I'm going to spank you."

"I . . . but is it going to hurt?"

"A tiny sting." I lean in and nuzzle her neck. "This is just about you and me and pleasure. I'm not going to hurt you. Okay?"

"Yes," she whispers. "Yes, okay."

I move to her side, viewing her profile, my cock resting at her hip and belly, one leg in front of her, the other in the back. Her bound wrists rest in front of her chest and I don't move them, to give her the leverage of the wall when I spank her. One of my hands flattens on her belly, the other goes to her head, forcing her to look at me. "Now is the time you need to trust me."

"Ironic, now that I really don't have a choice, do I?"

"I'm not going to hurt you," I repeat, sealing the promise with a brush of lips against lips, my tongue caressing past her teeth, licking into her mouth in a gentle seduction meant to echo my words, meant to calm her nerves and excite her arousal, to erase her fear. "You even taste stubborn," I murmur, sliding my fingers between her legs, lightly teasing her clit. "*Don't* trust. That's the rule you need to learn. No more. No one. Ever. The one time I did, I ended up tied to a chair."

"I can't live that way."

"You don't have a choice." I squeeze her backside, then command, "Don't trust *anyone*." Not giving her time to argue, I slide my fingers between her legs, into the slick heat of her body. She gasps and then moans. "You're wet," I observe, desire thickening my blood right along with my cock. "You're about to be wetter."

"What does that mean?"

I dip my fingers lower, deeper, distracting her and intentionally shocking her. I slap her backside, not hard, not even close to what I would do in an erotic game, but it's a message. It's about possibilities, about open doors she can never shut again, and I don't stop at one. I repeat the action. Another smack, and another, until I reach five. When I'm done, she is panting, and my fingers take over, stroking her, teasing her until she shatters for me, her body quaking with the impact.

I bring her down, waiting until she slumps slightly, moving between her and the wall, fitting my cock between her thighs, and laying her on top of me. She buries her face in my shoulder and I press my hands to the side of her face, tilting her face forward. Her cheeks are flushed, but it's her glassy eyes that do me in, that make my intentions waver. "Tell me I didn't hurt you."

"No. No, it wasn't pain. It was . . . I was helpless . . . vulnerable and . . ." Her voice trails off, the red in her cheeks darkening.

"And what?" I press.

"Exposed, and yet aroused. I was turned on, and I don't even understand why."

"Because it's sexy, baby. You have no idea how much I want to be inside you right now, but you need to understand the message I was sending you. I wouldn't do anything but please you, but someone else might not be so nice. You can't take risks, no matter what the circumstances are. Don't trust."

"Does that still include you?"

"Yes. I'm toxic, Gia. I will bleed poison into your life. I'm going to get you to safety, but then I'm gone."

"That's why you hid from your sister."

"Yes."

She studies me a long few moments, searching my face, and there is a shift between us, a spike of passion, a darkening of the mood in the most erotic of ways. "Untie me," she says. "I need to touch you. I *need* to touch you, Chad."

A rush of wild emotions beats on me from all directions. I feel responsible for her. I feel the impact of the decision I made years ago, and how it's bled into her life. My fingers flex on her face. "Tell me you understand first," I demand.

"More than you can imagine," she whispers, and I don't know what it means. I want to know what I sense she's hiding.

"Untie me," she repeats. "Please. And yes, *please* means please do all those things you said to me before. Please make me scream your name. Please make me never forget who you are."

Her words crash over me, stirring more of those dark emotions I'd awoken with, and that I live with every day of my life. I kiss her, and it's deep, passionate, tense with all the emotions I've suppressed since waking up from that nightmare raging to the surface. The only means to my relief is this woman.

I tear my mouth away from hers, and for a moment, we just stare at each other, and I don't know what it is that's between us but it's far more real than anything I've felt outside of pain in a very long time. I reach between us and unbuckle the belt, quickly loosening it and tossing it away. The instant it's gone, we are kissing again, her fingers delicate, soft and warm on my skin, and yet somehow as demanding as I feel.

My fingers close around her neck, under her hair, and I pull her mouth to mine harder, kissing her, consuming her, and finally I am touching her freely, exploring her body, her breasts, her nipples. I turn our bodies so her back is now against the wall, lifting her leg, sliding my cock along her core and pressing into her. Driving deep. Hard. Burying myself in the farthest part of her. Our eyes lock and hold, and the shift between us, that connection I've felt ever since she walked into the interrogation room, blossoms and grows. There is heat in my blood, heat in my chest that I do not want to feel. But it's here, alive, real, and it stretches between us, a tight band of desire that snaps.

Suddenly, we are kissing again, and I grab her backside and pick her up. Her legs curl around my waist and I carry her to the mattress, laying her down, going down on top of her. And then I am driving into her, pumping and thrusting, my hand still under her, arching her into me. *Fucking*. We are fucking, and it's that wild, primal, animalistic rush that I need, that she needs. And she's making these soft, sexy sounds that drive me insane but they travel through me, too, whispering in a way no other woman's soft sounds ever have. I'm fucking her, trying to get to that dark, oblivious place where the woman doesn't matter, only the sex does. But I can't. I pull back slightly, burying my face in her neck, forcing my body to slow down, to calm. Inhaling deeply, I slow down to allow her to get to the same place I am.

I cup her breasts, licking her nipples, sucking and teasing. I kiss her neck, her ear, her shoulder. Her fingers tangle roughly in my hair and a soft, desperate plea of "Chad," follows. It's then that I kiss her again, then that I drive back into her, and there's a new edge burning between us. We are grinding and touching and practically trying to get under each other's skins.

Too soon, it seems, she digs her fingernails into my back and tenses. A second later, she spasms around me, milking my cock, and I drive into her one last time and explode, shaking with the intensity of my release. Time floats away, and I am spiraling into that sweet oblivion that is the moments after great sex.

Slowly, I come back to the room, to Gia, to the natural scent of her that is pure, sexy woman. The feel of her beneath me makes me not want to get up, and that's when I know this was more than a fuck session. And that's not only new to me, it's trouble. Forcing myself to pull out of her, I stand up, not looking at her as I turn away, snatching up my jeans and walking to the bathroom. I rid myself of the condom in the toilet and lean on the wall, trying to figure out what the hell is wrong with me.

I just met this woman. I can't have an attachment to her. I won't. I don't. I push off the wall and put on my pants, walking into the bedroom.

Gia's standing by the wall we fucked against; her back to me, her naked, gorgeous backside in full view as she tugs the dress over her head. But it's not her gorgeous body that does me in. It's the tension radiating off her, slamming into me. It twists me in knots, punches me in the chest. *Fuck!*

I go to her, grasping her elbow and turning her to face me. "Are you okay?"

She laughs nervously, her cheeks flushing pink. "You stripped away every reserve I own and then told me that I can never be that vulnerable ever again in my life. Of course I'm okay."

Sarcasm. Nerves. I'm coming to know this pattern. "This, us, fucking like we did, it was an escape for both of us."

"Right. I get it. And the lesson of it all was that the next time I get naked with a man, he could tie me up and hurt me. Have a gun handy."

The idea of her having sex with another man sits uncomfortably in my chest, and I don't like it. She isn't mine and she never will be. "Sex is a necessity of life," I say. "It's going to happen. Be cautious. Be aware. And don't turn it into a relationship. When someone works themselves beneath your defenses, you're in trouble."

"Is that what happened to you?"

My walls slide into place and I release her. "If you have pants that fit and tennis shoes, change. We're going to be walking a few miles." I turn away from her, grabbing my shirt and tugging it over my head.

"Chad," she whispers.

"I've made a lot of mistakes, Gia, all with consequences others have paid for." Turning to face her, I add, "And you aren't going to be one of them. Go change." When she doesn't move, I want to go to her. I know I have to make sure that's not an option. "I am that guy you accused me of being. I will do just about anything for a rush, and cash. You stay around too long, I might sell you. *If* the price is right."

She pales, her shoulders slumping as if I've punched her, before she rushes to the bathroom and shuts the door. And it takes everything in me not to punch the wall.

SEVEN

FIFTEEN MINUTES LATER, I eye the clock on the nightstand that reads 11 a.m. and curse myself for being a good hour behind my planned departure time. Eager to get packed up and out of this rat trap, I secure my gun in my ankle holster and try Jared again. I'm listening to it ring, ready to throw the phone against the wall, when I hear the bathroom door. Glancing up, I find Gia standing at the end of the bed, her long brown hair brushed sleekly again, her lips glossed, and if I'm not mistaken she has on some makeup. She's wearing black jeans and a red Mickey Mouse T-shirt with red Keds, or whatever the hell they're called, to match. I'm struck by two things. She looks completely different and still adorably, impossibly sexy. What the hell is the deal with the shirt?

"Fuck me," I grumble, removing the phone from my ear and discarding it. "Did the kid just want you to silently scream for everyone to look at you? Is there any other option in the Walmart bag?"

She folds her arms in front of her, and I don't miss how carefully she avoids eye contact as she says, "There seems to be a fictional-character theme that includes neon green and hot pink."

"Of course there is," I say, regretting the large bills I handed the kid to avoid a high-profile, drawn-out checkout. "Put a hoodie over the top." I toss an empty duffel in her direction. "And put whatever you want to take inside that. Keep in mind that you can shop for better choices when we get to where we're going and get settled."

Her gaze meets mine, and the vulnerability of the woman I'd bound and fucked, or even the woman who'd darted into that bathroom, is nowhere to be found. This one is coolly reserved, absolutely composed. "Which will be when?"

"We'll arrive late tonight if things go right."

She studies me for a beat, then another, and I think she will ask the obvious question, but she does not. Instead, she simply walks into the bathroom and quickly returns with the Walmart bags in one hand and the hoodie in the other. She sets the bags on the bed and slips the hoodie over her head before picking through the purchased items and choosing a few things to stuff in the duffel.

"Done," she declares.

I toss the small cash bag on the bed in front of her in obvious invitation for her to take it. She looks at it, and then me. "Aren't you afraid I'll run? You did tell me that you'd sell me if you got the chance."

"Rest assured, you're of more value with me than not, right now. I told you, you're helping me take down Sheridan." I step closer, bringing us toe-to-toe, giving a cue at how badly I want to pull her to me and fuck her all over again. "You try to run, *I will* come after you."

"I have no doubt," she replies tightly, and there is a new detached coldness to her voice that tells me my promise to sell her if I got a whim to didn't sit well. It puts a distance between us that should please me, but it doesn't.

"Then we're clear," I state.

"Crystal," she confirms.

Neither of us looks away, and what ensues is a battle of wills mixed with enough sexual heat to have me ready to say screw it and strip her naked again. And *that* would be yet another mistake I can't afford. Gritting my teeth, I grab the one duffel bag I'm taking with us. "Let's go," I snap, walking to the door and opening it.

She doesn't move. "Where are we going on foot?"

"You'll find out when we get there."

"Right. Of course." She closes the distance between us, surprising me by stopping in front of me, her blue eyes burning into mine. "Just so you know. That lesson you wanted to teach me. Learned."

I told her not to trust anyone, including me. For a man who likes to get his way, success sure bites, like a bitch on too much caffeine and sugar.

Following her outside the door, I note that the year-round warm Texas weather is leaning toward hot. Putting on my baseball cap, I say, "No one would wear a hood on a sticky day like this. Stuff your hair under the back of the hoodie so it's not obvious you have long hair."

She does as I say while I pull the door shut and motion her forward. We start walking and she crosses the strap of the duffel bag over her chest and shoulder, while I do the same with mine. Gia goes to my right, next to the highway, and I grab her arm and pull her to my left, where she's safer. She folds her arms over her chest and keeps walking.

We walk a short path along the highway and then enter a row of stores and restaurants. "We'll get food when we get back on the road. I don't want to risk being recognized."

"Understood," she says, still staring straight ahead. "I guess I can't ask how we're getting back on the road, so I won't."

I motion to a shithole car lot next to a hamburger joint. "There's your answer."

"We're buying a car?" She stops walking and faces me.

"I have a plan for everything, remember?" I take her arm, telling myself it's out of the need for urgency, not the need to touch her again. "We're out in the open. We need to move." I start walking, taking her with me. She double-steps to keep up and we cross the parking lot of the restaurant. "Keep your head down," I say as we pass several people exiting a car in the lot.

"Can Sheridan's reach really be so far that he can get to us on the street?"

I keep it straightforward and honest. "Yes."

"That's it?"

"Money won't bring back the ones you love, but it can do a lot to destroy those you don't." We reach the edge of the car lot and I lift a rope with flags hanging on it for her to slide under. She darts underneath and I follow, an uneasiness coming over me that has me stopping and scanning the area for trouble.

"What is it?" she asks, looking around as well, not nearly as discreetly as I am.

I grab her hand and walk briskly toward the back of the small, gray concrete building that's no bigger than the double-wide trailers so popular in parts of Texas. Scanning as we round the corner, I stop, backing against the wall where I have a bird's-eye view of the entire perimeter and pull Gia flat against me.

Glancing over her shoulder, my gaze travels to the other side of the lot, where a grandpa in a polyester suit and cowboy boots who I assume to be a salesman is chatting it up with a middle-aged couple in jeans and flip flops. The salesman seems to sense my attention and waves. "I'll be right with you."

I give him a wave in return and fix my gaze on Gia, my voice tight, my jaw tense. "Don't ever make it obvious that you're looking for signs of trouble. That draws attention you don't need."

Her fingers curl in my shirt. "You think there's trouble?"

"I'm always cautious," I say, choosing not to tell her that the hair on the back of my neck is standing on end. "And you need to be, too."

"That's not an answer."

"Talk later in the truck. Not now." I turn her to face the lot, hands on her shoulders. "The basic white one in the corner. Tell me why I'm picking that truck?"

"It's the only big truck on the lot, and you like big trucks."

I rotate her to face me again. "This is a lesson. Everything is a lesson, and it's about life or death. Texas is truck country. In other words, it's easy to blend in with a truck. The repeating theme of my message being *don't stand out*."

She sucks in a breath and lets it out. "Right. Don't stand out. I'll learn."

"You need to learn quickly."

"I know, and I'm sure it gets easier."

"You can't let it get easier. If it does, you'll make mistakes, so make sure it doesn't. And after six years, I know from experience that making sure it doesn't takes a concerted effort. You will be tempted to feel like the storm has passed."

"You keep mentioning six years." Her hands close down on my upper arms, her voice going raspy. "What happened six years ago?"

I arch a brow, aware of the salesman's approach, while Gia seems oblivious. "You didn't know it was that long?"

"That long since what?"

"Since that bastard killed my parents. And Gia—"

"Six years," she repeats. "Chad—"

"Sorry about the delay." The sound of the salesman's voice is my cue to wrap my arm around Gia's shoulder and turn us to greet him as he adds, "Can I help you folks?"

"I'll take that white truck in the corner."

The man's brow furrows. "You mean you want to test drive it?"

"No," I correct. "We'll take it. How much?"

"Five thousand."

"I'll make it six if you can get us out of here in fifteen minutes." His eyes go wide, and I quickly explain away any suspicions I've created. "We were headed to Austin to get my sister away from her dickhead husband who beats her, but my BMW broke down. The part for the repair won't be in for a week, and I'd counted on beating that man's ass by sundown."

He arches a brow. "You carry around that much cash?"

"Asshole is a computer programmer with some hacking skills, and my sister is scared shitless of the bastard. I'm making her throw away her credit cards and stay off his radar while I deal with him. This will deplete that money, but I'll replace it when we get to her."

Gia surprises me by adding, "He's horrible." She presses her fingers to her eyes. "She and I are like sisters. I'm sorry. I'm scared for her."

"Oh, honey," the man says, clearly convinced and sympathetic, and I don't blame him; she's practically sold me on the story. "Ain't nothing I hate more than a woman-beater. I'll get you out of here in fifteen, and you keep that extra thousand." He opens the door and waves us inside.

My hand goes to Gia's waist, guiding her into the building, and while I don't like people at my back, the old man included, I like them at Gia's even less. I just hope like hell that acting performance she gave doesn't mean I'm one step away from a knife in my back that she's holding. Following her down a narrow hallway, we enter a bullpen-style office setup with two steel desks, one on each side of the door, facing the plate-glass windowed front wall that gives me a full view of the lot.

In unison, Gia and I step inside the door to the right and let the salesman pass by. He steps behind the desk on the left and opens a drawer while Gia surprises me by asking, "Is there a ladies' room?"

"That door we just passed in the hallway," the man offers.

I give her a warning look, and my eyes narrow at how bloodshot her eyes are. "What are you doing?" I ask softly, wondering how the woman who didn't even know why I picked a truck became this one.

She steps to me and flattens her hands on my chest, kissing my cheek. "Breaking down and needing this truck has me flustered. I just a need a minute."

I grab her head and lean in near her ear. "Don't try to play me. You won't like the results. I'll be watching the door."

"Good," she replies. "I really don't want to be alone right now."

I want to know what that means, but she pulls back, and considering we have an audience, I have to let her. But I don't miss how her lashes are lowered to become an effective shield that leaves me incapable of reading her intentions. I allow her to escape.

"Okay," says the salesman, still standing behind his desk. "I have the paperwork and the keys." He offers me his hand. "I'm Jeff, by the way."

The bathroom door shuts, and I step forward and shake his hand. "Thanks for the help, Jeff," I say, leaving out my name, a habit I've perfected over the years.

"My pleasure." He releases my hand and motions for me to sit. I comply simply because it gives me a good view of the bathroom.

"I'll need identification and the cash."

Removing my wallet, I adjust my chair to profile the front window and the door Gia should exit from any second, laying the ID that reads "Kevin Moore" on the desk for Jeff to review. "The money after the contracts," I state.

"Not a problem." He glances at the ID. "Mr. Moore."

Ten minutes later, I've signed the contracts and we're about to exchange cash for keys, and Gia has yet to appear. A blue Chevy four-door sedan pulls into the lot and Jeff sighs. "That would be my wife with my lunch." He pushes to his feet. "Let me go get rid of her."

I follow him to his feet. "That's not necessary. We'll be leaving anyway. Let's count the cash."

He hesitates. "Counting money in front of my wife is a negative for me. I need to get rid of her. I'll be fast." He doesn't wait for an answer, heading for the door, but not before he snatches the damn keys. Cursing the delay, I walk to the bathroom door and knock. "Gia, we're leaving." She doesn't respond immediately and unease rolls through me. "Gia—"

The door swings open. "Sorry," she says, swiping hair behind her ear, her eyes bloodshot, skin pale. "I'm not feeling grand. Are we ready to go?"

Whatever is going on with her, I don't like it, but this isn't the time to figure it out. I grab her hand and lead her back into the front office, and scan for Jeff, who isn't anywhere to be found. Neither is his wife's car. A frisson of unease goes down my spine.

"Where's the salesman?" Gia asks.

"Good damn question," I murmur, walking behind the desk and opening drawers. "Bingo," I murmur, grabbing keys with a tag that reads "Blue Dodge." Walking to the window, I scan the cars and find no signs of life. I do find the Dodge, and it's sitting in the center of the lot, blocked in. "Fuck."

"What's happening?" Gia asks, moving to my side.

"Nothing good," I assure her, offering nothing more.

Focused not on her, but on getting us out of here alive. The back door gives me no visual. The front makes us targets, but the cars are lined up close to the exit, offering good coverage.

"They found us, didn't they?" she asks from beside me.

I reach down and remove my gun from the ankle holster, barely glancing at her as I instruct, "We're going out the front door and between the two cars to our right." I turn to face her. "You go first so I can cover you. Get down low and stay that way."

"Low," she agrees. "Happily."

"Now," I say, opening the door without giving her time to develop a case of nerves, or us time to end up trapped, if we aren't already.

She goes down low and darts forward, and I follow, unzipping my bag and holding my hand with the weapon inside, where it won't be seen, as I do. In what feels like about a hundred heartbeats, though it's more like ten, we are between the two cars.

"Keep going," I encourage, urging her to the next row of cars, and toward the rope that divides the lot from a McDonald's. If we were seen, it's the predictable way to go, which means we can't hesitate or we'll be toast.

Gia seems to understand as well, driving forward and under the rope. I follow and in unison, no words needed, we head to the row of parked cars and kneel between the first two. I check the locks on some sort of Jeep. She checks the doors on a pickup.

"Here," I say when mine opens, and wasting no time, she climbs inside the side door and scoots over, going low. Again I follow her, settling the bag between us, my gun at easy grip range. Praying the owner doesn't show up when we're in the car, I quickly yank the dash panel off and connect wires, bringing the engine to a start.

"Chad," Gia says urgently, and I glance up to find that two men wearing gloves, both Mexican, I think, with the hard edge of hired professionals, have just cleared the rope.

I put us in gear, back up, and hit the accelerator.

EIGHT

NEVER LOOKING BACK, I force myself to keep a steady foot on the Jeep's gas pedal rather than gunning the engine, trying not to stand out, my mind already processing the magnitude of target a stolen vehicle makes us in a fairly small city. Driving around the other side of the building, I exit onto the main road, and then my foot goes heavy as I pull away from the restaurant and weave in and out among several vehicles to gain some much needed coverage.

"What just happened?" Gia asks. "I went to the bathroom and—"

"Don't talk," I snap, trying to put this all together. Either Jeff screwed me or Gia screwed me, and Gia was in that bathroom a long damn time.

"Chad—"

"*Don't fucking talk*, Gia," I growl, pissed at the idea I've been stupid with her all over again. She must get that I'm serious, because she doesn't push. But I plan to, and soon. She can count on it. Detouring to the highway to get out of the immediate view of any cops looking for the Jeep, but knowing it's still a sore thumb, I have a destination I can't bypass. I also can't trust Gia with the location.

"Get down on the floorboard," I order.

"What? Why? Are we—"

"Just do it, Gia."

She inhales and does as I order, wisely keeping her mouth shut. I focus on the road, and ten miles later, I exit in an area that is heavily residential and take several turns to bring us smack into middle-class Lubbock, rows of basic houses side by side. Pulling up to a redbrick residence, I park at the curb.

"Don't ask," I say, sensing Gia is about to speak. I grab the duffel. "Let's go." I climb out of the Jeep and keep my hand in my bag, over my gun. Juan Carlos has reasons to be loyal to me, but that doesn't mean he's alone. I round the Jeep and meet her at her door, where she is looking exceedingly uncomfortable.

145

"What are we doing?" she asks.

"Calling in a favor," I say, closing my hand around her arm as I start walking.

"Then this is a friend?"

"I told you," I say as we stop at the front door, "I don't have friends." I ring the bell. "Just people less willing to fuck me over."

She glances at my hand on her arm and then at me. "Why are you so angry with me?"

"That is a conversation for another time."

"Please," she encourages. "I need some insight into the ever-changing playbook that is your mood."

The door is opened by a thin Mexican woman in jeans and a T-shirt. "*Hola*, Maria," I greet her. "Is Juan Carlos in?"

"He isn't expecting you. He doesn't do drop-ins."

"I'm certain if you tell him it's me, he'll be fine with the visit." She opens her mouth to argue and I toughen my voice and order, "Tell him I'm here."

She frowns but disappears, shutting the door. Without looking at Gia, I say, "It's your playbook we're going to discuss."

"Good. I need one of those."

I look at her then. "We both know you have one. You're going to open it to me."

"I told you I'll help you with Sheridan."

"Deflection will get you nowhere," I say.

"Deflection? What am I deflecting?"

Maria reappears. "Go to the backyard." She shuts the door on us, and I grab Gia's arm again and start walking.

"You know I'm not making a run for it, right?" she demands. "Where would I go?"

"Not a conversation for here and now." We cross the driveway, where a shiny new black Escalade is parked, and hit grass again as we travel to the back gate. I open it and pretty much set Gia in front of me, following her and shutting us inside.

"Chad—"

"Save it," I bite out, grabbing her arm again and walking toward a small building, a converted garage turned into an office, about a hundred feet away. At the door, I don't bother knocking. I simply open it and step inside, taking Gia with me and releasing my hold on her as I kick it shut.

Juan Carlos sits behind a fancy mahogany desk, his long dark hair in a ponytail, a scar down one cheek that I had the unfortunate experience of witnessing him receive. "Chad, my friend," he greets, standing and offering me his hand.

"Stay here," I murmur to Gia, stepping forward and shaking hands with him, as he adds, "I hope my sister wasn't too much of a bitch to you."

"She was just the right kind of bitch to protect you. How much did that Escalade out there run you?"

His hands settle on his jeans-clad hips, a ring carved with the Mayan sun symbol on his left hand, which I happen to know is invaluable. "A cool hundred Gs. Isn't she a beauty?"

"I'll buy her for a hundred and twenty Gs."

"What? No. I just brought it home. You need a vehicle, I'll get you a vehicle."

"I need it tonight. Now."

"This is why you came to me?"

"And I need documentation for the woman."

"That'll take time. I can get you a vehicle and the identity by tomorrow night."

"We both know your ID packets are done and ready to go."

"For a substantial upcharge. I don't want to charge you extra."

"Then don't."

"I'm a businessman."

"How much?"

"A hundred and fifty thousand for the identity."

I whistle. "That's steep."

"Wait until tomorrow night. I'll get you a car and a reduced fee."

"Tonight," I insist. "On credit, of course. You know I'm good for it."

"I also know you're always cheating death by one step."

Not about to argue that truth, I reach in the bag, grab a wad of cash and toss it onto the desk. "That's a down payment."

He glances down and seems to do a mental calculation before opening a drawer, flipping through folders, and choosing one. He sets it on top of the desk and opens it for me. I glance down at the Texas driver's license with a rather unattractive brunette female who's a stretch as Gia, with a name that reads "Ashley Woods." "When do we get her picture to replace this one?"

"Now." He grabs his cell phone and dials, speaking in Spanish to his sister before refocusing on me and confirming what I've already understood.

"Maria's headed over here to take her photo, which will replace the current ones in all public databases in about seventy-two hours. We'll need several different looks to ensure the effectiveness of the cover story. As you should know by now, your price includes a family history, college degree, and a track record that reaches all the way back to birth."

"Social Security card?"

"Of course. And a birth certificate. As always, you receive everything you need to make the person she is now disappear."

The door behind us opens and I shift to put Juan Carlos in profile as I watch Maria enter. She quickly moves behind the desk, giving us her back as she and Juan Carlos talk. I motion to Gia and she steps forward. "Thank you," she whispers.

"For what?"

"I couldn't have afforded to do this without you."

Ignoring the punch in my gut at the vulnerability of her words, I stiffen my spine, refusing to let down my guard with this woman. "I need you alive to help me. This was for me, not you."

A stunned look slides over her face, replacing the appreciative one of moments before. "I see."

"Good," I approve. "Then we're clear."

"No, nothing is clear at all—but then, maybe it never will be again." Her chin lifts in the now familiar way I've come to expect from her, an act of bravado she doesn't feel. Or maybe it's just an act, period. "What do I need to do?" she asks. "What's next?"

I grit my teeth at the bite of pain I sense in her words, and resist the stupid need to comfort her, taking her arm again, and turning her to face Maria and Juan Carlos. "She's all yours," I say, but the way Juan Carlos's eyes flicker over Gia, the interest in their depths, leaves me regretting those words.

Maria motions for Gia to follow her through a door, Juan Carlos behind them, and a wave of protectiveness overcomes me. It's laughable that I would feel such a thing about a woman who must have decided she couldn't manipulate me, so she'd just turn me back over to Sheridan to save herself. It's logical. It's what has to have happened, so fuck her and any discomfort she might feel in that other room. I even turn for the door before I stop dead in my tracks, cursing and crossing the small space between me and her, telling myself her safety is in my best interests—I'm simply protecting an asset in the war against Sheridan.

Entering the room, I find Gia sitting in a chair facing me while Maria brushes her hair, an array of make-up and hair tools everywhere. Gia's eyes meet mine, and the bond that I sense between us has me cursing again. It's not real, I remind myself, any more than the name on those IDs we're buying. Maria steps between us, breaking the spell of the moment, and I let out a breath I seem to be holding in. Leaning on the wall, Juan Carlos joins me, a camera in his hand as he waits on the women.

"Who is she to you?" he asks.

"Just another curve in the ever-winding path that is my life," I say, wishing it were that simple, somehow knowing it isn't.

"Who'd she piss off?"

"Me," I say.

"She got in the way of you and a prize, then."

"What's mine is mine," I confirm, embracing my reputation, "and right now, that includes her."

"Her?"

I throw a look at Juan Carlos. "That's right. She belongs to me. And so we're clear, there is no 'even' where she's concerned. You hear of anyone looking for her, I don't care what price they offer—you keep your mouth shut."

"I don't stay in business by running my mouth."

"We both know you like money."

He lifts his hand, indicating the ring. "I wear enough money on my left hand to leave any time I wish."

"I wondered about that. Why don't you?"

He laughs low and cynical. "A woman. Isn't it always? If I ever convince her I'm not a monster, maybe she'll actually run off with me."

"Indeed," I agree, thinking that's exactly what happened with Meg, and will happen with Gia too, if I let it. But what stands out in my mind are the words *a monster*. It's the way I imagine Amy will see me when she knows I caused all of this.

Maria motions to Juan Carlos, and I follow him toward the women. We hover over Gia, and she doesn't look at me or Juan Carlos. "Gia," I say softly, her gaze lifting to mine, and I see the uncertainty, the unease in her eyes, and somehow it's okay for me to put it there, but not anyone else. "We need to be on the road in fifteen minutes," I tell the group.

"Then let's get the first photo done for the driver's license," Juan Carlos says. "I'll get that document doctored while Maria takes a few for school records and things of that sort—unless you want to tell me the lady's real name, in which case I can hack her existing records."

Gia's eyes go wide and I answer, "No. Take the photos."

"Very well," he concedes, motioning for Maria to step back as he aims the camera at Gia, and says, "Smile, pretty lady." She doesn't smile. He doesn't seem to care. He shoots several photos and then waits for Maria to pull Gia's hair back and help her change her jacket.

After four clothing changes, I've had enough. "We're done," I say, pulling Gia to her feet and tugging some sort of red jacket off her shoulders as she whispers, "Thank goodness." I lace my fingers with hers and walk to the outer office to find Juan Carlos working at a computer. "Time's up," I tell him.

He rotates in his chair and hands me a folder. "Everything you need."

I take it from him. "Keys?"

He fishes them out of his pocket and hands them to me. I accept them and lead Gia to the exit, urging her outside as I pause and glance over my shoulder. "I left you a present at the curb. You should get rid of it quickly." I step outside and shut the door to the echo of his string of curse words.

Wordlessly, the air thick and awkward between us, Gia and I rush through the backyard and open the driver's-side door of the Escalade. Gia steps in front of me and climbs in the door, and damned if I don't get a nice, long view of her backside that I know is even better naked than in those jeans. I follow her inside and she settles on the floor.

"You don't want me to see how to get back here," she says as I start the engine.

"That's right," I confirm.

"You think I had something to do with what happened at the car dealer."

I back out of the driveway. "I told you, Gia. I can't afford to trust you."

"So I'm right. I didn't have a phone. And even if I did, if I really was working for Sheridan and this was all one big ploy to earn your trust, why would I call him to tell him where you were?"

I hit the brakes and put the vehicle in drive. I cut her a condemning look. "I guess you figured out that I won't be manipulated."

"And what? I wanted to go ahead and let him kill me for failing and get it over with?"

"Or you're naive enough to think helping him capture me again will save you. It won't." I hit the accelerator.

"I had no phone, Chad," she hisses.

"You were in that bathroom a long damn time, Gia."

"I told you—"

"You were feeling sick. You seem just fine now."

"I'm not you, asshole, and I don't know if I'll ever be fine again." I watch her turn to rest her back on the seat, curling her knees to her chest. "Maybe you should stop blaming what happened on me in time to stop it from happening to us again."

"There is no 'us' and you'd be smart to remember that," I reply sharply. But as I find my way back onto the highway, on edge, I replay her warning in my head. My mind retraces every second at that car dealership. I've lingered on Gia as the guilty party because those goons were on us too soon after the salesman exited for it to have been his doing. But even if Gia somehow had a phone, I'm not sure she had time to call Sheridan and have those men arrive that quickly, either. Over and over I replay the events, with something hard and sharp biting at the back of my mind. I shove it away. I deny it.

Two hours into the drive, we're continuing our way to Denver, crossing through New Mexico's high desert country, and my mind hasn't slowed down yet. Gia, however, is breathing deeply, somehow sleeping on the floorboard she never even tried to get up from. That sharp, biting possibility I've been fighting is making me crazy, making me want to crawl out of my own skin. Finally, after what seems like miles and miles of nothing, a secluded rest stop appears. I quickly pull off the road down a tree-lined path to find a deserted parking area that is nothing more than a dirt road with a wooden, cabin-like structure next to it.

Parking, I sit there behind the wheel, my nerves jumping, as Gia stretches. "Are we 'here,' wherever it is we're supposed to be going?"

I exit the Escalade without answering, slamming the door shut. By the time I round the hood, Gia is exiting as well. "Oh, good," she murmurs. "I really need a bathroom."

She's adorable, pretty, so damn innocent—which could all be a façade, only it doesn't fucking feel like one at all. I start walking toward the deserted building and she quickly catches up with me, taking the wooden steps to a porch that divides the men's and women's bathrooms.

Gia stops at the door to the women's restroom and faces me. "I guess we're double-teaming this again?"

I grab her and pull her to me. "Why were you in that bathroom?"

"I was weak. It all hit me and I started to cry. I'm not a crier. But I just—"

I kiss her, my fingers slicing into her hair, my tongue licking into her mouth. I need her. I need an escape, and I want nothing more than to yank her jeans down and fuck her right here, right now. She moans and wraps her arms around my neck, and I mold her close, trying to suppress what my mind is telling me. I lift her, my hands around her backside, carrying her into the bathroom.

As I shove her against the wall, our lips part and she whispers, "I hate that you hate me."

It's a jolt of reality that I need, and I set her down, turning away and leaning on the sink, my head dipped low, my breathing heavy. I do hate, but not Gia. I hate Sheridan, and Amy is going to hate *me*. *Amy*. I repeat her name in my head, willing her to be alive, and forcing myself to face what I've been avoiding. If Gia didn't call Sheridan and the salesman didn't either, that leaves only one option—and it's trouble.

Shoving off the sink, I remove the back of the cell phone, removing the SIM card and breaking it in half. Next I do the same with the phone, before walking into one of the stalls and flushing both down the toilet. Exiting I find Gia standing there, looking stunned. "What just happened?"

"I stopped blaming you. We need to go, and now." Her eyes go wide, and I close in on her, urging her out of the bathroom and down the steps. "Now," I say again, and she takes off running, with me on her heels. Inside the Escalade, I start the engine and back us the hell out of what could easily become a trap.

Pulling onto the highway, I am not pleased to see just how few vehicles are on the road, leaving us standing out like a sore thumb. "You think we were tracked through your phone," Gia states.

"Yes," I confirm. "I called from that number over and over, and didn't block my number."

"You think that means the person you've been calling betrayed you?"

My fingers tighten around the steering wheel. "No. I don't think he betrayed me."

"Oh." She pauses a moment, and adds, "This doesn't mean he's dead. It doesn't mean your sister isn't safe, either. It doesn't."

While her words are meant to offer comfort, I reject what will only make me weak and soft. "The only thing we know for certain is that you and I are alive, right here and now. Everything else is a question. And I do mean everything."

NINE

GIA AND I are two hours from Denver when I start grilling her, wanting to take advantage of anything she might have learned about Sheridan after a year of working for him. I have her describe every visitor, every employee, every interaction she had with anyone and everyone. I ask a ton of questions about anyone who might resemble Meg, but get no answer that makes me believe that Meg has visited Sheridan or communicated with him, when I know damn well that she did. Sheridan is too smart to make many mistakes, but too human not to make any.

By the time we hit the Denver city limits, I've stopped at a store to buy a phone and spent a good portion of time focusing my thoughts on a person of interest. A fortysomething, attractive blond woman who, per Gia's claims, started visiting Sheridan a month ago.

"They were intimate?" I ask. "You're sure?"

"Oh yes. Very sure."

"You saw them showing affection?"

"No. It was a vibe when they were together. A way that they looked at each other. The length of time they were behind closed doors together, often for hours."

"And you never knew who she worked for?"

"No, and I could never get to the sign-in register to find out who she was."

I arch a brow. "Why would you try?"

"Honestly? I don't know. There was just something about her that seemed odd."

"Odd. Okay. Did anyone else ever join their meetings?"

"Never. This isn't much help, is it?"

"It helps."

"But we don't know who she is."

"I'll find out."

We reach the exit that leads to Cherry Creek, the fast-developing area where I bought a number of investment properties years before—and the location where I've hidden

Amy—and I tell myself to pass it by. I'll be looked for here, but I can't seem to care. I exit and stare at the road, completely still and focused, but adrenaline pulses through me, my heartbeat pounding in my temples.

"Chad," Gia prods gently. "What's wrong?"

That she can read me so easily is a sign that she's slipped beneath the walls I've erected around myself. "Aside from the present delay," I say, stopping at a light, "who said anything is wrong?"

"Your mood. The exit. What am I sensing? Are we close to your sister?"

I cut her a look. "If my sister is where she's supposed to be, yes." The light changes and I turn to the left and down the street leading to what should be Amy's new apartment, but I keep going, passing it and the hotel directly across from it. I want to stop, but I have another destination in mind. "Stuff your hair in your jacket again," I order, grabbing the baseball cap and putting it on before taking another left.

"If you were betrayed, Chad, Sheridan could know where Amy is. Please tell me your plan isn't just to barge in and grab her. They could be waiting to grab you and her together."

"If Sheridan knew she was here, he'd already have her."

"You don't know that. Maybe she was a backup plan. We're both too tired to think through this clearly."

"There is no 'we.' "

"There *is* a 'we.' I'm here, and believe it or not, I put my life on the line for all of this."

I pull up in front of the Inn at Cherry Creek. "If he hasn't found her yet, I'm not wasting a moment that might let him. Grab your bag." I pop the door open and the doorman greets me, as does one on Gia's side. I give the man a nod, snag my duffel, and unzip it, palming him a large bill as I quietly say, "Keep my vehicle at the side of the building with the keys inside." He gives the tip a glance and his agreement is adamant and instant.

Gia rounds the hood of the vehicle and I lace my fingers with hers, leading her forward. "Chad—" she begins urgently.

"Kevin, while we're here," I tell her softly. "And you're Ashley, but I'd prefer you just not speak."

I don't have to turn to look at her as we enter the elegant boutique hotel's lobby to feel her glower. She steps in front of me, her palm flattening on my chest, and damn it, my skin burns beneath her touch. "What about a trap?"

I cover her hand with mine. "You're asking for attention we don't need. We'll talk upstairs."

Her expression tightens, but she steps to my side and we walk to the high marble counter.

"Good evening," the sixtysomething, gray-haired attendant offers.

Forsaken

Giving the man a nod, I pull my wallet from my jeans pocket, sliding a credit card and a fake ID onto the counter. "We'll be staying two nights."

"All we have available is the executive suite."

"Fine."

"The cost—"

"Is fine." I look him straight in the eye, letting him see the various bumps and bruises on my face. "And yes to everything you're going to offer. We had a car accident two days ago, and my wife is feeling under the weather. I'm eager to get her to a room, where she can rest."

The man's eyes widen and flicker to Gia. "I'm sorry, ma'am. We'll get you checked in quickly. I'm glad you're both okay."

"Thank you," Gia says, going along with the story. "I— *we*—do appreciate that."

I grimace at the jab but say nothing, and true to his word, in all of five minutes, the man has us on an elevator. Gia turns to me, and I to her.

I stare down at her, this woman, this stranger who could be an enemy, and while I do not want to be a fool, I don't believe that to be true anymore. And there is something about her and us I don't understand. I only know that whatever it is she stirs in me, it is raw and ripe with some kind of deep, cutting hurt, and yet somehow sweet, when I'd

163

thought nothing could ever be sweet again. She is also the only reason I detoured to a hotel before going to my sister's apartment.

"Chad, we—"

"Kevin," I remind her, lacing my fingers into her hair, and without conscious thought, I am pressing my mouth to hers, and for a moment there is just her, us, and a caress of lips that could so easily, *too easily*, turn to white-hot passion.

The elevator dings softly, destroying those few seconds of peace I'd found in Gia, and that I'd needed more than I'd realized. I lean back, refusing to look at her, refocusing on what is important, on why I needed that moment of peace, on the possibility that I may soon discover my sister isn't here.

Lacing my fingers with Gia's, I lead her with determined steps to the end of the hallway and open our door. The executive suite contains a living area with a flat-screen TV above a fireplace and a bedroom on either side.

"What is the plan?" Gia asks. "What are we doing?"

"*We* aren't doing anything. And you know the plan. I'm here to get my sister."

"*Now?* Where? How?"

"You know I'm not telling you that."

She makes a sound of frustration. "You have to have a plan that doesn't include charging in and grabbing her."

"I'm not grabbing her. I'm taking her to safety."

"Oh, God. You don't have a plan. I'm repeating myself here, but they could grab you and her together. Maybe that's the idea. Maybe they didn't have her, and they want her. Maybe they're following us."

"The only way that would happen is if you're involved, and I'm hoping like hell that's not true."

"I'm not involved, but that doesn't mean they aren't watching her. Maybe they left her free in case you escaped, or they planned to show you pictures or videos of her to threaten you, but you escaped before they could. Please, Chad. Think about this. Don't go and get killed."

"Because I'm all that's keeping you alive, right?"

She flinches. "Asshole. For your information, right now I feel like I'm the only thing keeping *you* alive."

I shrug and turn. "I'll be back."

"I'm going with you."

"Not a chance in hell."

I don't have time to argue with her. I drag her to the bathroom and shove her inside. "If I'm not back by the time the maids find you, I'm dead. Take that bag of cash strapped over your shoulder and the rest in the duffel I'm leaving behind, and get the hell out of here. I'm not taking the Escalade, so it'll be here if you need it. And don't scream to get attention. It might be the wrong kind of attention, the kind that gets us both killed."

"Don't do this," she demands, and I shut the door, grab a chair from the desk behind me, and shove it under the doorknob.

"I'll be back," I promise, silently swearing to myself that it will be with my sister by my side.

"Chad! Wait! I need to tell you something."

I pause. "Yes?"

She's silent several beats before she says, "Please don't get killed. Please come back."

The plea is desperate, passionate, as if she really does give a damn about me. And damn it to hell, it's hard to leave her behind, when I'm not sure I'll ever see her again.

WHEN I EXIT the hotel the doorman is quick to turn in my direction, but I hold up a hand, waving him and the use of the Escalade off. My walk through the high-end neighborhood is short. I travel a few blocks past little shops and a busy cross street filled with restaurants and a towering new high-rise under construction. This, like another half-dozen locations where I've acquired properties across the country, is meant to allow me the option of a safe haven if needed, while I slowly amass resources using the deeply disguised holding companies I've always known we'd need to stay off the radar of Sheridan and his cohorts.

With each step I take, I think of Amy. I haven't seen my sister, *really* seen her face-to-face, in six years. The idea of holding her and telling her that I love her has me shaking inside. The range of emotions we'll both feel if she's in the apartment I set up for her will be extreme and surreal, and while there will be relief and happiness for us both, I know her anger will come hard and fast. But I'll deal with it. If she's alive and well and I can touch her, hold her, if I can know she is safe, she can bust my chops all she wants. *Please be there*, I think. *Please be angry and give me hell.*

My heart races as I cover yet another block, and I start to relive that moment almost two months ago now when Jared called me from overseas. He'd intercepted chatter from Sheridan's camp that had made it clear that the job Amy had taken in a New York museum had attracted their attention and tied her to our past. I'd missed that communication myself, and I still don't know how. But Jared had found it, and he was too far away to help. That one problem had forced me to tell Meg about Amy for the first time. I wonder now if the timing was all a setup, a way to get me to expose Amy's location, but I refuse to believe Jared was involved.

My pace quickens, the certainty that I'm about to find

out if Amy survived my captivity turning seconds into what feels like hours. I enter the apartment complex foyer and skip the elevator, opting for the service stairs. I'm on the second floor in a flash, bursting through the doors and charging to the door that should be Amy's. I knock when I want to kick the door down. I knock some more until, with a shaking hand, I reach in my pocket and find the key I'd made years before. When I stick it inside the lock, it doesn't move.

Cursing under my breath, I dig in my pocket again and pull out a picking tool I'd grabbed from my bag somewhere in New Mexico and make fast work of opening the door. Before entering, I arm myself with my gun, and step forward. Shutting the door behind me, I stand there and listen for any noise, any sound that might tell me someone is here. I hear nothing. Not a damn thing. Inching forward, I bring the completely empty apartment into view. I'd had it furnished in case Amy needed it, but those items aren't here now, and neither is she. Where the hell is the furniture? Where the fuck is my sister?

I scan for clues, anything to tell me where Amy is, and my gaze catches on a note pinned to the wall. Rushing toward it, I stare at the plain white sheet of paper that contains only a typed phone number—as good as a ransom note.

I growl, pounding the wall over and over until my knuckles bleed. Time ceases to exist until I somehow come back to myself, to the room, and to my senses, and search the rest of the barren apartment. When I'm sure I'm alone, I shove my gun in the waistband of my jeans under my shirt and snatch my new phone that I picked up on our way to Denver, dialing the number typed on the piece of paper, pacing as the line rings. Once. Twice. Four times, and then a voice mail beep, with no outgoing message.

"Call me back, motherfucker," I order roughly. "And if you hurt one hair on my sister's head, I swear to you I'll scalp you and bring popcorn to snack on as I watch you bleed to death." Ending the call, I stand there, inhaling heavily, as if my sense of smell might tell me if my sister was ever here. Logic overcomes me and it hits me that smell can't, but neighbors could.

Aware that I'm in danger, practically inviting Sheridan to grab me again, I can't seem to give a damn. Even if Amy wasn't here, Meg would have told Sheridan that this is where I'd planned to take her.

Still. Don't. Give. A damn.

Exiting the apartment, I start knocking on doors, and two apartments down, a little old lady answers. The woman, who can barely remember what her own apartment number is, offers no help. I'm fucked.

Giving up this strategy, I take the stairs, exit the apartment building through the foyer, and cut to my left, stopping at a cell phone store. Hesitating only a moment, I decide a few stops will give me a chance to find out if I'm being followed. Quickly, I cross the road, hitting up the retailer for several more disposable phones, which I buy with yet another fake credit card and ID. I'm out of the door and walking again, taking a different route to the hotel than I'd followed on the way to the apartment.

My nerves are jumping, my skin crawling as if eyes are on me, though I find no signs that I'm being tracked. Trying to find the source of my discomfort, I weave through the neighborhood, walking inside several stores in a mall, where I intend to let darkness fall before I depart. With a new hat on, I finally exit back onto the street, and that sensation of being watched has eased. Returning to the hotel, I enter through its restaurant and a side door into the lobby.

It's nearly eight in the evening when I take the elevator to our secure, key-coded floor and enter the suite, where I immediately hear "Chad! Is that you?"

"Yes. Who do you think it is? The bogeyman?"

"If his name is Sheridan then yes."

Damn. I pace a few more times. I seem to be good at pacing. I'm good at a lot of things that don't mean shit right now. I need to fix that, and fix it now. I need to find my sister. I need to destroy Sheridan. Angry, I grab the chair in front of the door and shove it aside.

"Oh, thank God," Gia gushes, flinging her arms around my neck. "You're in one piece."

Stunned by her greeting, by the way her sweet curves meld against me, I fight the heat that rushes through me, untangling her grip and pressing her hands against the wall. "Tell me what you know about my sister," I demand.

"*Nothing*, Chad. I told you that. Is she—was she—"

"You know I didn't find her."

"I wanted you to find her. I was terrified for you."

Anger expands in me, seeping into my veins, and on some level, I know it's not about Gia at all, or maybe I just fear it will be about her. I don't want to trust her and be wrong. "You barely know me."

"I know you're in pain. I know what being alone feels like, and I know that's what you feel right now."

Alone.

It's a word that pierces my heart with guilt. It's what I know my sister has felt for six long years. I was all she had, the only one she could count on, even if she didn't know I was there—and I failed her. The pain is a seed that grows and expands inside me in an instant, and suddenly, or maybe not so suddenly, the idea of being betrayed by Gia is not as biting as the idea of failing her as well. My hands come down on her face, and I stare at her. "I have money and re-sources to hide you, and I promise you, no one will find you.

But I won't be there with you. I'm poison to anyone near me. You can't forget that. *I can't* forget that."

I don't give her time to reply. My mouth closes down on hers, my tongue pressing past her lips, stroking and stroking again, in what is instantly an aggressive, searching kiss. She moans, and I swear the sound of her moan shatters a piece of my soul that is already bleeding for my sister. In this moment, it feels like all I have left is this woman.

I let go of her wrists and her arms wrap around me again and she is small and delicate and somehow brave and bold at the same time. The touch of her, the taste of her, it's like a rush of anger, passion, and need combusting inside of me, feeding the same in her. One minute I'm kissing her and she's kissing me. The next we are naked and on the bed, her pretty pink nipples in my mouth, my cock buried deep in her sweet, tight pussy, and I am thrusting into her. There was no beginning to this. I don't want there to be an end. There is just us, and I'm kissing her and fucking her and she's just as ravenous. Just as needy. I am lost in this woman and her moans and soft touches, and she has become the only piece of heaven I have left.

"Chad," she whispers, and in that instant my name matters more than her moans. It tells me that she knows who I am, *really knows*, because I've hidden nothing from her, shown her all of my good and bad and terrible self.

I answer her by licking into her mouth, softly murmuring, "Gia," letting her know that I too am lost in the moment, but I know who I'm lost with.

Her leg wraps around mine as if I've given her the answer she seeks and now she's fully committed, no holding back. My hand slides under her perfect little ass and I squeeze, lifting her, thrusting into her. Once again, I'm different with her than with the string of nameless women I've known, kissing her, unconcerned about the emotional bullshit that too much intimacy is to me. Gia tastes like the indescribable flavor of escape wrapped in sweet honey. And when she locks up around me, arching upward, her fingernails digging into my shoulders, her sex clenching around me, I am beyond control. I thrust into her, pushing deeper, and when her body clenches around me, spasms milking me, I too am tensing, shuddering with release. Time and space fade in and out, and I cling to that hazy, wonderful place where nothing but pleasure exists.

Like a hard slap in the face, the room returns, and with it the moment I wanted to escape that seems eternal. Reality is here, and so is the wet, wonderful feeling of being buried inside her that represents a huge mistake. "Fuck," I whisper. "We didn't use birth control." I am off her in an instant, closing the space between me and the bathroom, and grabbing a towel that I toss at her before I'm back to pacing.

"Fuck. Fuck. Fuck." She says nothing, and I glance at her un-moving, sitting with her back to me on the edge of the bed. "Why aren't you saying anything? The last thing either of us needs is to bring a baby into this hell."

Still she says nothing, calmly standing to retrieve her jeans. Frustrated, I close the distance between us, my hands on her shoulders as I turn her to face me. "What about this being a problem don't you get? I am a target. I can't raise a child."

"You don't have to."

"Like hell. If you're pregnant—"

"I'm not. I can't . . . be pregnant."

I blink and shake my head. "What? What does that mean?"

"It means," she rasps, her voice quaking with barely con-tained emotion, "I had an infection when I was eighteen. It left me infertile."

The pain in her confession is palpable, a deep cutting blade that clearly inflicts itself on her over and over, the way my guilt does me. And on some level, it's the same, that sense of not having a family, of never being able to even try. "Gia—"

"Don't offer sympathy that you know doesn't help. I don't want to bring kids into the hell that's become my life anyway." She jerks away from me and I reach for her, turning her to face me again, but somehow I lose whatever I intended to say. What am I supposed to tell her? That alone is better, when I know it sucks? That it gets easier? Because it doesn't. It never gets easier.

"Gia—"

"I said don't," she snaps. "This isn't new to me, and if anything, the 'why me' I've asked myself too many times now has an answer. A child would have made this so much more complicated."

There are no words of comfort I can give her. They'd be false promises, lies. They'd be hope, the kind I have for my sister, despite the doubts I have of her safety. "You are going to survive," I vow. "I'm going to make sure of it."

"Yes. I will survive, but we both know it's not because of you. You're going to get what you need out of me, and then send me away with cash and a new identity. Let's keep this real. The sex is just sex, a way we're both coping with our situation."

I despise every word she's just spoken, when I should embrace them. Instead, I want to make us both forget they exist. I need, and I don't even know what I need anymore. I grab her pants and toss them aside, tangling fingers in her hair. "Sex is how we cope?"

"You know it is."

"Then let's do a little more coping."

"Yes," she whispers. "Let's."

My cock thickens with her approval, my body hard and hot. I can't get enough of her but I'm damn sure going to try. I lower my head, anticipating the taste of her, the moment I will once again be inside her, when suddenly my cell phone rings. I pause, lost in a haze of lust, in a burn for this woman, but the ring sounds again, jolting me back to reality.

Blood pumping fiercely, I release Gia, scrambling for my pants, cursing myself for leaving my phone unattended. Relieved and scared shitless of what I'm about to hear, I dig it out of my pocket and hit the Answer button in time to hear, "I'm calling you back, motherfucker."

TEN

AT THE SOUND of Jared's voice, the tension in my spine eases only a fraction. "Tell me my sister's alive."

"She is. And she's safe. For now. But we need to talk."

"Define 'safe.'"

"No imminent threat."

"Where is she?"

"Do you really want to do this on the phone?"

"How likely is it that anyone else saw me go to that apartment?"

"The apartment itself, zero. I have it wired with cameras

and a silent alarm. You were the first mouse in my trap, but I reset it to see who else might come calling."

I open my mouth to ask if he means Meg, but glance at Gia, who's naked and hugging herself, and I hesitate to bring Jared here for reasons I can't explain. "1732 Wazee Street in half an hour." I end the call and Gia is already getting dressed. "The contact I've been trying to reach left me a number at my sister's apartment. We need to go and meet him."

"We?"

"I have a safe house near here where we'll stay until we decide what comes next."

"Then why come here at all?"

"I knew the maid service would rescue you if I didn't come back from that apartment."

She tugs her shirt over her head. "I don't know if I should thank you or tell you you're crazy."

"Neither." I sit down and start putting on my boots.

Gia sits and does the same with her tennis shoes. "So your sister's alive?"

"He says she is."

"You don't believe him?"

I stand up and grab the duffel. "I need to see her with my own eyes."

She nods and pushes herself to her feet, sliding her bag

over her shoulder. "I would, too. Chad. How much do you trust this person we're meeting?"

"I trusted him with my sister's life."

"Right. Of course."

I narrow my gaze. "Why?"

"Because greed is a terrifying thing. What you have, or what people think you have, represents the kind of power that changes people."

"And you know this how?"

"We all know it in our core. It's humanity." She draws in a breath. "You said you'd sell me if the price was right. What would this man do if the price is right?"

My gut clenches and I grab her and pull her to me. "I was trying to make sure you don't trust anyone. I was trying to keep you alive."

"I got the message. You're a treasure hunter. I'm just lucky enough to be worth nothing to anyone—unless Sheridan simply wants to punish me for betraying him. But your sister is another story. She means everything to you, and Sheridan knows that. This man we're about to meet knows that. Meg knew that. Even I know that. Listen to your own advice. Trust no one. Not even this person we're going to meet now."

"He protected my sister."

"Who is the best way to get to you."

"He doesn't even know what Sheridan is after."

"If he's good enough and smart enough to be worthy of protecting your sister, do you really think he didn't dig in and find out?"

"Sheridan hasn't exactly made this public."

"You think that he couldn't have found out, Chad? Trust no one."

"Including you, sweetheart."

"I'm not asking for your trust. I'm demanding your brains. Use them. Now."

"Why does this matter to you?" My fingers dig into her arms and I give her a shake. "Why?"

"Because," she hisses without any hesitation, "if you really have the cylinder, and if it really works, it could save our world as easily as it could destroy it, and that's all in your hands. And mine, too, if I can influence you to protect it."

"And if I have it? What do you want to do with it? Whose interest are you servicing?"

"Not yours, if you want to sell it to the highest bidder. It can't be sold. It can't be given to anyone who will abuse it. I don't know what the hell to do with it—but I know you can't sell it like you said you'd sell me."

"I'm not selling you or it."

"You have it. Tell me."

"Trust no one, baby. No one."

Her fingers curl on my shirt. "Convince all of them, whoever they are, that you don't have it—or else they will never stop coming."

"You think they're going to believe that?"

"Make them believe it."

She's shaking. Her lips, her hands. Her entire body. I stare down at her, this woman who has managed to spell out the backup plan I've worked on for six years and never perfected, any more than I've figured out what the hell to do with the cylinder.

"Right. I'll just tell them it's all been a big mistake, and we'll all go our own sweet ways. If that was possible, don't you think I would have done it before now?"

"They thought you were dead," she argues. "You didn't have to tell them anything before now."

"Obviously they didn't think I was dead, or they wouldn't have kept looking for me."

"All the more reason to convince them you don't have it. Including whoever we're going to see now. It won't be easy, but there has to be a way."

I glare back at her. "What's your story?"

"It's not my story that matters. It's yours."

I study her another moment, like I'll see some answer in her face I don't find. Shoving my hair back under my baseball hat, I say, "Let's go," and dig cash out of my bag, stuffing it into my pocket for easy access. I also stick the gun in my waistband, instead of my ankle holster.

Gia notices this gesture, eyeing the gun a moment before she tugs the hoodie over her head and tucks her long dark brown hair underneath without me telling her to. We stare at each other again and I don't fucking know why, any more than I know why I'm not walking. We just are. We're staring and standing and not moving. And then I'm moving.

With a low growl, I cave to the ever-present need to hold onto her, lacing her fingers with mine, and leading her to the door. We step into the elevator and still I keep her close. Exiting the elevator, I'm on alert, on edge, and I blame Gia. Granted, I'm always there to some degree, but she has me ready to drop and roll with my gun drawn.

I fork over a big tip to the doorman and when he offers to escort us to the side of the hotel where the Escalade still waits, I wave him off. My instincts are buzzing, and this time it's not about Gia and her warnings. This is a sense of awareness I've lived with even before Sheridan, when I first started walking the line as a treasure hunter. The same instinct that made me damn good then, and even now, at getting away with things others cannot. I have a sense that a wrong move now will be lethal, like there are eyes all around me, and Jared's claim no one else saw me at that apartment isn't true. It was a risk, one I could have made more calculated had I not been fucking emotionally coming apart at the edges over my sister's well-being. I'd been in the moment, not the big picture.

Following Gia to the passenger's-side door of the Escalade, I hold it open and ensure she's safely inside before quickly moving to the driver's-side door. Climbing inside the vehicle, I lock the doors and start the engine. Every nerve ending in my body is jumping.

"Chad—"

"Later. When I know we're safe."

I pull onto the road and my sense of unease increases. I veer into the neighborhood behind the hotel and start weaving through the streets. When I see no signs of trouble following me, I turn onto a main highway and head the few miles downtown. Still, I'm cautious, and travel down another residential street—and notice the dark sedan from two streets back. Abruptly, I put us in reverse and back toward the vehicle. It starts backing up and I shove us into Park and draw my gun.

"Chad!" Gia calls out.

"Lock the door," I order, exiting the Escalade and shutting her inside.

The sedan stops moving, idling, and I rush at it, closing the distance between it and me, but the hair on the back of my neck stands up at the same moment I hear the sound of fast approaching motorcycle engines revving. I glance over my shoulder as the glass shatters on the passenger's side of the Escalade. *Gia.* Forgetting the sedan, I turn and start running, rounding the vehicle as Gia's scream pierces the air. A man, or I think it's a man, in leather and a helmet is leaning into the Escalade while another waits on a motorcycle nearby, holding a gun in my direction.

Fuck him—if he kills me he can't get the cylinder, and I don't back down. I shoot at his tires and miss. He revs his engine and comes at me. About that time, Gia is hauled out of the truck and I tackle the man holding her. We go down on the ground, and I curse as I land on the bottom, my head hitting the pavement, along with my gun, which bounces away. A fist comes down on my face, followed by another.

"Chad!" Gia shouts, and I'm terrified that the other man will get to her before I can.

"The gun!" I shout, grabbing the jacket of my attacker at the same moment I ram my knee into his groin.

The sound of a gunshot splits the air, and the man on top of me rolls off. As tempting as it is to go after him, I roll in the opposite direction, coming to my feet to find Gia holding the gun. I take it from her as both of the men mount their bikes and speed off.

"Inside," I order urgently, ushering her toward the Escalade.

She hesitates at the edge of the glass-covered seat and I grab her, all but tossing her across the seats. She yelps, no doubt from the glass that also digs into my jeans-clad leg, but I'll take 'alive and with me' over 'dead or with someone else' any day.

I throw us into Reverse, finding the black sedan nowhere in sight, hearing the sound of sirens in the not-so-far distance.

"Why the fuck were they after you, Gia? Sheridan doesn't want revenge on you badly enough to ignore me."

"I don't know. And who says they were ignoring you?"

"They were after *you*, Gia," I say, putting us in Drive and accelerating. "And now our damn license plates are going to be hot all over again."

"They weren't after me," she insists. "That makes no sense."

"No. It doesn't. Does it? Trust no one? Nailed that one." I glance down to find her hand bleeding. "Fuck."

She curls her fingers into her palm. "I reopened my cut. I'm fine, but your eye is swelling again."

I rip my shirt over my head and toss it to her. "Wrap it. And you're not fine. Nothing is fine." She's right. My eye is swelling again. Fuck me, and fuck all this shit. I round a corner and pull onto a main downtown street, then take two more turns. Finally I pull into the driveway of what was once a brewery and is now a six-thousand-foot apartment building with a tech center. I key in a code and the garage doors open. We enter the two-deep, four-car garage and a white pickup truck follows us inside.

"Who is that?" Gia asks urgently. "Is that your friend? Please tell me it's your friend."

"We're about to find out," I say, lowering the garage door and exiting the Escalade with my gun drawn. Rounding the hood, I target the driver's door, watching as it pops open. But even before I see the man's face, his light brown hair tied at the nape and the orange UT Longhorns T-shirt is a dead giveaway.

"Nicest greeting you've ever given me." Jared laughs, shutting his door and settling his hands on his jeans-clad hips. "Should I remind you that I got an invitation, and I wasn't the guy that uglied up that pretty face of yours or stole your damn shirt?"

"We were attacked a mile back," I say, and I can't seem to contain the accusation in my voice as I add, "You were the only one who knew we were here, and where we were going."

"There's no way anyone found you through me. No one saw me. No one saw you at the apartment. I'm sure of it. And who the hell is 'we,' and do you trust that person?"

Something is off. Really off, and I don't know what, but

it can't be Jared. I've known him for eight years, and he's never failed me. That only leaves Gia. "I haven't decided," I say, holstering my weapon and moving to open Gia's door. She twists around to face me, her legs dangling from the glass-covered seat. I stand in front of her, an unmoving wall, and tell her, "We need to talk."

"Right. I was almost kidnapped or killed or whatever that was, and now I'm sensing I'm the enemy again. Why don't you just tie me up and torture me, the way Sheridan did you?"

"Don't tempt me."

My hands come down on her waist and I lift her over the glass, setting her on the ground. Her bloodied hand comes down on my chest. "Where's the shirt?"

"I dropped it."

I reach around her, retrieving it and wrapping it around her hand in a knot. "That talk," I say when I'm done, "is going to be free of bullshit."

"Yeah, like you're capable of that."

"What the fuck does that mean?"

She throws a look toward Jared and then back to me. "Alone," she says. "We have that no-bullshit talk alone."

My lips thin. "Alone it is, sweetheart, but get ready to tell all, because we both know you haven't." I grip her elbow and lead her toward the door. Jared is leaning against the wall, one booted ankle crossed over the other, his gaze sweeping over the blood on my chest before he arches a brow. "Talk about liking it rough."

"You aren't funny, asshole," I growl, and for some unexplainable reason, I pull Gia in front of me, putting myself between her and Jared, like he's the problem, not her. Keying another code in to the panel on the wall, I still feel safer with Gia in front of me than behind. I urge her forward and follow her through a laundry area that leads to a kitchen with a low-hanging stainless-steel ventilation hood dangling over a stone counter. Still holding Gia's arm, I scan the furnished living area to the right and the dining area to the left, finding nothing but two years of dust gathered since my last visit.

Motioning to the winding black metal stairs in front of us, I lean into Gia and say, "The master bedroom is to the left. There's a first aid kit under the bathroom sink. I'll be there in a minute."

She doesn't move. She turns and faces Jared as he joins us in the kitchen. He scowls. "Something you want to say to me?"

A second passes. Two. Three. "Nothing," she finally replies, turning and running up the stairs.

Jared whistles. "What was that, and who the hell is she?"

Trust no one. The words play in my head. The sense of

unease I am feeling with Jared is like removing the last piece of security I had left in this world, and it's pissing me off. I march past him and enter the laundry area, keying in a code that will put this place on lockdown if anyone tries to come or go without another matching sequence of numbers.

Returning to the kitchen, I find myself confronted by Jared, who gives me a big hug. "I thought you were dead, man."

I return the embrace, relief seeping into my bones. He's a friend. A real friend. Gia might stir unfamiliar emotions in me, but I share a history with Jared. "They can't kill me," I tell him.

He breaks away and stares at me. "What is it you have that they want so badly?"

I step back from him, and we both lean on the counter, facing each other, him arching a brow. "You aren't answering. Talk to me, man. What are they after?"

"More importantly, where's my sister?"

"Back in New York and safe, I promise."

"New York isn't safe."

"Denver wasn't safe. Not with Meg here, working damn hard to get close to her. And let me show you just how big a problem that was." He reaches in his pocket and pulls out his phone, flipping it around to show me a picture that has me grabbing the cell from his hand.

"Rollin," I growl. "That bastard is supposed to be dead."

"That's what we all thought. The question now becomes, does Daddy Dearest know he's alive? He hasn't shown up on Sheridan's radar at all."

"What about Meg? Has she? Where is she now?"

"Gone. She followed Amy to New York, wreaked a little more havoc on her life, and then disappeared. I've tried to find her."

"At least tell me you got the clue I left for Amy and gave it to her."

"That I can confirm. I gave her the clue, and she found the letter you left for her, and the list of Sheridan's business partners and their many sins. She went to Sheridan and promised to turn him and his partners in to the authorities if they didn't leave her alone. And her new fiancé went one step further. He hired a hit man and promised Sheridan that everyone on that list would be dead if anything happened to Amy or anyone close to her."

"Fiancé? What the hell are you talking about? I haven't been gone long enough for her to have a damn fiancé, let alone one she trusts enough to involve him in this."

"Long enough for her to fall in love and get pregnant."

"*Pregnant?* Amy's fucking pregnant?"

He gives a grim shake of his head. "No. She miscarried, and she didn't handle it well."

And I wasn't there for her. The idea that she has been alone, and turned to some stranger out of desperation, shreds me. "Explain how and why she ended up back in New York?"

"That's where her billionaire fiancé, Liam Stone, lives."

"Billionaire? She got pregnant by a man she just happened to meet the night she was on the run, and he just happens to be a billionaire?"

"I agree, it's hard to swallow. But Liam Stone claims he loves her, and he's pretty damn convincing. And his résumé, if you want to call it that, is impressive. Protégé of a famous architect and famous as one himself. He not only makes a fortune from his own work, he inherited a fortune from his adopted father, who was also his mentor."

"And he met Amy how?"

"They met on her flight to Denver."

"That's a little too coincidental for my comfort."

"He has to have a corrupted agenda? While I agree again, there simply isn't proof, and he did go for Sheridan's jugular with that hit man."

"Which could have been an act to convince Amy to trust him. And who says he has to be working with Sheridan? There are plenty of people outside of Sheridan's circle who want what he wants, all of whom would use my sister against me to get it."

Lisa Renee Jones

"Which is *what*, damn it? What was worth the slaughter of your family, the risk to your sister, yourself, and now me? What's the problem here? Why not just give them what they want? Because I've never known you not to take money for anything. It's time to tell me what this is about."

"It's time for you to get out. Tell me what I need to know, and then get as far away from me as you can."

"It's too late for me to disappear. Liam knows I'm in this, and so does Sheridan."

My jaw clenches. "I didn't want this for you."

"Yeah, well, we both know I didn't want this for me, either. There's a reason why I didn't join The Underground. But I'm in now, deeper and deeper every single day. Give them what they want—or tell them where to get it themselves."

"It's not that simple."

"Why?"

I stand there, knowing I should tell him the truth, trying to force the words that just won't come. Telling myself it's to protect him, I say, "I need to deal with a situation. I'll be back in a few, and I'll want to see everything you have on Mr. Liam Stone, and anyone who's been anywhere near my sister since I've been gone."

"I assumed as much." He glances at the blood on my chest. "And your . . . situation. Does she have a name?"

"Her name is 'My Problem, Not Yours.'" I don't give him time to argue, turning and rushing up the stairs, not about to lose sight of what I know in my gut: Gia's no secretary, and she's about to tell me the whole truth and nothing but the truth, so help me God. Reaching the bedroom door, I open it and step inside a room with brick walls and steel beams across the ceiling, a huge king-sized bed in the center. And sitting on the end of it is Gia, my shirt still wrapped around her hand and a gun, one of several I have stashed in the room, lying across her lap.

ELEVEN

CAUTIOUSLY, I SHUT THE DOOR. "I see you found my stock-pile of weapons."

"Now we're even," she replies. "You have one, and so do I." I step toward her. "Don't," she warns.

"Why?"

"Because you want the gun, and I'm not letting you take my only way to protect myself."

"You don't have to protect yourself from me. I pulled you out of the arms of that attacker today, remember?"

"To serve a purpose. To serve you."

"I thought we agreed that we both want to destroy Sheridan."

"You want my help until you don't need me anymore. Then you'll do just what you promised and sell me to the highest bidder."

"I don't have any reason to sell you."

"You'll find one."

I narrow my gaze. "Why did those men come after you?"

"Do you have the cylinder?"

"You're deflecting. You also told me to convince everyone I didn't have it, and I assume that includes you."

She stands, holding the gun on me. *Do you have the cylinder?*

"Don't you think I'd have sold it by now if I did?"

"I don't know. Would you?"

"Why do you care so much?"

"I have nothing and no one because I tried to protect it. You know this." She scrapes her teeth over her lips. "Fine. Don't tell me. Just answer this. Did you mean it when you said you'd do anything for money? When you said you'd do anything for a price?"

"Why? Are you offering?"

"Don't keep playing word games with me. You said you'd do anything for money, but you also said you turned down five hundred million because this was bigger than the money." Her voice is quavering, laced with some mix of emotions—anger? Fear? "Which is it?" she demands.

Fear and anger. Yes. That's what I see in her, but there is pain, too, heartache, like what I'd seen in her face when we talked about children. Whatever is going on here is far more personal than she's letting on.

"Gia," I murmur softly. "Put down the gun."

"Answer me, Chad!"

I close the distance between us and cover the gun with my hand, aiming it past my body. "Gia."

"Damn you. I just want an answer."

"Tell me why this matters to you," I order.

"I told you—"

"The real reason, Gia. The reason I see in your eyes, in the shaking of your hand. The reason that you gave up everything. The reason those men were after you."

She releases the gun and sinks onto the bed. I go down on a knee in front of her, and set the gun on the ground, out of her reach. "Talk to me," I order softly.

"I'm not a secretary."

"I knew that."

"I was working on a top-secret project, which I destroyed before I helped you escape."

"Re-creating the cylinder?"

"Yes."

"How'd you get on that team?"

"I won awards and trained with some cutting-edge chemists in the field of clean energy. It was a topic that my father . . . lectured on frequently. It was his passion. Now it's my passion, and my way to stay connected to him. The idea that an oil company would want to change the world, to be a part of the change they usually stifle, however naive it obviously was, appealed to me."

"How close was he to creating a new cylinder?"

"It could have been a year or decades, but I thought we had a seed of something that felt special. It wouldn't come together, though."

My hand closes down on hers where it rests on her knee. "Did you really burn your work, or did you take it with you?"

"I burned it."

"Would you tell me if you had it?"

"You didn't even know about this when you said you'd sell me to the highest bidder—so no, I would not make myself sound more valuable to you or anyone. For what it's worth, though, I didn't keep it. There wasn't time. But anyone on that team has knowledge that Sheridan doesn't want shared with others. So this isn't just about me betraying him. It's about what he thinks I took, and can give to someone else. Ironically, if you give him what he wants, I won't matter anymore—but that defeats the entire reason I did this. It would make an evil man the most powerful person on this planet."

"If I were going to do that, I would have done it six years ago."

"Did he think you sold it to someone else? Is that why he killed your family?"

"I told him I couldn't find it, but he said that someone inside The Underground—the group of treasure hunters I worked with, men who were supposed to be like blood family—had betrayed me and told him I had it."

"Do you?"

"You've asked that over and over, and each time, I don't answer. Let's break the perpetual cycle. Right now, we need to deal with your hand, and Jared has information on my sister that I need."

"I can wrap my hand," she insists, and I should let her, but I'm already leading her to the bathroom, and for reasons I can't explain, I need more from her. Something. Anything. Just . . . more.

We enter a room where steel sinks and a sunken tub are enclosed by brick. Everything about this place is a modern money tank that is part of a massive portfolio I've stock-piled.

"Chad—"

I cut her off by turning her to face the counter, cranking the water and unwrapping my shirt from her hand to stick it under the flow. I'm aware of my body wrapped around hers, of how small and feminine she is. When our eyes meet in the mirror, the connection I feel jolts me beyond reason. I don't know what it is about this woman. Maybe it's timing, maybe it's some good in her that I sense when I'm simply so damn bad, but she gets to me in every possible way.

"I need to know," she whispers.

"You don't need to know," I insist, turning off the water.

She grabs a washcloth and turns to face me, her uninjured hand branding my chest. "I . . . do . . . I . . ."

Her objective is lost as somehow my wet hands settle on her waist and our mouths are far too close. The air thickens around her, the heat between us burning with demand. I want to kiss her, to strip her naked and escape this hell, if only for a few minutes. But I fight the urge, trying not to muddy the waters that are already thick with sludge. This can't happen. *We* can't happen.

"No," I say, to this, to us, and to her need for answers I won't give her.

"Just *no*? That's not a good enough answer."

"It's the only one you're getting." I step away from her, feeling the ache of not touching her far too deeply, and reach inside a steel cabinet, setting a medicine kit in front of her before moving to the sink beside her to clean up my bloodied chest.

Silent seconds tick by, and I am far too aware of the intimacy of our sharing the bathroom, quickly wiping down my skin and walking to the closet to grab one of the T-shirts I have hanging inside. I return to the bathroom, still pulling it over my head, to find Gia standing in my path, arms folded in front of her.

"We aren't staying here," I announce. "My sister's in New York."

"That's good, right? She's safe?"

"Depends on how you define *good*. In the short time I've been away, she's managed to get engaged to some billionaire architect."

"Do you think he's a setup by Sheridan?"

"I'm sure he is. That's why we aren't staying. I'm going after her."

"Am I going with you?"

"Yes."

"And the man downstairs?"

"Jared," I say. "Yes. He's going with us."

"Who is he to you?"

"He looked after Amy while I was gone. He's also probably one of the top twenty hackers in the world, and the entire reason we were able to manipulate death certificates and records to disappear six years ago. He's been close to Amy and her fiancé the past few months, and at this point, she doesn't even know I'm alive."

She blanches, holding up her hands. "Wait. Your sister thinks you're dead? Why would you let her suffer that way?"

"Because Sheridan will use her against me if he gets the chance, and together we're a bigger target. It had to be this way."

"Are you going to tell her now?"

"I'm going to do whatever I think keeps her safe. Right now, we're going downstairs to connect a few dots with Jared and make plans. Don't tell him about the cylinder. I'll tell him when I'm ready."

"How can he not know about it if he helped you hide Amy?"

"I had no reason to tell him why we were in trouble. Amy and I were dead to Sheridan. He was out of this and safe, just monitoring pings with certain keywords for me from a distance. I'm going to have to tell him the truth, but right now I want him focused on Amy, not on a million questions about the cylinder. I'll tell him the truth before he has time to hack your personnel file."

She studies me a moment. "What happens when you get your sister back? Does he make everyone disappear again until Sheridan finds one of us and kills us? Because Sheridan will keep coming for us—and now that he knows you're alive, it won't take six years for him to find you, or us, this time."

I grab her and pull her to me. "I told you. No one else dies because of me. He's not going to have time to hunt me down. I'm hunting *him* down this time, and I won't settle for anything less than his total annihilation."

"If that's a promise, I'll take it."

"It's a promise, sweetheart." And before I can stop myself, I seal it with the intense kiss I'd denied us both only minutes before, tasting her deeply, passionately, and telling myself it will be our last. Finally, I force myself to set her aside before I make that one last time really damn unforgettable. "Jared is waiting on us downstairs."

We stare at each other, the heat of that kiss burning around us like damning flames, ready to consume us. *We can't happen*, I remind myself, grabbing her hand, the touch scorching my palm, but I don't let it stop my progress forward, leading her to the hallway and down the stairs.

Entering the kitchen, we find Jared standing at the stone island in the center of the room, a coffee cup, a laptop, and a file sitting in front of him. "I see you found the coffeepot," I comment, my hand protectively at Gia's back.

"The beer was older than the coffee, so coffee won," he

says, but it's not me he's focused on. It's Gia. "And you would be?" he asks, giving her a once-over.

"Gia," she supplies, and rather than avoiding him, she leans on the counter across from him. "And you're Jared. I've heard all about you."

"And yet I've heard nothing about you," he counters. "How'd you end up with an asshole like Chad?"

"The same way she ended up with an asshole like you," I assure him, claiming the spot next to her. "She was in the wrong place at the wrong time."

"I was working for Sheridan's company," she supplies. "I overheard Sheridan talking about Chad and something he wanted from him. Next came the order to torture him, and I just . . . acted."

His gaze flickers between us. "Did you know each other before this?"

"No," she says. "I acted in the heat of the moment, without thinking about the consequences."

Jared's brow furrows. "If you thought he was in trouble, why not call the police?"

"Sheridan's very powerful. By the time the police came and investigated, Chad would have been moved, and I would have been fired and probably called crazy."

"It's complicated," I assure him, spooning a shit-ton of sugar into my coffee. "And we don't have time for me to explain it to you right now. Bottom line, Gia made decisions, and Sheridan thinks she knows more than she does. Right now, I'm focused on Amy and getting her away from Liam Stone."

"That's no easy task. He's possessive, and protective, and keeps her guarded. Add to that the fact that she's in love with him and won't walk away, and you have a problem."

"She's not staying with Liam fucking Stone. For all we know, he's holding her for ransom, like bait, and I'm the fish."

"That might be true," he says, "but you aren't going to convince Amy of that easily. She'll fight leaving Liam. And she knows you're alive, Chad. Or, she knows you were a month ago. I had to play your voice mail to me to get her to trust me. You can't just leave her a note and a warning this time."

Gia's hand comes down on my arm. "She's going to be hurt," she warns. "You need to tread cautiously, because she could withdraw from you rather than welcome you. That could push her closer to Liam, and give him more control over her."

The idea of hurting Amy, of her hating me, continues to tear me to pieces, but I will endure her wrath to save her. To know she's alive and well. "Her safety has to come first. I'm going after her. Now, tonight."

Gia turns to me, gripping my arm tighter. "Sheridan will

expect you to go after her. You can't just charge in and grab her."

"I told you. I always have a plan."

"'Grab her, run, and deal with the aftermath later' is not a plan."

"It will be if I say it is."

TWELVE

TRYING TO ARRANGE A FLIGHT that I can be certain won't make it onto Sheridan's radar turns into a nightmare and uses a shit-ton of resources. Aside from cash, I end up calling in a favor from someone who had dirt on someone who had dirt on the pilot. It's nearly five in the morning when we reach the private airstrip a good hour outside of Denver from which we'll take a private jet to New York City.

With a computer case on my shoulder and the folder of Jared's notes and photos inside it, I follow Gia inside the luxury plane with leather seats, a lounge area, and televisions. To say I'm irritable and tired is an understatement, but after hours of grilling Jared about Liam Stone and everything he's witnessed these past weeks, I can come to only one conclusion: I need to get to my sister now, not later.

My hand comes down on Gia's back and I direct her to a seat by the window, quickly joining her. We're both buckling up when Jared stops in front of us. "If you're done grilling me, I'm going to the back to try and get some sleep."

"We'll have in-flight internet. I'm going to dial in and do some research, but I'll save the questions until after you get your beauty sleep."

He holds his hands out to his sides. "What can I say? I hack better when I'm beautiful. And seriously, man. You need rest. When was the last time you slept?"

"About four hours in two days," Gia answers for me, "and before that catnaps while tied to a chair for I don't even know how long."

"Go away," I order Jared.

Jared laughs. "Night-night, Prince Charming." He gives Gia a sympathetic look. "You're welcome to join me in the back of the plane if he gets intolerable."

He disappears and I grimace at the empty space he occupied moments before and say, "You aren't going anywhere with him."

"You act like I'm your possession. Or . . . like you don't trust him."

The engine roars to life and with it, something dark snaps inside me. I rotate to face her, my hand sliding under her dark brown hair to wrap the back of her neck. "I don't trust anyone," I say, lowering my head, bringing our mouths one hot breath apart, "and until I say otherwise, you *are* my possession. Do you have a problem with that?"

"Would it matter?"

"Don't answer my question with a question."

"Fine. For reasons I can't define, no, I do not have a problem with that, but my answer is subject to change at any moment."

And for reasons *I can't define*, I don't want her answer to change. I kiss her, and it's a demand for something, anything, which only she can answer; my need for this woman is seemingly the only outlet for the guilt I've lived with and can no longer manage to contain.

"Well then," she whispers when our lips part, "I guess I'll stay sitting right where I am."

"Yes," I say, my voice gravelly, my body tight. "You will."

I don't let go of her. I don't *want* to let go of her, but I don't cave to my craving for another kiss, either. Instead, I find myself simply inhaling, drawing in the scent of her—no perfume, none of the fakeness that has haunted my life these past six years, just utterly seductive. Now I want that kiss. Now I *need* it, but suddenly the plane lifts off the runway, jolting me back to the reality of the hell on wheels we're living. *Hell, everywhere we go*, I think.

I release Gia, facing forward, running my hands down my jeans, and I am suddenly certain that everything that's just happened is a product of the all-too-familiar thrum of energy that it's time I admit is an old friend. It's a part of me that I've lived with for a good few years since the fire. Trying to shake it off, I set my computer bag on the ground, reaching inside to remove the folder.

Gia shivers beside me. "Do you think they have blankets on this plane?"

"I'm sure they do," I say, unhooking my seat belt to stand up and open the overhead bin, where I hit the blanket jackpot. I stand still a moment in thought, wondering why Jared making a joke about Gia had set me off the way it had. He's been a close friend and a protector of my sister while I was gone. What the hell is wrong with me?

Grabbing a blanket and two pillows, I slam the compartment shut, rejoining Gia, who eagerly covers herself as I buckle back in. "There might be a little Prince Charming in you after all," she teases, snuggling under the cover.

"Only if you have a fucked-up idea of Prince Charming," I assure her, shoving pillows down beside each of our armrests for later use. Reaching for the file, I flip it open on my lap. Gia shuts it, her hand resting on top of it and my legs. "You've spent hours going over that file and the data and photos inside. We both have. Tellar Phelps, security guard, ex-military: Buzz cut, tall, muscular. Melody Ethridge, a new friend of Amy's: Blond, twenty-eight, high-end real estate agent. Likes to shop."

"Her brother," I say tightly. "Derek Ethridge, Liam's best friend and a wealthy real estate investor who has put to-gether financial investment packages tied to the Middle East and the oil industry."

"He also gave Liam a reason to be in Denver when he met Amy."

"So Liam could design a downtown development. Right. It's certainly a good alibi."

"Alibi? He didn't commit a crime by bumping your sister to first class to meet her, Chad. It's actually pretty romantic."

"It's convenient. It's all very convenient."

"A major downtown development, which Jared vali-dated as real, would require someone with Liam's design credentials. And there's proof in the file that it's a real devel-opment. Those kinds of massive projects don't come to-gether without effort."

"If this was a setup meant to make me expose my sister, it could have been planned for a long while."

"How would they have known you were going to send her to Denver in time to plan it? Did you detail that to someone before the last minute?"

"Why are you trying to protect Liam Stone?"

She lifts the arm and turns fully to face me. "I'm not protecting him, but I see how much you care about your sister. She's not going to feel like you do, though. She's going to feel joy that you're alive and then anger that you left her alone. If you're not careful, you'll push her away, and that only gives Liam more power over her. And if he really loves her, and she loves him, it could drive her away forever."

"I'm not trying to be her hero, Gia. I'm trying to save her life. If Stone turns out to be a good man when this is over, she can be with him."

"Will it ever be over? I'm not sure it will. Think about this. You can't just go in there and kidnap your own sister."

"Why the hell not?"

"She'll be furious."

"And alive, Gia."

"Even if Liam Stone isn't the bad guy here, Sheridan is going to expect you to go after your sister. We now know that he knows where she is. He's going to be watching her, but he won't touch her until you show yourself."

"Even if that's true for now, it won't be for long. Sheridan knows I'm alive. He'll find a way to use her against me. I have to go after her, and I've told you before: I always have a plan, and this time will be no different."

"Earlier you said that plan was grabbing her."

"And it still is. My way, on my terms, and safely. Now go to sleep. We have hours in the air."

"I'm not done arguing with you, but I do need sleep. And so do you." She hits the button to recline my chair and then lies down on top of me, pulling the blanket over us. And it feels good, dangerously good, and a warning bell goes off in my head. Meg didn't cloud my judgment, but Gia could—if I let her. Still, I don't move her away, the fingers of one hand digging into the arm rest, those of my other hand curling by my side. "You don't trust me, but you'll sleep with me?"

She tilts her head up to look at me, surprising me when she reaches up and runs her fingers over my several days' worth of stubble. "I never said I didn't trust you." Before I can reply, she lays her head back down.

"Gia—"

"We're both too tired to argue," she says, without looking at me, her fingers curling on my chest, "and I'm definitely too tired to win. Let's sleep." She peeks up at me. "But for the record, I didn't say I do trust you, either."

She lowers her head again and I have no idea why, but my lips that never curve do so now, undoubtedly hinting at one of my rare smiles. And once again, it's because of this woman.

I LIE STARING at the ceiling of the plane, the sweet weight of Gia on top of me somehow overriding my plans for revenge. I find myself replaying those moments in the hotel room when I'd been buried inside her, lost in nothing but her. Kissing her—and it's with the memory of how she tastes on my lips that I finally fade into sleep.

Slumber predictably delivers a nightmare, and I wake with the touch of the tires on pavement and the taste of ash and vengeance on my lips.

Gia stretches, and I run my hands through her wild brunette mane, and I swear, I am so damn on edge that I want to drag her to the back of the plane and mess it up even more. She frowns as her eyes meet mine, surprising me when she reaches forward, stroking a lock of hair from my eyes. "I see the anger in your eyes."

I cover her hand with mine. "It's always there."

"I understand, and don't even think about telling me I can't. You don't know me well enough to say that." There is a raw ache in those words, a sense of her dealing with how alone she is now; something I understand more than I wish I did.

She tries to remove her hand, but I hold on tight. "I

want to know you, Gia. Everything about you—but I can't. You know that."

"I'm not asking you for anything except what you promised."

"Which is what?"

"Sheridan's destruction."

There is a deep-seated anger roughing up her voice, shadowing her eyes, and for the first time, I'm clear-minded enough to question just how deep this need to destroy Sheridan runs for her. "What aren't you telling me?"

"We've been through this."

"No, I don't believe we have." The plane stops on the runway and, not about to linger inside where we could become targets, I add, "We'll be talking again later. Count on it." I stand up and turn to find Jared pounding away at his keyboard, unaware in a way he has never been. He doesn't even realize I'm staring at him. Abruptly, his gaze lifts and meets mine, and there is something in his eyes, a warning I can't read. But he's sharp, and I know he'll have checked on Gia. I just hope like hell that the truth he discovers matches what she's shared with me.

The door to the plane opens behind me and I step into the aisle, giving Jared my back as I allow Gia to exit in front of me. The pilot steps into view, and he and I exchange a look of understanding about the need for his silence before I join Gia where she has paused at the top of the stairs.

"Let's move," I urge, my hand again going to her back, an action I'm making a habit of and can't seem to stop.

"That SUV—"

"I arranged it."

She sighs with relief, clearly more on edge than she let on in the plane. Peering over her shoulder, she confirms my conclusion. "I'm really nervous about being here."

"I always—"

"Have a plan," she finishes.

"That's right." I smack her ass and she yelps. "Now move. Lingering isn't smart."

For once, she doesn't argue, hurrying down the steps. Jared takes the spot behind me, and I glance at him over my shoulder. "Anything I need to know?"

"Not urgently," he comments at my back as I clear the final step, a reply that tells me he doesn't want to speak in front of Gia, which means I'm not going to like what he has to say.

"IT'S HORRIBLE," GIA says, sitting up on the ride through Brooklyn toward Manhattan, reacting to the poverty-stricken neighborhood around us.

"The crazy part about it," Jared replies, "is that people live in poverty here on an income that would make them middle-class elsewhere."

"Why stay, then?" Gia asks. "I don't understand."

Jared runs his hands down his jeans-clad legs. "If there's one thing hacking has taught me, it's that people stick with what they know and understand. And really, how would anyone living this close to the edge ever get to another city or state? They have no resources to start over."

Gia gives me a concerned look. "Tell me we're not hiding in an area like this."

"The complete opposite," I assure her, "but there are plenty of areas like this in the city."

Her thoughtful gaze returns to the window. "I don't think I'm going to like New York."

"You'll like it," I promise. "You have to focus on the good, and forget the bad."

She twists around to face me. "Forget? You say that like it's easy, or even right."

"You have to find a way to let go of certain things."

"Like the past?"

"Yes. Like the past."

"You make it sound like it's easy when I know you don't believe that. It's not."

"No. But it gets easier."

"I don't want it to get easier," she whispers, turning away, and her pain is present between us, alive and real.

I'm glad I wasn't with Amy to feel her pain, but not out of selfishness—rather, it's out of fear I wouldn't have been strong enough to tell her no when her safety was at risk.

We fall back into silence, and I'm strangely aware of Jared's presence, as if he's waiting for me to comfort Gia. As if he's damning her, or me, or both of us, for what he believes is a relationship based on some sort of weakness. The idea that it might be condemnation based on something he's found in her past grinds through me and suppresses my urge to reach for her.

It's another forty minutes before we defeat traffic and reach midtown Manhattan, where I have the driver stop at a corner near a number of luxury department stores and a major subway stop. I pay our fare and send him on his way, covering our trail by never letting anyone see our endgame.

"Shopping time," I explain as Gia looks around, her blue eyes big with the same wonder all first-time visitors to New York experience in the crush of people amongst towering buildings. "We need to be prepared for anything. That means we both need a full wardrobe and suitcases befitting our final destination, which is a money-driven neighborhood. And we need it all quickly."

"And you didn't allow the driver to know where that destination is," Jared comments. "Smart."

"It's better than stupid," I retort dryly.

"Yes," he says, giving Gia a quick look before adding, "it is. Especially considering we still don't know how Sheridan found you in order to insert Meg into your life."

Gia reacts instantly, stepping closer to him. "I'm not Meg, if that's what you're inferring."

"Just making conversation, *Gia*."

"I don't trust you any more than you trust me," she replies.

"Good thing you aren't the one handing out the cookies at the party, then. I'd hate to get denied a good snack."

"Enough," I snap, irritated that Jared didn't keep this between him and I, even more so that he's choosing to do this now, where it could escalate into attention we can't afford. "Let's make this quick," I say, grasping Gia's arm and stepping forward, setting us all in motion.

Jared eagerly falls into step with me while Gia double-steps to keep up, stumbling and falling. I twist, grabbing her waist to catch her and stand her up. Our eyes lock and hold, and she doesn't have time to hide the uncertainty, the hint of fear, in hers. Things I can't dissolve with words. "You okay?"

"I'm just fine. A perfectly peachy New York tourist."

I have no idea why, but I laugh, and then she laughs, and the tension of the confrontation is gone. Lacing my fingers with hers, I ignore Jared, and start walking again, all of us falling into step.

"I'm surprised you're touching me after his accusations," she murmurs for my ears only.

"I told you: If you die, it will be my choice. I'm keeping you close enough to make that decision myself."

"Thanks for that comforting thought."

I offer her nothing more. Not until I find out what's at the root of Jared's attack.

FOR THE NEXT hour we shop, and I douse every objection Gia offers over the expense of our purchases. I need us ready for any event, action, or travel, without another outing, and I press to ensure that's what I get. Finally, we've spent enough to buy a luxury car, but have managed to acquire full wardrobes for all three of us, along with accessories and various beauty products for her. When all is said and done, we each pack a brand-name suitcase with shopping bags, and I arrange delivery of the rest of the items. From there, we take the subway to one of my ministorage units, where I fill an extra suitcase with a duffel stocked with weapons that I make sure Gia doesn't see.

It's late afternoon by the time we take another few trains and arrive at our true destination, the Two57 residence inside the elite high-rise Park Hotel. We stop at the edge of the eighty-story building and Jared glances up, letting out a long whistle. "This is Liam Stone living."

"More importantly, it's an extremely profitable rental property I purchased years ago. It's also been vacant for the past three months. Until now."

Moving forward, I hand the doorman one of my fake IDs along with Gia's, motioning for Jared to show his, all of which I've arranged to be on an approved list through my broker, who wasn't loving me at four this morning. "My girlfriend and my best man are here to visit me for a few days."

The doorman, an ex-military type I'll appreciate more after we're inside, scans my various cuts and bruises and doesn't warm to us.

The attendant makes a phone call, reading off our IDs, before he finally thaws and greets me with a "Welcome home, Mr. Wade and company. Can I take your bags?"

"Yes, please," Gia gushes, smiling at him, and for the first time, the man seems to soften a bit. I let her accept our ticket.

"Gorgeous," Gia murmurs as we enter the fancy, Vegas-style modern lobby, with marble floors and low-hanging oversized lighting, as well as a lobby desk I intend to visit on my own.

"The security outperforms the decor," I promise her, my hand again finding its way to the small of her back, as I pause us a few feet away from the counter and hand Gia back her ID, which I accepted from the attendant. "Show them this when they ask for it. You're my girlfriend, Ashley, who lives with me." She starts to look at the ID and I say, "Don't. Slip it in your new purse."

"Ashley," she repeats, doing as I've ordered. "No more Gia."

"Gia's a rare name," Jared comments, strands of his long light brown hair draped around his face where they've escaped their confines. "It's not one you can keep without notice."

"It was my mother's name."

There's a sadness in her that I understand, and wish I didn't. "Which makes it all the more dangerous right now," I reply.

"Took the words right out of my mouth," Jared agrees. "I'll keep an eye on the front while you get the keys."

Pleased to have an extra set of eyes, I lace my fingers with Gia's as we step to the counter.

"Our rental agent should have left us a key," I say, sliding my identification onto the counter.

Noting his curious inspection of the various facial injuries that I don't intend to explain, Gia laughs and says, "He looks horrible, doesn't he? That's what he gets for refusing to do the dishes."

The attendant, an older, distinguished-looking black man, frowns while I laughingly insert, "It was a bar brawl. You should see the other guy."

She nudges me. "Stop it. It was a car accident. Sorry. We've just gotten so many looks, and we're a little giddy from travel."

The man starts laughing. "Oh, well, I hope everyone was okay."

"Everyone was fine, or we wouldn't be making a jest of the matter," Gia smoothly assures him.

"Excellent," the man replies and gives me a nod. "Let me get those keys, Mr. Wade and . . . Mrs. Wade?"

"Not 'Mrs.' yet," I say, "but I'm working on remedying that."

We receive another smile and the man turns away to go to a small alcove and key some information into a computer.

Elbow on the counter, I face Gia, intending to compliment her, when she softly asks, "Won't Meg know this place?"

"No. She knew far less about me than she thought she

did. I bought this apartment under a holding company and we're simply the newest renters."

She tilts her head, studying me a moment. "You really never let her in until you were desperate to save Lara."

"Amy," I correct. "That's who she's become to me, because that's who she had to become on her own."

"But you stayed Chad?"

"I've been many people."

"Who were you to Meg?"

"I dared to be Chad to Meg, but it didn't matter, now, did it?" I ask, digging for that hole Jared may have found. "Meg knew who I was from the moment I met her, and she played the poor, desperate, beaten woman that day in the subway station."

I watch her, looking for some flicker of unease, but I get more. "That's how she got you?" She sounds shocked, appalled even. "She played desperate and beaten? No wonder you don't trust me. That's despicable."

My relief is instant. I don't know what Jared discovered, but if Gia's acting, it's an Oscar-winning performance, and I would be the first to give her the statue. "Do you expect less from anyone associated with Sheridan?"

"I thought he was a good man. I won't lie about that—I did, Chad. I was completely fooled. I was a fool."

Every bit of relief I'd felt is gone. The torment in her

reads like a confession and an apology I don't want to hear. "What are you saying?"

"Mr. Wade," the attendant says, surprising us, "the real estate agent actually only just called when our office opened this morning. We changed the locks on the apartment, as is standard procedure, and the maintenance team is bringing me the keys. They're on their way to the lobby now."

"Understood, and more than acceptable," I confirm, considering I'd woken the broker I use for several New York properties early this morning. "Our decision to take this property over another was rather sudden."

"You're welcome to go to the coffee shop off the lobby to wait, if you like, and I'll find you."

"We'll do that," I reply, wrapping my arm around Gia's neck, and turning us to face Jared, who is standing in a corner, arms over his chest, legs wide as he watches the door.

Seeming to sense our approach, he glances up and meets us in the middle of the lobby. "We're supposed to wait on the key in the coffee shop."

"I'll keep an eye on the door," he replies. "I'm on edge just being in this city."

Giving him a nod, I turn Gia and myself toward the coffee shop, and we enter and sit in a corner, where a waitress quickly takes our order. And while I fully intend to redirect Gia to the topic of her confessionlike statement before our arrival, she beats me to the punch. "I'm nervous like Jared, too, Chad. I can't help it. We're targets."

"We're fine, Gia. I need to know what you were talking about back there."

She straightens, shoving her dark brown hair behind her ear. "What? I don't know what you mean."

"You really thought he was a good man. What did he convince you to do?"

"It's not what I did; it's what I could have done."

"What does that mean?"

"You didn't hear the conversation I did. The man has a God complex. If he gets the cylinder, the world will not be the same. The idea that I was helping him, even looking up to him, is just . . . it's hard to swallow. He was like a father figure to me."

"A fucking *father figure*? How close to him were you?"

"He took the time to get to know all of us on the team."

"How many were there?" I ask.

"Four."

"Only four? So you knew him well?"

She shakes her head. "No. No, that man I overheard talking was not the man I knew. The man who killed your parents is not the man I knew. He showed us a façade of a man who was all about honor and changing the world for the good."

I laugh bitterly. "Right. All about changing the world for the good. Or rather, his good. How did he get close to you?"

"Our group had weekly dinners. I feel stupid, but he's a gifted deceiver."

The coffee arrives and I wait for the waitress to leave, finding Gia's eyes clear again, as if she's regained control. "Why do I feel like you're still not telling me everything?" I lean closer to her, my voice soft, but firm. "I told you, Jared is the best hacker on the planet. He's going to look into you, Gia. I'll find out what you don't tell me."

"Mr. Wade," I hear, looking up to find the hotel attendant. "Here are your keys." He slides a small envelope in front of me. "We've left a concierge services menu in your apartment, along with a variety of property information. I had your luggage sent up already. Is there anything else I can do for you?"

"We have a few retail deliveries that should arrive soon."

"I'll make sure they're sent up promptly."

"Thank you very much."

The man departs and I stare at Gia, needing the truth, no matter how brutal it might be. "If you started out as an ally of Sheridan," I begin.

"You're an ass," she whispers fiercely. "You tell me not to trust you and yet you demand I do in all kinds of ways. And then when I dared to share a part of my heartache over this, what happens? You accuse me of basically donating my body and soul to Sheridan's efforts to be the most powerful man on the planet." She stands and I follow her, lacing my fingers with hers and stepping close, our breaths mingling.

"Hurting you is the last thing I want to do. I just don't want to get burned."

Her gaze jerks to mine, her hand flattens on my chest, and I know she must be able to feel the racing of my heart. "I don't either."

"This was the wrong place for this. Let's go upstairs, where we can be alone."

She lowers her chin, no longer allowing me to see her eyes. I want her to look at me, to let me see that the answers she hasn't given me aren't going to make her the enemy. But there are too many people here, and the window of opportunity is lost.

"Come on," I say, deserting our coffees to lead her toward the shop exit. I stop dead in my tracks as we clear the line crowding the entryway and see Jared talking on a phone.

"Who would he be talking on the phone with that you consider safe?" Gia asks beside me.

"Not a damn soul."

Seems I've been busy worrying about the wrong person.

THIRTEEN

I CHARGE FORWARD and Gia keeps pace with me. Jared seems to sense our approach, ending his call and punching a few buttons, which does not diminish my growing anger before he starts toward us. We stop toe-to-toe, him explaining his actions before I can demand answers.

"I have alerts set up on Liam Stone, Sheridan Scott, and every member of the consortium Sheridan works with, and my program leaves me voice mails." He shoves the phone in my direction. "Take it. Check."

Despite knowing he'd had time to erase any evidence, I

don't hesitate to take the phone, determined to catch anything he might have missed. Glancing down at the screen, I confirm the message alert, but a frisson of my initial unease lingers and I don't stop there. I go to his call log and check for anything further, but then, he could have cleared his log in expectation that I would look at it.

Still, I scan it, and it gives me nothing. I should be comforted. This is Jared, the man who helped me save, and hide, my sister. It's then that I realize my "trust no one" philosophy hasn't been as pure as I thought. Until this moment, I trusted Jared.

Eyeing my longtime "friend," I hand him back his phone, watching as the anger seeps into his brown eyes. "You asshole," Jared accuses in a low, vehement tone. "I see what's in your face. How can you think that I'd betray you, you son of a bitch? I exposed myself to Liam Stone, and thus Sheridan, for *you*, and I don't even know your damnable secret." His gaze flickers to Gia and back to me. "Do you want to talk about what I just found out here, or elsewhere?"

It hits me then that he doesn't trust Gia any more than I would a stranger in the mix, and he's been investigating her. I'd expected it. I knew it was coming. And I hate the dread I feel in my gut right now over what he might have found out. "Upstairs," I reply.

We stare at each other for two hard beats, and then in

unison we turn and start walking toward the elevators. I have the strong need to separate him from Gia by putting him on my left and Gia on my right, where I hold onto her arm. Inside the elevator, no one talks, the explosion seeming to wait to happen until we are certain to be free of recording devices.

Finally, we're on the forty-ninth floor and we enter the two-bedroom, four-thousand-square-foot apartment, walking across black hardwood floors toward the floor-to-ceiling windows with huge white beams at the corners. Stopping in the center of the room, Jared and I face each other. "The master bedroom is behind me, Gia. Jared and I need a few minutes."

"Yes, but—"

"You're next," I say, not liking the idea that she feels any need to preface this conversation with her own statement.

I sense her hesitation, but she grabs at least one suitcase from beside the door and rolls it toward the bedroom. I wait for the door to shut, and when it does, Jared immediately demands, "I need to know what I'm dealing with here."

"And I need to know what you just found out."

"Among other things, Liam Stone, a man known to be rather reclusive, is making a rare public appearance on Friday night, with his fiancée by his side."

I blink at the unexpected news that has nothing to do with Gia. "Why, and where?"

"A fundraiser for the governor's upcoming reelection campaign. It's not his type of event. No event is his type of event. And Wes Wells is on the guest list."

A chill goes down my spine at a name I know to be part of Sheridan's consortium. "That can't be an accident."

"The question is, does Liam Stone know Wes is attending? No. Scratch that. The real question here is, what the hell am I involved in, Chad?"

I run a hand down my face and walk to the window, resting my hands on a small wooden handrail there. Jared joins me and the two of us stare out across the city, where trees and buildings jut upward here and there.

"Sheridan, the consortium, and who knows who else believe that there's a cylinder that creates enough clean energy to render all other forms of energy, oil included, unnecessary. I don't have to tell you what kind of power a cylinder that creates enough energy to power the world would have. If it's in play, a second device wouldn't even be needed. And of course I don't have to tell you what being the only person to possess that kind of power would mean to Sheridan."

"He hired you to get it?"

"Yes," I confirm.

"And?"

"And I told Sheridan I couldn't find it the day of the fire. Rollin offered me five hundred million dollars for it and I told him I can't give him what I don't have."

"Do you?"

Responding to the weight of Jared's stare, I cut him a look. "Someone got to the man who had it before me," I say, and it's the truth—just not all of it. "Rollin accused me of having it. He said someone in The Underground told him I did."

"Who?"

"I didn't tell anyone in The Underground anything about this, and Rollin didn't name names. But he and his father clearly thought I was entertaining bidders, since he tried to kill me and everyone in my family."

"You couldn't give it to him dead."

"I couldn't give it to anyone else, either. He wants to know who has it now, but in the meantime he's trying to duplicate it. Gia isn't a secretary. She's a chemist who was working on a project to attempt the recreation of the cylinder, with no success thus far. She thought he was going to use it to save the world. Then she overheard him talking about my captivity and saying he was going to use it to hold the world hostage. That's how she got involved."

I expect him to lash out at Gia, but instead Jared asks, "Why is he so convinced you have it?"

"It hasn't shown up," I repeat. "Do you know how many people would do just about anything to get it?" And knowing that could include Liam Stone, I straighten, facing Jared. "Does Stone have access to the party's guest list?"

Pushing off the rail, Jared turns to me, his hands on his hips. "Not officially, but generally Liam Stone can get just about anything he wants."

"No. He gets what he's allowed to get." And just that fast, I'm angry—or maybe it's not so fast at all, but rather a festering black spot that's been growing since Jared's return that I didn't want to acknowledge. I grab Jared's shirt and shove him against the railing over the window. "Why didn't you get my sister out of Liam Stone's hands?" I demand, realizing now how much that's been under the surface, bothering me since he told me about Stone.

He grabs my arms. "I've seen what you haven't. She won't leave him unless it's in captivity. I'm sorry, Chad, but I had no idea if you were ever returning. Me locking her away in a cage was too far for me to go. You want to go after her now, fine. But you need to understand that that man has a hold on her, and he won't easily let go of what he considers his."

"*His*, my ass."

"He has more money and power than you do, and as harsh as the truth is, he has her trust. You're going to have to earn it back—and it's going to be a war."

The truth of those words crushes what's left of my heart and I let Jared go, running my hand down my hair. I can't lock Amy away eternally. I have to deal with Liam Stone, but I'm going to have to do it after I know she's safe. "I need a way to get to her before Friday night."

"I'll start working on it." He glances toward the bedroom. "I hacked Gia's personnel file at Sheridan's company. Her story matches what you just told me, but there's no mention of a top-secret project."

"That's because it's top secret."

"Four people. That's all that special team comprised, and Sheridan handpicked them all."

"None of this is news to me," I say, relieved it's the truth. "But those other three members will be working to re-create what Gia destroyed. We need to know who they are, and what their motivations are."

"I'm working on making files on the others, but my point wasn't about them. The bottom line here is that Gia was close to Sheridan by being a part of this project. Now I see her getting close to you. She could be another Meg."

"We don't know where Meg came from, or how she found me. We know where Gia came from."

"And we need to know those things about Meg, too. I need everything you can give me from your life before she found you. But that still does nothing to tame my worries about Gia."

"Gia's not another Meg, for all kinds of reasons, and I have no intention of letting anyone screw me over again. On that note, Gia and I need to have a conversation sooner rather than later." I turn to leave.

"Be careful, Chad."

I consider a number of replies, none of which I'd accept if I were him, so I opt to scrub my jawline that's in desperate need of shaving and simply say nothing. I cross the room to enter the master bedroom, likewise wrapped in windows, and Gia greets me at the door, her pale skin like ivory, her dark brown hair draping her shoulders, and worry etched in the furrow of her brow. She is beautiful. She is here. She is mine, if only for now, and I have every intention of keeping her.

I kick the door shut and she takes a step backward, giving me space I do not want. "You have to know that party is a setup. You can't show up there."

"I take it you listened in on our conversation."

"Yes. I did. Chad—"

She yelps as I grab her, rotating her to press her against the door, trapping her legs with mine. "He hacked your personnel file."

"Of course he did. I don't trust him."

I tangle rough fingers into her hair, tugging just enough to force her blue eyes to mine. "He doesn't trust you."

"Like you?"

My answer is a deep, hungry kiss. The taste of her, addictively sweet, fills my senses, stirs a craving for more. *She* makes me crave more. Escape. Passion. That indefinable sense of needing what only she can give me. She moans, a soft, sexy sound I feel in the tightening of my body, the burn in my limbs. My free hand caresses her hip, her waist, the curve of her breast, and I want nothing more than to be lost at sea with this woman, floating on an ocean of waves, so far away from the rest of the world we can't be found. But I have to settle for here. Now. Lost in her. *With her.*

Only, she's not *with* me. I feel it in the tentative caress of her tongue, the uncertainty and reserve of her fingers barely flexing against my chest, and I tear my mouth from hers. "I fucked up in the lobby. But Gia, in a very short time, you've gotten inside my head and under my skin in a way no one else has. You know the real me, and that's dangerous for both of us."

"Dangerous. Right." She shoves against my chest. "Let me off this wall."

"Gia—"

"It's my turn to say stop talking. I *can't* take the back

and forth we have going on. You tell me not to trust you, and then use other words to demand the opposite. I can't be this conflicted about you and us when I'm struggling with all I've lost."

"When I tell you not to trust me, it's not about the here and now. It's about the future, after the dust settles. You can't be with me. I will always invite danger. I am a part of a world you can't understand."

"I'm a part of this world now, too, and I need to understand to survive."

"You aren't. You can't be. I won't allow it."

"You can't change what already is. You think that if I'm out of your sight, I'm safe? That's a fantasy, Chad, and I'm not willing to live in a fantasy that could kill me. I want to fight Sheridan. And I want to protect the cylinder, which I know you have." She balls her fingers around my shirt. "It's not enough to convince him you don't have it. One day this world might need it. You have to come up with a way to make sure it gets to the right person."

"And who is that?"

"I don't know. We have to figure that out. We can. Together."

We stare at each other, the sound of our breaths mingling together, the sun starting to dim beyond the windows, like the resistance I once had to this woman. "I want your help. I even need it, but I won't lie to you anymore. You need to know that the first chance I have to make it happen, *I will* get you out of this."

"If I don't want to go?"

"You'll go."

She inhales and lets it out. "And never see you again."

"It has to be that way."

"If I resist?"

"Then we'll go to war," I assure her, "and I'll win."

"If you send me away, I'll go after Sheridan on my own."

I lean back, pressing my hands on the wall beside her. "That would be foolish, and you're not foolish."

"So is your thinking that you can take on something this big on your own. And don't say you have Jared. I told you I don't trust him, and some part of you doesn't either. You didn't tell him you have the cylinder. You didn't even tell him what you were hiding for six years."

"What he doesn't know can't get him killed."

"That's bullshit, Chad. They'll kill him to get to you, just like they'll kill me, or your sister. You do have to destroy them, and I don't even know how you do that."

"I'll figure it out."

"Damn you and your stubbornness," she hisses. "You're going to end up dead."

"Well, I can promise you that if I do, no one will ever

find that cylinder," I say—finally admitting for the first time, to anyone, that I have it.

Her eyes blaze with pure fury. "And so the smartass returns. You think joking about your death is funny?"

I slide my hands to her hair. "Now *you* need to stop talking. Right here, this moment, is about just that: the moment."

"This moment won't erase the facts. This is bigger than you and me. I have to be a weapon if I can be."

"But not another loss," I declare. "You give me the information. I risk myself. End of story." She opens her mouth to argue and I silence her with a kiss, and I swear I can almost taste the blood I won't let be hers, almost hear the piercing scream of my mother's agony in my head. I cup Gia's head, deepening the connection between us. Needing again. Demanding. Taking. Relieved when she goes from stiff and unyielding to wildly responsive, her tongue stroking mine, her hands sliding under my shirt, her palms soft and warm. Her touch is somehow like a calm summer breeze on a hot Texas night and at the same time it's the fire that makes it hotter.

But Gia isn't calm. She's all over me—kissing me, touching me, possessive in her own right, as if she is trying to hold onto me beyond the moment.

In a rush of movement, I manage to undress us both, picking her up to carry her to the bed. We go down together, and I intend to be on top, but we end up side by side, staring at each other, and I'm lost all right, lost in the deep pools of torment in her eyes.

I grab her and shift our bodies, pressing the thickness of my erection between her thighs. I tangle fingers in her hair and lead her gaze to mine. "Gia."

She leans in and kisses me, and there is a desperateness in her that I don't fully understand, but when she shoves on my chest, I let her push me to my back and climb on top. My gaze rakes over the view of her high breasts and pink, budded nipples. Her slender waist and curvy hips I grasp with my hands, anchoring her as she wastes no time, gripping me and sliding down my erection.

She takes all of me, in more ways than one, and I know that she doesn't know. I can't let her know. We've only known each other a short time. We're reacting to circumstances, to being alone, and being destined to stay that way. She feels she needs control. I've given it to her, allowing her to take the top position by way of demand.

But she surprises me when she leans forward, pressing her palms to my chest as she brings her cheek to mine and whispers, "Alone isn't better." It's gut wrenching.

I react instantly, one hand cupping the side of her face, flattening the other on her back, holding her to me. "And right now, we aren't alone."

She leans back and tries to look at me, but I don't let her. I force her lips to mine, licking into her mouth, breathing with her, drinking in the fear I sense in her, the desperation that is richer now, fuller in a way that can't be possible unless it's about passion and how much we need each other in this place, at this time. I start to move, cupping her backside, lifting my hips. The kiss deepens, maybe because of me, maybe because of her. I don't know. I don't care. I just want her, and this, and that escape into oblivion that I look for in sex and that she actually gives me. We become more frenzied, rougher in the way we drive our bodies together, and we can't kiss. She sits up, staring down at me, and her fear is gone, replaced by the burn of desire.

I watch her move, seduced by her body, her curves, the sway of her hips and the bounce of her breasts—loving the way her head drops forward, her long dark brown hair draping her ivory skin, the way she can no longer sit up and lowers those tight little nipples to my chest, where they rest against the wall of dark blond hair there, her face nestled in my neck.

We ride out what becomes a storm of need, a burn that has to be sated, grinding our bodies together, the sounds of pleasure and heavy rasps of breathing taking on lives of their own. I cup her backside, caress her breasts and tug roughly on her nipples. It seems to send her over the edge as she gasps, "Chad."

A moment later, her sex tightens around the thick ridge of my erection, and it is heaven and hell at once. I ache for the burn to become a rush of pleasure, a release, and I loathe it for the ending it's sure to become. And it does. Her body spasms and spasms some more, and I can do nothing but respond, pressing her down against me as I thrust upward. Once, twice, and then the explosion, the pleasure—the darkness of release that is eternal and not long enough—and then, too soon, the end.

Gia has already collapsed on top of me, both of us exhausted, sated. For a minute, maybe two, I just hold her, before rolling her to face me. We don't speak at first. I'm not sure either of us wants the return to reality, and with it, our battle. But finally, Gia ends the silence. "Alone isn't better."

God. This woman could make me forget why alone *is* better. I reach up, stroking hair from her eyes. "Gia—"

The doorbell rings and I'm on my feet in an instant, tugging on my pants and grabbing my gun from the holster at the foot of the bed. I open the bedroom door to find Jared already at the door to the apartment. "Delivery," I hear from the hallway before Jared says, "Yes. We were expecting you."

I lean on the doorframe, willing the adrenaline rush in my body to calm. Jared turns to look at me over his shoulder, giving my naked chest and low-hanging, unzipped jeans a look before shaking his head in frustration. He really doesn't trust Gia, and I really have to face the facts that Gia can't yet fully comprehend: In a world where a delivery makes me draw a weapon and I question everyone and anyone, including a longtime friend and the woman in my bed, being alone *is* better, and trust doesn't exist.

FOURTEEN

HOURS LATER, all three of us have showered and thrown on casual attire. The sun has set long ago behind the skyline, darkness a cloak beyond the floor-to-ceiling windows of the main living area. The marble coffee table is the command center of our hours of work piecing together anything that might be of value to defeat Sheridan and protect Amy.

Stretching, I lean back on the ottoman I'd pulled to the end of the table a good hour ago, watching Gia tab through something on her computer screen while she nibbles on a slice of pizza. Seeming to sense my attention, she arches her brow with a questioning look. I answer by lifting my chin toward Jared, who is sitting on the opposite side of the couch from her. "Just wondering how you're surviving the stench of his anchovies."

Jared glances up from his computer, but doesn't stop typing. "I guess she doesn't have your delicate little nose."

"Chad's right," Gia says, crinkling her nose. "They stink."

"Spoken like a person who ordered 'just cheese' pizza," Jared responds. He seems to have grown more comfortable with Gia as we've shared information, and she's become comfortable with him as well.

"Anything that's furry and stinky should not go in food," Gia fires back. "And it's funny how *furry* and *stinky* remind me of Sheridan. I just finished typing up everything I remember about the year I spent with the man. The dinners. The conversations. The people in his life. I just e-mailed my notes to both of you at the addresses you gave me. I'm GiaGia@Gmail.com."

"GiaGia?" I ask, and it's my turn to arch a questioning brow.

"It's a memory," she explains.

"Gia, you know—"

"That I'm not Gia anymore," she finishes. "Yes. It's a free e-mail address on Jared's protected remote server. Let me cling to my past where I can safely."

"There is no place to do it safely. I didn't make those kinds of assumptions, and I still don't know how I was located and targeted by Meg."

"So far I can't find a clear answer to that," Jared adds, "and I know you've looked as well, but I'm not exactly focused right now. I just fed a personnel list for the facility Gia worked at into a program I created, as well as the guest list for Friday night's party. The program will flag certain criteria I've coded it to look for, but it's going to take a few hours. I can speed it up by not running anything else at the same time." He pulls another computer out of his briefcase. "Good thing I have a backup computer." He glances at me. "I've done this previously with Meg and come up dry. When I couldn't find anything on her electronically, I followed her to a restaurant and bar in Denver, played the social game, and left with her fingerprints. I've done a few jobs for the FBI, and I managed to get her details run through their system without leaving any record the search was done. Nothing turned up. She doesn't exist."

I'm blown away by everything Jared's done, feeling like a shithead for doubting him. "Thanks, man. Seriously. I didn't even have time to leave you money when I disappeared. I swear you will be repaid generously in every possible way."

"The only payment I need is for this to end. And I'm pissed as hell that Meg escaped my radar. She was in Texas at the same time we were, and then she was just gone. No sign of her again, and she's the only link we have to Rollin. And it makes me nervous as hell to know he's a dead man walking around out there somewhere, a license to kill from his fictional grave."

"The upside," I say, "is that I can have the honor of putting him in his real grave."

Jared turns his computer toward Gia. "You're sure you don't remember seeing Rollin before?"

Her brow furrows. "You know, now that I see a larger shot rather than the cell phone photo you showed me before, there *is* something about him, but I don't know what. Maybe . . . a photo on Sheridan's credenza, perhaps?" She shakes her head. "But I'm not really sure. I didn't exactly get invited to his office to chitchat about his personal life."

"Why *did* you go there?" I ask.

"For my interviews. For a couple of team meetings. I think maybe four times."

"What about when he hosted all those weekly dinners?" I press. "Did he talk about anything personal at all?"

"He asked us a lot of personal questions as we ate, and seemed genuinely interested in the answers. But once the food was cleared, it was all about the research progress."

"This really shouldn't be news," I say. "Sheridan is a smooth operator who is never foolish."

"He left a door open, and Gia overheard a conversation that led her to help you escape," Jared reminds me. "That sounds pretty foolish to me. Greed and desperation create screwups. And six years is a long time for both things to fester."

"Yes," Gia says, averting her gaze to punch a random key on her computer. "Six years is a long time for it to fester."

Sensing a shift in her mood, I tilt my head to study her, but she leaps to her feet, tugging her teal T-shirt over her snug black leggings, and announcing, "I need a soda. I put some of the beer from the grocery order in the fridge earlier—anyone want one?"

Jared lifts a finger. "I'm in. I hack better with a buzz."

Gia arches a brow in my direction, but I don't miss how she doesn't quite make eye contact.

Lifting a hand, I decline. "I hack better with caffeine. Another Coke for me."

"Coke it is."

She turns and hurries away, her pace a little too fast to be casual. "Chad hacks like my kindergarten teacher," Jared yells over his shoulder at her. "Better get him Kool-Aid."

"Since when did you grow a sense of humor?" I ask, not sure why I haven't let the friendly banter bait me into admitting just how good at hacking I've become.

"Since when did you lose yours?" he challenges.

"Six years ago," I snap, the question setting me off for no logical reason.

He gives me a level stare. "Which is why you have to end this."

I nod, still trying to shake off the irritation I don't understand while he's already moved on, keying a couple more strokes before adding, "I just sent you the list of party attendees, but remember, it's going in my program tonight. I wouldn't bother to analyze it too much until the program finishes."

"The party is a setup," Gia says, setting the drinks on the table and sinking back to the floor, her strange energy from a minute before seemingly gone, leaving me to wonder if I'd imagined it. Or, considering how touchy I am with Jared, maybe I just absorbed it. "Anything too convenient," she continues, "or too good to be true almost always is."

"I'm not denying it reads like a trap," I assure her. "In fact, I'm certain that's exactly the case." I look at Jared. "This consortium member on the guest list lives in Houston," I say, having studied each member quite extensively. "Can we find out when he arrives for the party?"

"One step ahead of you," Jared responds. "He's out of the country at present, and his return ticket is a week out."

"That pretty much confirms the trap, and that Sheridan is watching Amy," I conclude. "And Liam's a little too close to the situation for my comfort."

"Liam is too close to *your sister* for your comfort," Gia comments. "That means you aren't objective. Don't let him be a distraction from a real threat, like you did me."

"I don't trust Liam any more than Chad does," Jared interrupts, "and I haven't made that a secret to Amy. I can use that to get to her. I'll call her and tell her I have information about your whereabouts and will only talk to her. She'll agree, but finding a way for her to ditch Tellar Phelps is going to be the issue."

"That's the bodyguard?" Gia asks.

"Yes," Jared confirms, "and a damned good one at that."

Fighting an urge to pace, I say, "Tell her *no one but her* means no one but her. Tell her I'm in a life-or-death situation. Fuck, man. Tell her whatever the hell you have to. Just get her free of Liam and Tellar."

He reaches into a briefcase and sets another folder on top of my pizza box. "You need a reality check. These are shots I took while watching them. I find when I'm at a distance that I miss things that I see later in photos. And they tell a story: Namely, that Amy won't cut Liam out of the information loop."

Gia moves to sit on the ottoman next to me and I open

the folder, suddenly staring down at a close-up of my sister, feeling like I've just taken a punch in the chest. It's then that I realize that watching her from a distance, seeing her and knowing she was alive, had quite possibly kept me sane all of these years.

Gia's hand slides to my leg, warm and welcome, and I can almost feel Jared's eyes on us but I don't give a shit. "She looks like you," she observes. "Her hair is much blonder than yours, but she has the same defined cheek-bones as you, and you both have the same remarkable pale blue eyes."

"She looks exactly like our Swedish mother," I say, hating the memory of Amy braiding her hair and wearing dark-rimmed glasses for years after the fire. I laugh sadly. "My father called the two of them Twinkies. Amy loved it. So did my mother."

"What'd he call you?" Gia queries.

"Same thing as you. *Asshole.*"

She laughs, and I swear there is some kind of a musical, sweet quality to it that takes just enough of the edge off to allow me to turn to the next photo, a shot of Amy with Liam. My sister is looking her normal, sweet, innocent self in a floral dress of some sort, her arm latched around that of an impeccably dressed Liam Stone. She's laughing up at him, and the joy in her expression is something that I've not seen since before the fire—and he, in turn, is looking at her like he's the wolf and she's dinner.

Shutting the folder, I glare at Jared. "I've seen enough. I get the idea. He's possessive and she's head over heels. She'll want to believe Liam is good even if he's the devil himself."

"He might *actually* be a good man," Gia argues.

"And I might be Prince Charming," I reply dryly, eyeing Jared. "You say Meg told her that Liam's life was in danger to lure her away before. So let's go that route again. Tell her he's in danger again and you can't risk him taking the wrong actions. She can't tell him about the meeting."

Gia makes a frustrated sound and flips open the folder, holding up the shot of Liam and Amy. "What do you see in this photo?"

"What I cannot unsee," I snap.

She glowers. "I'm serious, smartass. What do you see?"

"A man who wants to fuck my sister."

"Fine. Be stubborn. *I* see a man in love. Completely, totally in love."

I glance at the photo and back to her. "I still see a man who wants to fuck my sister, and could easily fuck her over. So what the *fuck* is your point?"

Her glower turns to a scowl. "'*Fuck. Fuck. Fuck.*' Will you *fucking stop* with the F-bombs, and think beyond your caveman-brother routine? She loves Liam. You say she feared for his life once before. If you put her through the hell of that again, she's going to be furious. Don't push her away before you get her back."

"She's going to hate me no matter what, so, no harm, no foul. At least she'll be alive to do it."

"You just said that the party setup confirms Sheridan's people are watching her. She's safe while they wait for you to make a move. And if Liam Stone is in love with her and she with him, what's to stop them from holding him for ransom, or even killing him, to get to you through your sister?"

"Liam Stone has proven he's capable of taking care of himself. We'll warn him to tighten his security." I eye Jared. "I need an option that doesn't include you alerting Amy of anything in advance."

"Amy has a doctor's appointment every Tuesday and Thursday."

"What kind of doctor's appointment?" I ask, immediately thinking of her miscarriage.

"She's being treated for the blackouts she's apparently been having for a while now."

"Blackouts?" Gia asks. "What kind of blackouts?"

I inhale and let it out. "Post-traumatic stress disorder. She's battled it off and on since the fire, but honestly, I'd thought she'd have beat it by now."

"She had, too, for a while," Jared confirms. "They seemed to be retriggered by recent events."

"Right," I say, the reminder that I wasn't there for her again feeling like a bullet to the chest. "All the more reason to protect her," I reply. "Does Liam go with her to the appointments?"

"He drops her off and goes to the bank," he informs us. "And then they meet up at the coffee shop next door. But Tellar is always with her."

"Does he go inside the doctor's office?"

"I don't know," he says. "And I can't hack that answer for you. The thing to do would be to watch from a distance on Tuesday to figure out the routine and act on Thursday. That gives us tomorrow to focus on our many loose ends, like Meg and Rollin."

Gia grabs my arms. "Please think hard about what your next step is. You and Amy are the ones who will feel the outcome of what you do next, Chad. Can you really live with Liam Stone ending up dead if he's truly the love of Amy's life?"

I stand up and walk to the window, hands settling on my hips, and stare out over the lit-up Manhattan skyline without really seeing it. Liam Stone is a problem that could create more problems, and a whole lot of heartache, for my sister.

Gia steps to my side. "You okay?"

"Fucking beautiful," I murmur.

"She's safe. Sheridan is waiting on you. Faster is always better."

But she's wrong. And I believe Jared is right. Six years has bred greed and desperation in Sheridan. "If I don't show up to that party, Sheridan will try to flush me out rather than risk losing me again. In other words, seventy-two hours from now, my sister could well become a target, and if Liam Stone is involved in this, then he could be the one to pull the proverbial trigger."

WE FIND OUR way to bed at nearly four in the morning, and I fall asleep with Gia curled at my side, feeling the warmth of her body as a cushion against all things cold and icy in this world. I think I can't sleep. I'm certain I can't, but then somehow I'm in the middle of a nightmare, aware on some level that I'm asleep but unable to escape.

Smoke burns my lungs and I choke, shouting for my sister. "Lara! Lara!" I wait, the flames licking across the spare bedroom floor, eating away at the carpet and any time I have left. I wait, though, listening for a reply that doesn't come, the heat burning my skin without touching me. Now my fear is shifting toward my parents, still trapped in their room, the sound of the fire trucks still too distant. I grab a tree limb that juts toward the house, using it to haul myself onto the roof and feeling sick as I observe flames consuming the opposite side of the house. They're gone. My parents are gone. But Lara might not be.

I grab the tree again and don't even think about the drop, jumping to the ground, my bones rattling with the impact. That's when I see Lara, flat on the ground, with my neighbor and trusted friend huddled over her. I'm rushing toward her when a glint of something to my right catches my eye. I stop, searching the line of trees and bushes separating us from another house. I go low and move back to the edge of the house, where the flames have yet to consume it, smoke billowing just above my head. And I wait. The glint comes again and I don't wait for another confirmation. Whoever set that fire is watching.

I gasp and sit up, my heart thundering in my chest, but I am still in that nightmare, replaying the moment I'd found the bastard who'd set the fire, plowing him with my body and going down on top of him. Remembering the struggle and my hands on his throat. Choking the life out of him, and enjoying it. Fucking loving it.

"Chad," Gia says softly, and I become aware of her lying next to me, her body pressed to mine, her hand on my chest over my thundering heart, the moon casting a warm glow over us from outside the windows. "I'm here," she murmurs. "You're here, not there."

I grab her hand and look down at it, so small and feminine, so fragile, and I don't want her to be hurt. Not by Sheridan and not by me. She needs to understand how bad this is, how deeply embedded in hell she's become. "I killed the man who set our house on fire," I confess, without looking at her. "I choked him to death and then threw him in the burning house. My only regret is that I didn't throw him in alive."

She surprises me by climbing onto my lap and cupping my face, and when I look into her eyes I find understanding, not condemnation. "He would have killed again. He might have come after you and your sister."

"That wasn't what I was thinking. I just wanted him to die for killing my family."

"No one knows how they'll respond in the midst of that kind of hell. No one can judge until they've lived the same nightmare."

She presses her lips to mine, a whisper of unspoken acceptance in the touch. I expect that burning need to fuck away my edginess to overcome me, but it does not. Instead, there is only a calm I do not remember feeling in what seems like a lifetime, a sweet sense of rightness that only she, it seems, can stir. I roll Gia to her side, me on my back again. She settles on my chest, her leg tangled with mine, her hand on my heart.

By the time I'm drifting back to sleep, I decide that she's right. Alone isn't better, but with the smell of smoke still burning in my nose as if I really was in that nightmare, I know that sometimes it's the right thing to be.

MORNING COMES, AND as tempting as it is to visit the house where Amy is living, I resist, aware of the many eyes that will be on her, looking for me. I won't risk being spotted and ruining my chances of getting her out of Manhattan safely. Instead, Gia and I research Liam Stone, looking for connections to Sheridan, or anyone who would want the cylinder. At least where Liam Stone is concerned, I am both relieved and concerned when we find nothing to better aid my decision as to how to handle him and Amy.

Worse, perhaps, is Jared coming up with the same result of "nothing" as he digs for more on Rollin, who we both worry is a sleeping giant that could come back to bite us in the ass. Why fake his death? Where is he, and what is his role in all this?

By late evening, the three of us are sitting at the glass-topped kitchen table, eating grilled chicken sandwiches we've ordered from the concierge service, and going over the plan for the next day. By the time bedtime arrives I'm keyed up, eager to see my sister again, even from a distance.

I use Gia to burn off the energy, but I'm starting to realize that what I do with her is not the kind of fucking I'd do with other women. It's not a blind lust I use as an outlet. It is passionate, burning-up-the-sheets sex, punched with every piece of emotional baggage I own and actually allow Gia to see. When it's over, we are sated, exhausted, and I am certain I will sleep peacefully, but I do not. I have the nightmare again, the memory ripping at the frayed edges of my mind and doing more damage. This time, though, I somehow manage to wake without disturbing Gia.

For two hours, I stare at the ceiling, thinking through every option I have to end six years of hell, until I can no longer stand to circle the problem without answers. I quietly slip away from Gia and enter the bathroom, decorated in the same black and gray as my mind. Bypassing the oval black tub that tells me the designer was in a really fucking bad mood when he got to this room, I turn on the shower and step in. Before I can pull the glass door shut, Gia steps inside, wrapping her arms around me.

She tilts her chin up to look at me. "You aren't okay, are you?"

In a blink, I have her against the wall, burying myself inside her, trying to drive away my demons. But though it's fast and hard and wild, it's only a small escape, one that doesn't erase the memories of those nightmares, and I know why. I pull out of Gia and stare down at her. "To answer your question: No, I'm not okay. I'm about two days from telling my sister I'm the reason our parents are dead."

It's the first time I've said it out loud, and I swear the words linger on my tongue like boiling acid. And suddenly I am angry at Gia for understanding me instead of hating me.

I turn away and reach for the door. "Chad," Gia says, confusion etched in her voice.

"We need to get dressed," I say without turning. "Dress to blend in with a crowd if you need to." I step out of the shower and grab a towel, leaving her the way I should have in the first place. *Alone.*

GIA AND I manage to manipulate our shared personal space in awkward silence, and by eight thirty, I'm sporting a one-day shadow again and I've dressed in black jeans and a plain black tee. I've just finished strapping on a shoulder holster when Gia exits the bathroom wearing a pair of snug navy jeans and a simple navy long-sleeved blouse, gaping as she watches me insert a handgun in the holster.

"I thought all we were doing today was watching the surveillance feed Jared hacked from the truck you bought yesterday?"

"We are," I say, disposing of the gun again, "but you can never be too prepared. That's exactly why I told you to dress to blend in. Wear that long, black, knee-length jacket with the hood we got you. It's cold outside, and it lets you disappear if you need to."

She hugs herself. "You're making me very uptight."

"Good. You need to be. This isn't going to just go away." I walk to her, towering over her, proving to us both that I can be around her and not touch her. "The cold, hard fact is that if I convince Sheridan that I don't have the cylinder, you become more valuable. And no matter how guilty I feel about starting this, it doesn't help you for me to pretend that isn't the case."

"I don't need you to make things pretty for me, Chad. I don't even know where that would come from. And there were three other people on the team, but frankly, if I have to be the bait that we use to take that man down, that's exactly what I'll do." She pauses, her jaw setting. "With or without you."

"Responding to that will not get us out of here on time,

so I won't." I glance at the black Gucci watch that I'd bought to replace the one Sheridan's men had stolen from me. "We need to move now."

"I thought Amy's doctor's appointment was at eleven?"

"It is, but this is Manhattan. You don't just get a parking spot, and we want plenty of time to test the cameras." I begin to turn and she grabs my arm, and damn it, my sex clenches in automatic reaction. "Today is about observing, right?"

"Yes," I confirm. "Today we watch. Thursday I get my sister."

She studies me for several beats, weighing my reply. "Good," she finally says. "Because we still need to talk about how to handle Liam Stone."

Having no interest in talking about Liam Stone, I tap my watch. "Grab the jacket and let's go," I say, dislodging her hand from my arm and leaving the room. Stepping into the living room, I see Jared waiting at the door, his long hair in some sort of funky bun at the back of his head.

"What's with the bright green Fighting Irish T-shirt?" Gia asks before I can, stepping to my side.

"I'm blending in, as instructed," he replies. "There's a large Irish community in New York City, and a number of pubs near the coffee shop."

I don't approve of this strategy, but we're on too tight a

clock for me to argue. I herd everyone to the elevator and the valet parking area, where I've had the Ford Explorer I'd purchased yesterday pulled around already. With Jared driving to leave me free to exit quickly if need be, and Gia in the back seat, we drive around for an hour looking for parking. Finally, I bribe someone to give up a curb spot directly across from the coffee shop.

Once we're parked, Jared sets up a laptop on a cradle beneath the radio, the screen split into quarters to show various portions of the medical building and coffee shop. At ten forty-five, Liam Stone's Bentley pulls up to the building, and instinctively my hand goes to my weapon, every muscle in my body tense. Gia's hand goes to my arm, a silent warning to steady myself, and it's unnerving how well she reads me. But then again, my hand on my weapon isn't exactly a sign that I'm feeling relaxed.

The passenger's-side back door opens and Liam steps out of the vehicle, towering over the hood, but rather than move away and allow Amy's exit, his body encloses the small space, preventing it. He scans the area around them while the driver's door opens and a man in a suit, sporting a military-style buzz cut, emerges, his demeanor unapproachable and ready for battle.

"Tellar Phelps," Jared murmurs, watching him discreetly taking in his surroundings. "They don't seem like men who believe they've negotiated safety. Maybe someone warned them we might show up," I comment.

It's in that moment that Amy steps out of the Bentley, her long blond hair lifting in the wind over the collar of some sort of trench coat. My hand that was resting on my gun goes to the door.

Still holding my arm, Gia settles a second hand on my shoulder. "She's safe. That has to be enough right now."

I inhale a hard-earned breath and force it out, watching as Liam pulls her to him, possessively kissing her hard on the lips, before Tellar offers her his arm. Tension travels up and down my spine and I ball my fist over the door handle. Liam remains unmoving, watching Amy and Tellar until they enter the building. Once she's assumedly safely inside, he rounds the hood of the car, coming fully into view, his suit and his carriage screaming *regal, rich bastard*, a little too like Sheridan for my comfort. Once he's at the driver's door, he opens it, but he doesn't disappear into the car as I expect. Instead, he pauses and scans the area around him again, his eyes running over our car, stopping, and lingering a moment before his attention shifts.

Gia lets out a loud breath. "Did he see us?" Gia asks. "He seemed like he knew we were here."

"No," Jared insists as Liam slides into the driver's seat,

pulling into traffic. "He'd never leave Amy if he knew we were here."

"At least now we know he drives himself to the bank," I observe, running my hands down my legs and relaxing marginally. "A flat tire at the bank on Thursday would be well timed."

"So you're going to just steal her away from Liam?" Gia asks, her voice thick with disapproval.

"I'm going to do whatever feels right after I finish making my observations," I reply.

"You can probably pay some kid in the area to stick a nail in his tire or pull some wires discreetly," Jared suggests as if Gia hadn't said a word.

"A stranger isn't reliable," I say, watching the computer screen as Tellar enters the elevator with Amy. "Fuck. The man is stuck to her like glue."

"The coffee shop seems to be our best bet," Jared suggests.

I axe that idea. "We need more time in between us and Liam and that means finding a way to reach Amy inside that building, while he's dealing with his meetings and whatever car trouble we manufacture."

"Sheridan probably has access to the building's security," Gia reminds me. "And it's you he really wants, Chad. You have to be careful."

"She's right," Jared agrees. "I should make the contact with Amy. They aren't looking for me. I can go into the building Wednesday night and stay the night. I'll wait in the doctor's office, where there won't be cameras. But we'll need a distraction to get her out of the building."

We all seem to contemplate that, tossing out ideas, and waiting for what seems like forever for Amy to appear again. Finally, she reappears on the footage and exits the elevator into the lobby. Tellar is by her side, laughing at something she's said. He replies and she stops walking as she bursts into laughter.

"Looks like the hard soldier isn't so hard after all," I observe.

"He's close to Amy, and he's a bit of a clown with his friends," Jared explains, "but don't let that fool you. He's dangerous."

Amy grabs his arm, as if to steady herself, wiping away tears, smiling larger than life as she and Tellar begin to walk. *She's close to Tellar.* She has friends, something she hasn't dared in years. She's happy, and if I don't shatter her world again, Sheridan will. "Damn it, Amy," I murmur. "Never let your guard down."

"She can't help it," Gia replies. "She's human, just like you, Chad."

"No," I say tightly. "Not anything like me. She deserves

to be happy, but it can't be here, like this, while she's being hunted."

"Which is why we're going to end this, this time," Jared promises.

Amy and Tellar exit onto the street, and he guides her close to the building, putting himself between her and us, and anyone else. Thirty seconds later, they disappear into the coffee shop and we turn our attention to the computer screen again, watching as the two of them order coffee and sit down together, laughing and chatting away. There's absolutely no chance of getting to Amy with him on top of her this way.

I frown as an unfamiliar redheaded woman approaches the table, stopping to talk to my sister. "Who is that?"

"Her doctor," Jared comments. "She was in the file."

"No," Gia says, her voice oddly raspy as she adds, "She wasn't."

I frown, realizing she's right, which seems like an oversight that Jared doesn't usually make. The woman laughs and turns slightly, giving us a look at her face. "Oh my God," Gia murmurs. "Can you zoom in? I need to see that woman's face."

I twist around to look at her. "What is it, Gia? Who is she?"

"I think . . . I . . . *zoom*, Jared," she orders. "*Please*. Now, before she leaves." Jared does as she demands, and the minute the redhead's face is fully in view, Gia grabs my arm. "The woman I said was visiting Sheridan. That's her."

"You said she was blond."

"She was, but that is either her or her doppelganger. They're using the doctor to try and get information from Amy about you and the cylinder."

That icy cold I haven't felt in days is back, and I am frozen inside. "The question is, who is 'they'? Liam Stone, or Sheridan and his consortium? Rollin, maybe? All of the above, or someone else? I'm not waiting until Thursday. We get her now."

Jared pops his door. "I'll walk in and tell her I need to talk to her in private." He doesn't wait for a reply, exiting the SUV, and I curse, grabbing the beanie from my pocket and pulling it over my head. I quickly follow him, meeting him at the hood of the vehicle. "The back door of the coffee shop opens to Fifty-first Street," he says as I step in his path. "Amy and I will meet you there."

"How are you going to get her to the door?"

"I'll figure it out. Just be there. Liam will be back any minute." He dashes through traffic before I can stop him.

"Damn it to hell," I curse, rushing to the driver's door, and claiming the seat behind the wheel as Gia climbs into the front to join me.

"Are you sure this is a good idea?" she asks.

"No. No, I am not sure this is a good idea." I start the engine. "Watch for Jared while I watch traffic. I have to get to the side door to pick up Amy. Tell me when Jared enters the coffee shop." I look over my shoulder, trying to find a gap in the traffic to pull onto the road and seeing none.

"He's inside," she announces. "But Chad, the Bentley is back, and Tellar just exited the building. I think he's going to trade places with Liam." She turns to me. "You need that distraction we talked about now. I'll make one." She opens the door. I reach for her, but it's too late. She's out of the SUV, and I shout, "Gia, get back here!" but she slams the door back into place.

"Fuck me," I curse, cutting into traffic, promising myself that I'm going to lock Gia up after this and throw away the key. Maneuvering into traffic, I cross three lanes and eye my rearview mirror in disbelief to find Gia talking to Liam and Tellar. She's cleared a path to free Amy, but at what cost?

Dread heavy in my stomach, I cut right onto Fifty-first Street and pull into the service lane, identifying the coffee shop door, and wait. Wait some more. And then it feels like I wait some more, when really it's only a minute. Maybe two. Okay, three. It has to be fucking three minutes.

I get out of the SUV and my fingers curl by my sides, debating my next move and then launching into action, running for the door. Once I'm there, I enter into a hallway and run smack into Amy and Jared. Amy gasps. "Chad. I . . . I . . . "

She bursts into tears and wraps her arms around me, and while this is the wrong place and time, the emotions that overwhelm me are second only to those I'd felt the night of the fire. I hug her, holding on so tight I'm not sure how she can breathe.

"We need to move," Jared warns.

He's right, and my hands go to my sister's arms, lifting us apart. "He's right. We have to go."

"Go? Where? Why? Oh God. Is it really you? How is it you?"

"I'll explain everything, but not here. It's not safe. We need to go somewhere else." I turn her toward the door, ready to get the hell out of this place, when I hear a voice.

"She's not going anywhere without me."

I stiffen and look up to find myself staring into the piercing blue eyes of Liam Stone. The door to my right opens, and I catch Tellar's entry from the corner of my eye. Jared is to my left, and Liam directly behind Amy.

And one person is missing: Gia.

FIFTEEN

LIAM'S VOICE ECHOES AROUND US, seeming to bounce off the walls and repeat. Amy is the first to break the spell, whirling around to face him, and wrapping her arm around mine.

"Liam. This is my brother, Chad." Her voice trembles, quavering as if emotion is consuming her the way it threatens to me. "He's really alive. Can you believe it? He's really alive."

"And trying to kidnap you," Liam observes, never taking his eyes off of me.

I don't take my eyes off him, either, but I'm aware of

Tellar to my right and Jared to my left. "Go find Gia," I order Jared, before speaking directly to Liam. "I'm leaving with my sister."

"What?" Amy asks, releasing me and folding her arms over the pink lace bodice of her dress. "I'm not leaving without Liam."

"We're leaving, Amy," I assure her. "Together and alone." She sways toward Liam and I grab her arm. "We need to leave. Now."

She jerks her arm away. "You can't come into my life six years after you left and just grab me and run. Liam is in my life, and he's staying. And he'll help you if you let him. He's safe. He can be trusted."

"No one is safe," I assure her. "Not for us. And everyone who suddenly comes into our lives has hidden agendas. Believe me, I had my Liam, and I paid the price."

She hugs herself, and I can almost see her withdraw from me. "I hate that you went through something so horrible. I know how lonely it is in this life we were forced into, but Liam isn't the person who did that to you. He has no hidden agenda."

Unbelievable. Jared was right; she's been all but brainwashed by this man. "No hidden agenda, huh? Then why is your doctor working for Sheridan, showing up at his office in a wig?"

"She's a good friend," Amy says defensively. "An amazing friend who has put herself in danger to protect us."

I shake my head in disbelief. "What part of 'she's working for Sheridan' did you not understand?"

"She's right," Liam interjects. "Dr. Murphy is not working for Sheridan, but he thinks she is. His people approached her, and she came to us right away. We tried to discourage her from going along with them, but she didn't listen. She felt that being inside his circle meant knowing his plans, and protecting me and Amy."

I almost laugh at what is either ignorance or a blatant lie. "Sheridan corrupts at will. You might be convinced of her honor, but I'm not."

Liam's eyes sharpen, a flicker of anger in their depths. "Contrary to your obvious belief that I'd be careless with your sister's safety, I wouldn't trust Amy's care to an unknown. Dr. Murphy has been a longtime family friend, and a very close and personal friend of Alex's."

Amy launches into further explanation. "That's Liam's adoptive father."

"She also supplied some interesting intel on Sheridan's new business interests, which I've been monitoring—interests the consortium wouldn't be pleased with, and which could in fact divide and weaken them."

"And the wig?"

"She says he's become paranoid to an extreme," he replies. "Something has him shaken, and I have a few ideas about what."

I open my mouth to press for details, but Amy is already pleading Liam's case again. "Liam's one of the good guys. He helped me deal with Sheridan and that list of his allies you left for me. He hired a hit man and told Sheridan that if anything happened to me or anyone close to me, they would all be killed."

Feeling the clock ticking, I grab her arms and pull her in front of me. "A hit man won't stop Sheridan or anyone else on that list from using you against me when the time is right, and that time is now. You need to come with me. You can come back here when this is over."

"When it's over? Will it *ever* be over? I love you. I love you so much, but I'm not leaving Liam. If I'm wrong about him, I don't care."

Dread fills me, but my resolve is strong. "I don't want to hurt you, little sis, but I can't lose you either. Don't make me take you by force."

"You can't do that. I won't let you. He won't let you. It's my choice to stay, and I will suffer the consequences."

"This is bigger than you and me and our personal wants and needs. If it wasn't, I would have given them what they wanted a long damn time ago." I set her aside, holding onto her arm, my gaze colliding with Liam's. "We're leaving."

His jaw sets hard, his eyes glinting with steel. "Let me be crystal clear," he replies crisply. "You'll have to shoot me to get her away from me, in which case, Tellar will shoot you."

"And risk putting Amy in the crossfire? Not a risk a man in love would take."

"I've never met a trained sniper who couldn't pick a target," Tellar replies for him. "That includes me."

I glance at him, a cynical twist to my lips. "Sniper?"

"That's right," he confirms. "And a very skilled one."

"I'm a firm believer in karma, and that's a heartless job that doesn't scare me. It makes me want to shoot you."

Amy grabs my arm. *"Please. Stop.* Let's leave now. Together. In peace. Let Liam show you all of his research on Sheridan."

The clock is ticking, and while I'd assumed Jared would return, he and Gia could as easily be sitting ducks in the truck as we are here in this hallway. "For Amy's sake, I'll review the information, but on my terms. We leave together, in my vehicle, and we go to a location of my choice where you can make your case. You can bring the research to that location."

"We take two cars," Liam counters, "and Amy stays with me."

"Not a chance in hell," I reply. "You could call Sheridan or someone else to intercept us."

He hesitates a moment, then concedes, "We'll take your vehicle but I want to know our destination."

"An apartment I keep as a safe house near Rockefeller Center. You get nothing more."

"Pick a public place."

"Public is dangerous," I argue.

"Private can be, too."

"The Marriott Central Park," I say, every second feeling like an hour. "There's a bar with a view of the street and valet parking that can hold the vehicle by the door for the right cash."

"Tellar drives. Amy's in the back with us."

"Agreed," I state, "but we're plus two: Jared, who you know, and Gia, the woman who tried to distract you from coming in the door."

"And we should trust Gia why?" Tellar asks.

"Because I say so, Sniper," I snap, getting to what matters. "I'm the black SUV in the delivery zone. The keys are still in the ignition. You take the front guard." I raise my jacket, exposing my weapon. "I've got the rear."

Tellar and Liam have some sort of silent exchange before Liam reaches for Amy, and I reluctantly release her, allowing him to move her in between him and Tellar. Tellar pushes open the door and inches part of the way outside, scanning to ensure a safe departure, before announcing, "We're a go."

Liam's hands settle on Amy's shoulders, urging her forward, but she glances around him at me and whispers, "Please don't disappear."

"I'm not going anywhere, little sis," I promise a moment before Liam's big body blocks her from view, and the three of them step outside. Staying tightly on Liam's heels, I exit the building only seconds after him, scanning for danger, expecting to find Jared and Gia waiting in the SUV. By the time Tellar has safely escorted both Amy and Liam into the back seat of the vehicle, it's clear Jared and Gia aren't present, and a low burn is rising in my gut.

"Where's your plus-two?" Tellar asks, as I join him at the back door.

"Good question," I say, digging my phone from my front pocket. "Drive around the block until I figure out where to pick them up."

I expect an argument. I get a nod and a quick "Understood," that stirs suspicion, but then, what the hell doesn't in my world.

Surveying the area once more, hoping for any sign of Jared and Gia and finding none, I enter the backseat and slam the door shut, already dialing Gia, certain Jared can fend for himself. I get her generic outgoing message. I try Jared and it goes straight to voice mail. I dial again and my phone beeps with a call I try to pick up, cursing when it seems to go dead too soon. "Fuck," I curse, waiting for a message that isn't registering. Leaning around Amy, I find Liam and ask, "Did you see where Gia went when she left you?"

"Toward the side door where you parked," Tellar calls out. "She should have made it to the vehicle."

That burn in my gut is now on fire. My voice mail finally beeps and I punch the button, holding my breath as Jared's voice plays. *Where are you? There are men following us. I'm going into the subway to try to ditch them. If I can't find you . . .* It breaks off in static and comes back in: *coffee shop . . . we'll go to the apartment.* More static and then nothing.

I end the recording and for a moment, I am frozen in hell, living the fear that my best friend and a woman who has quickly come to matter to me could be lost. Throwing caution out the window, I grab the driver's seat and lean forward to talk to Tellar. "Do you know where the Two57 Tower is? Jared said that they were being followed and he'd go there."

Tellar eyes Liam in the rearview mirror and I curse, leaning back in the seat to replay the message on speaker. About halfway through it, Amy covers her mouth, and the unreadable Liam Stone hears it out before ordering, "Two57

Tower, Tellar. Now." Tellar cuts left on the next street and Liam glances in my direction. "Who is Gia? Is she a potential target?"

"She's a chemist who worked on a top secret project for Sheridan. She found out I was being held captive and risked her life to save me. Now she knows things he doesn't want known, and he will come after her."

"Like he has us," Amy says, her voice low, gravelly.

Drawing her hand into mine, I know now isn't the right time for explanations, but more and more it feels like tomorrow isn't a guarantee. "I started working for a group of treasure hunters—"

"The Underground," she supplies. "We know. Jared told us. What does Sheridan want from you?"

"Knowing what it is puts you at risk."

"Are you kidding me, Chad? You're actually going to try to keep this a secret? I've lived six years in hiding. I deserve to know why."

"I know that, little sis, and I'm not unwilling to share the details you want, but you have to understand that while you trust Liam and Tellar, I don't. I can't imagine you did at first, either." We stop in what looks like a traffic jam and my mind races with worry over Amy, and absolute fear for Gia and Jared. I look at Liam's hand on Amy's leg and my mind is made up. "I believe that Sheridan wants you alive. But I'm not confident he won't kill Gia and Jared to punish me. I have to get to them before it's too late."

She grabs my arm. "No. Please. No, you can't leave."

"I have to do this, Amy. Give me your phone so I can input my number."

She twists around trying to find her phone. "Oh no. I left everything at the table in the coffee shop because Liam was watching it."

Liam hands me his phone. "We'll meet you at the building. Call us if you need us to meet you someplace else."

I key in my number and dial it to log his number in my call log, handing it back to him. "Protect her or I kill you."

"Losing her would kill me," he replies, and when I look into his eyes, I think I might just believe him. I pray I'm right.

Grabbing Amy's hand, I kiss it and promise, "We're connected. We're always connected." I let go of her and reach for the door, her sob following me as I exit onto the street and force myself to shut the door. Digging my phone out of my pocket, I try to call Jared and then Gia, both calls going to voice mail. Street by street, I redial them both, and each time I hear a voice mail pick up, my insides twist a little more.

Ten blocks pass and I reach the door of the apartment, thankful to see the doorman I met on arrival present. "Did my fiancée arrive yet?"

"Not yet, sir. Do you want me to buzz you when she arrives?"

"Are you sure? Could you have missed her?"

"Impossible. I've been in this spot and supervising the rest of our team."

My jaw sets and I walk past him, my destination the security desk, where I have the attendant check the logs to ensure Jared and Gia haven't signed in. The answer is the same. They aren't here.

My cell phone rings and I look down at Jared's number. "Where the hell are you?"

"He's occupied at the moment," comes an unfamiliar voice that sends a chill rushing over my body.

"Where's Jared?"

"Occupied, as is the quite lovely Gia. Or is it Ashley now, as her identification states?"

My gut clenches. He has her purse, and Jared's phone. "Where are they?"

"The coffee shop, of course."

"I just left the coffee shop and they weren't there."

"*They* aren't there, actually. She is. I just left her there."

The line goes dead and acid burns through my veins the way Sheridan has burned through years of my life. Aware I could be watched, somehow I walk, not run, toward the building's exit, redialing Jared's number as I do. It goes straight to voice mail. Heavy-footed now, I burst through the exit of the tower to find Liam, Amy, and Tellar standing with the doorman.

"I got a call from Jared's phone," I announce, focusing on Liam. "They have him, and they say they just left Gia at the coffee shop. Get Amy someplace safe now. I'll call when I can." I don't wait for an answer, certain that seconds wasted could cost Gia her life.

Launching into a run, I dodge random people on the busy sidewalks, quickly crossing intersection after busy intersection, until Tellar appears by my side, announcing, "This is a trap. You know it's a trap."

"What the fuck are you doing here?" I growl.

"Helping you."

"Help me by protecting my sister."

"Liam has Amy, and I'm not going anywhere." We cross a busy street, dodging cars, and while I try to dodge him right along with them, it doesn't work. He reappears by my side, already running his mouth again. "Did you hear me? It's a trap. Whatever this is, it's a trap."

"Of *course* it's a fucking trap." Nearly at our destination, I force myself to slow to a fast walk, scanning for potential trouble. "It's also a ticking clock, with Gia's life on the line. They killed my family. They'll kill her."

"Let me go in after her," he says. "They aren't expecting me."

"That's not happening," I say, but right about the time I'm about to shove him against a wall and give him a knee he won't forget for ten years, I spy a cop on the corner and decide that's a bad idea.

"They could grab you the minute you walk in the door."

Once again, I'm forced to trust him. "Good thing I have a sniper at my back." We stop at the door. "I know my sister wants me to live, but no one else dies because of me. Gia comes first."

"As it should be," he says, opening the door for me. "Sniper at your back."

Another time, that statement would give me pause, but I don't allow myself to think of anything but Gia. Entering the coffee shop, every muscle in my body is stiff, every nerve ending on edge. I scan as I walk, confirming Jared and Gia are at none of the ten or so sparsely populated tables, continuing toward the hallway leading to the back exit. Entering the enclosed hallway where I'd reconciled with Amy, I find it empty, but my heart misses a beat as I catch sight of the bathroom doors.

"I've got this one," Tellar says, stopping in front of the

men's room and reaching under his jacket to hold his weapon.

At my nod, he enters, and uncaring of who I might interrupt I repeat his action with the women's bathroom, my hand covering my gun, dread in my gut as I push open the door to find the immediate area clear, both stall doors shut. Bending down, my heart stops beating as I find someone sitting on the floor and recognize the boots as Gia's. Straightening, I try to open the door. "Gia! Gia, open up." She doesn't reply and I jiggle the door harder, afraid to kick it open and slam it against her. Pushing my way into the unlocked stall next to hers, I climb onto the toilet and bring the stall below into view, feeling sick at what I find. Gia is bound and gagged, her head hanging forward, a needle stuck in her arm.

"Tellar!" I shout, lifting myself over the divider, feeling as if Sheridan is using a shovel to gut me right here and now. "Tellar, damn it!"

He bursts through the door. "I'm here."

"Call an ambulance. They injected her with something, and she's not moving."

SIXTEEN

I JUMP OVER THE STALL WALL onto the toilet beside Gia and unlock the door, which immediately opens in the other direction, and then drop to one knee to wrap Gia in my arms. She doesn't move, and I can't breathe. What if *she's* not breathing? I'm reaching for the syringe, wanting it out of her arm, *needing* it out, when I hear "Stop!"

Tellar bends down in front of me. "Some poisons are lethal to touch. Some so potent even gloves won't protect you."

"Poisons," I repeat, the word heavy on my tongue.

"Please, God, no." I reach down and untie the gag around her mouth, leaning down to thankfully feel a light rush of air. "She's alive."

"I could see her chest moving," Tellar says, shrugging out of his jacket and using it to remove the syringe.

Trying not to think about what a drug so lethal that it can kill by touch could do if injected, I untie her hands. She suddenly jerks and gasps, grabbing my shirt. "Chad. Chad. I . . . where am I? What happened?" She starts shivering. "Cold. I'm so cold."

"Hold on, sweetheart. I've got you." I maneuver to get out of my jacket and Tellar takes it, laying it on top of her, and I don't miss the absence of her jacket or her purse.

She looks up at Tellar, stares at him a moment, and then, as if she's just seen him, pulls back, shrinking against me as if she's just noticed him. "No. No. No. Who are you? No."

"Easy, sweetheart," I murmur, holding her tighter. "This is Tellar. Remember. Amy's security guard."

"I'm a friend," Tellar promises. "I called for an ambulance, Gia. Help is coming. Okay?"

"Yes," she whispers. "Yes. I . . . Amy?" She turns to me, her bottom lip trembling, tears on her cheeks. "Is Amy . . . okay?"

"Yes," I say, astounded by the selflessness of her worry. "She's okay. You're okay."

"No. No. I don't . . . promise me you won't make this for nothing. Promise me. My father . . . he . . ." She shivers and curls into me.

"I'm sorry, Chad," Tellar says, "but we need to talk about what to tell the police."

He's right. I hate him for being so fucking right. I hate Sheridan. I hate all of this, but I cup Gia's face, forcing her gaze to mine, and her skin is icy—so very icy. "Gia." She blinks. She shuts her eyes. "Gia, honey, listen to me."

"Listening," she whispers. "Can't open . . . eyes."

"You need to say you were mugged and don't remember anything. I'll handle the rest."

"My name . . . Ashley . . ."

"No. Be Gia. I'm Chad. Just say you remember nothing. I'll handle it."

"Thank you," she squeaks, more tears running down her cheeks.

I stroke the dampness with my thumb. "Why are you crying?"

"Scared. I'm . . . scared. "

"Don't be scared. I'm right here. Help is coming."

Sirens sound in the distance, throwing me back in time to smoke and fire and death. I cup her body to me, pushing myself to my feet. "I need to get her to the front door."

Tellar backs out of the stall, moving to the exit to hold it open. I rush out into the hallway and it's a blur. I don't see people. I don't see things. One minute I'm holding Gia, and the next she is lying on the sidewalk with emergency personnel all around her.

"What's her name?" a paramedic asks me.

"Gia. Gia Hudson."

A police officer appears, and Tellar and I are giving a statement when Gia starts shouting my name. I rush toward her, trying to get her to lie down, while she tries to sit up. The instant her eyes meet mine, she relaxes and I go down between two men, taking her hand. "I've got you. I'm here."

"Don't leave me."

"I won't," I promise, relieved as they start an IV. "As long as you don't leave me. You hear me? Don't leave me." But she doesn't answer, her lashes lowering, dark half-moons on her too-pale cheeks. She is unmoving, so still, that I watch her chest, savoring every tiny lift I find, every piece of evidence she's alive.

The next few minutes become a whirlwind that finds me in the back of an ambulance, Gia having no idea I'm there. I stare at the monitors as I had her chest, terrified by how slow her heartbeat is one moment, and how rapid the next.

"Why is that happening?" I ask the paramedic traveling with us, a surehanded man in his late thirties.

"Most likely an impact of whatever drug she was given. We're close to the hospital."

The implication being that she needs to be there now. Holding her hand, waiting for the drive to end, I promise myself I will never feel this helpless again. Never. Again. And while killing every member of the consortium had once felt like it would invite revenge seekers and more trouble, right now that plan sounds pretty damn good.

The ambulance stops and the doors are jerked open. I exit and watch as they rush Gia into the hospital, at least five people surrounding her, and there's no mistaking their urgency. The instant we are inside the building, she is rushed to the back room, and I am left staring at the double doors.

Alone.

"Any news?" Tellar asks, stepping to my side, and I can't believe the relief I feel at this stranger's presence.

"No news. She didn't wake back up on the ride over, and they seemed to be waiting for her when we got here."

"That's a good thing, not a bad thing."

"It means they knew she is in real trouble."

"No. It means they were making sure she never got into real trouble. I did a lot of years in Special Ops. With an unknown toxin, time is considered critical. And we acted quickly, and so did they—not to mention Liam's a huge donor here. He'll have a lot of pull to get her whatever she needs as fast as it can be received. I know you don't trust any of us, and in your shoes, I'd feel the same, but Liam Stone's a good man and he loves your sister."

"Chad!"

At the sound of Amy's voice, I turn to find her running toward me, and I want to wring Liam's neck for bringing her here when she should be hiding somewhere, protected. Safe. I fully intend to say as much, but she flings herself at me, hugging me, and I am so damn glad she is alive and well that I hold her and don't let go.

"How is she?" Amy asks, leaning back, hugging herself, and shivering. "I left my coat at the coffee shop."

My mind flashes back to the bathroom, to Gia curled against me. *So cold*, she'd said, and now I'm cold straight to the bone, yet somehow my frozen heart is being painfully thawed.

"Chad." I jolt again at the sound of Amy's voice, looking down and realizing her hand is on my arm, and I've spaced out while Liam fucking Stone has all but painted a target on her chest by bringing her here. "Are you okay?" she says, sounding worried. "Is Gia okay?"

"Gia wasn't good when they took her back."

"Do you know what drug she was given?"

"Not yet," I say."

Amy stares at me a long moment. "You love her."

Love. I repeat the word in my mind, but it settles in my chest, heavy. Painful. "Love isn't a word I've allowed myself to use with anyone but you in a very long time."

She studies me several beats. "But the possibility is there and won't go away."

"We barely know each other," I argue, though she is right when there's every reason for her to be wrong.

"And yet somehow she feels more right to you than anything has in six years. That's how it was for me with Liam when I met him. It was illogical. It was terrifying because of all the reasons I had to fear strangers. But it wouldn't go away. And I didn't want him to go away no matter how many times I told him I did."

"Yes, well, I'm not you. I don't deserve peace, and Gia doesn't deserve this world any more than you did."

"You deserve peace, Chad. You do. *You do*."

"I got us into this."

"No. I know more than you think I do. I overheard conversations and I've gathered some information. Dad borrowed money. Sheridan extorted him. Mom slept with Rollin, and I lived with knowing that by convincing myself that it was to protect Dad. And you started working for The Underground and tried to help. Sheridan's the monster, not you."

"I see Jared's been running his mouth."

"I needed answers. I deserve answers."

"I know that, Amy, but I'd prefer to be the one to give them to you. And you're right. Dad borrowed money from Sheridan to fund dig sites. Big sums of money he should have known better than to borrow. But I didn't know Dad was in trouble when I started working for The Underground. I did it for the high and the money I wanted. I even took jobs for Sheridan when Dad told me Sheridan was trouble. But when I tried to pay off Dad's debt, Sheridan insisted I do another job for him. He wanted me to find something for him that seemed innocent enough."

"Until it wasn't."

"Right. And once I knew what I had, I wasn't sure who to give it to and I'm still not. I think they knew, and it's speculation, but I'm fairly certain Rollin threatened Dad to get into Mom's bed and try to find out more about what I was doing. When he pressured me I told him I couldn't find what he wanted. He said someone from The Underground said I did."

"The Underground betrayed you?"

"I never told anyone about that job. Someone lied for the payout. And I promise you, if I knew who, they'd be dead."

Her brow furrows. "I'm confused. Who helped me hide, then?"

"A friend."

"So the tattoo wasn't for The Underground?"

"No. It was just a tattoo we got together one night out partying."

"Where is he now?"

"Dead, Amy. Everyone close to this dies."

"Oh God. Chad, I don't understand. If Sheridan thought you didn't have it, why kill him and burn down our house?"

"He must have believed I had it, and thought I was selling it to someone else."

"But . . . then he made sure he'd never get it either."

"I know. I've spent six years trying to make sense out of it. There is none."

"I need to know what it is. I need to feel like I have a reason to keep fighting this fight."

I reach up and stroke hair behind her ear. "And you deserve that and so much more. It's a cylinder the size of a pencil eraser that would make enough clean energy to make all other sources of energy unnecessary."

Looking confused, she asks, "Isn't that a good thing?"

"Yes and no. It would crumble industries and governments. It would make the one person who holds it in their hand capable of demanding anything. Doing anything."

Liam joins us and I give him a hard look. "We need to talk."

He gives me a nod and we move several feet away, but I

don't wait to lay into him. "What the fuck is she doing here? You're a damn prodigy architect, which means you're supposed to have brains. What part of 'they were herding us to one spot' do you not get?"

"Herding us, or trying to make us scatter like wild, scared animals? We had Amy cornered in that hallway, the three of us all willing to die for her, and they picked another target. Right now, she's safer right here with us."

"You want to know about 'right now'? *Right now*, Jared is most likely being tortured for information he doesn't have to give. When they find that out, they'll lash out again. Amy can't be here for that."

"I need to know what's going on."

I am not in the mood to explain anything to this man. "Ask Amy. I just told her the entire story."

"I need Gia Hudson's family!"

I whirl around, rushing to meet the fiftysomething gray-haired nurse near the double doors Gia disappeared through. "I'm Gia's husband," I announce as Amy steps to my side and asks, "How is she?"

"Disoriented, but stable and resting," the nurse reports. "We've started fluids to help with the nausea and to flush her system of any toxins." She hesitates. "We're waiting on your wife's test results, but I need to let you know that the syringe tested positive for arsenic."

Amy gasps, grabbing my arm as if she needs to be steadied. "Arsenic," I repeat, the word falling from my mouth like lead, impossibly heavy. Impossible to believe. "She was injected with arsenic?"

"It would seem likely, yes."

"What's the treatment for arsenic poisoning?" Amy asks.

More importantly, I ask, "What's the survival rate?"

"There are a number of drugs and protocols, depending on the toxicity," the nurse replies. "Right now, her condition suggests limited exposure. Let's hope that proves true." She offers me a clipboard. "We'd like to have you sign for consent. We feel like it's best to start treatment now."

"Without the final tests?" Amy asks. "Is that safe?"

"Time is critical with a toxin," the nurse explains. "We feel this is the smart choice."

Sold on fast action, I sign the documents and hand back the clipboard. "Start treatment."

"We'll be out with an update soon," she promises, disappearing behind the doors again.

I grab Amy's hand, keeping her close as I return to where Liam is ending a phone call. "Gia's stable, and the syringe was positive for arsenic. I need to know if Dr. Murphy can treat her, and I need to know now."

"She can, and she will. I already have Tellar working out the logistics, but she's only in if she feels she can treat successfully and we can get the medication." He motions to Tellar, who's talking on the phone a few feet away.

Amy gapes. "What? Are you crazy, Chad? We can't move Gia now. We don't even have her test results."

"I can hack her results," I assure her. "I can't bring her back from the dead, which is what she'll be if she stays here."

"What's the word?" Tellar asks, holding the phone away from his mouth.

Liam tells him, and he quickly returns to his call. "Arsenic. Low doses expected. Stable condition." He listens a minute. "Got it. On it." He ends the call. "Make sure they've started the meds before we leave, and take the IV bag with us. She said that should happen within half an hour. The big question is how we get her out of here."

"They've already started treatment," Amy replies, "which says this is dangerous. She needs hospital care."

"She needs to be somewhere safe," I counter. "This isn't it." I glance between Liam and Tellar. "We go big and bold. I pick her up and carry her out of here, only it's not Gia, it's a decoy. Tellar will have Gia and take her to a safe house, where we'll meet her."

"This is insanity," Amy argues.

"And I like it," Tellar adds.

"It's not ideal," Liam replies, "but I don't have a better

idea on such short notice. Derek Ethridge, a close friend of mine, is picking up Dr. Murphy. His real-estate holding company has properties in the Hamptons that are vacant in the off-season. We can use one of those. We need to decide who goes with Chad and who goes with Tellar."

Though it kills me to think about Gia being on her own with strangers, I know it's the right choice. "Everyone has to go with me or it'll look suspicious. Even Tellar. He puts her in the car with Dr. Murphy and Derek and then joins us at the front of the building."

"You don't have a decoy," Amy points out.

Tellar grins. "I know a girl named Coco. Don't let the name fool you; she's ex-Special Forces, and she'll do anything just to prove she can do it."

"Okay then," I say. "Try to reach her."

He powers up his phone and punches in a number. "Hey, Coco. I have a dare for you, but you have to be at Mount Sinai Hospital in thirty minutes." He pauses a minute and says, "Wear that under your coat and plan to leave everything behind. We'll make it worth your while. Great. Yes. See ya, honey." He ends the call. "Coco is in, and she has her own hospital gown. There's a story behind it that I'll tell everyone over tequila when we get to the safe house."

"Safe would be telling me those calls are not traceable."

"I'm a sniper, not a Sunday school teacher."

"Killing people and knowing how to stay alive yourself are two different things."

"Things which, I suspect, we both do well."

"Not well enough, or Sheridan and his cronies would be dead already," I reply. "How do you know Dr. Murphy's phone isn't monitored, considering her connection to Sheridan?"

"She has a disposable," Liam replies. "And so does Derek. Anyone Amy might need on an emergency basis has one."

Amy hugs herself and grimaces. "There's nothing about this plan that feels safe."

"There's nothing about leaving Gia here that's safe," I assure her.

"We need an exit plan," Tellar says. "I'll scout the building."

"Get me a computer," I say, "and I can hack the hospital floor plan and Gia's test results and treatment plan."

Liam glances around and then walks over to a man on a MacBook, speaks to him for a moment, and then hands him a wad of cash. He returns and hands me the computer. "Hack away."

Power. Money. Liam Stone has them. People who have them, like Sheridan, usually want more. Tuning out Tellar and Amy, I close one of the two steps between myself and Liam and stand toe-to-toe with him. "Circumstances dictate that I trust you. My sister's love for you dictates I trust you. But hear this, Liam Stone: Don't hurt my sister—or I will choke the life out of you and burn your body to ashes, like I did the hired hand who set our house on fire."

I turn and walk away, cranking up the computer and getting busy.

Liam, Amy, and Tellar are quick to join me, without comment about my confrontation with Liam. In all of three minutes I have hacked the hospital's computer system, and my first order of business is to pull Gia's file and download her test results, which I text to Liam to pass on to Dr. Murphy.

The reply is almost instant. "The arsenic levels are low," he reports, "but there's a second drug in Gia's system, a sedative used before surgery that frequently causes people to lose pieces of time."

I glance up from the computer, where I've just pulled up the ER floor plan. "That explains why she doesn't remember what happened to her."

"The good news is it doesn't impact the toxicity of the arsenic, and there is a plan for treatment. We just need to get Gia out safely."

That's something I'm ready to have happen now, not later, and I start the conversation about how to execute a plan with that result. Ten minutes later, we have plotted our exit strategy. Twenty minutes later, Derek and Dr. Murphy are at the side door by the ER. Liam and Amy are in the SUV that is pulled around to the front, and Coco has arrived. Petite, brunette, and proper-looking, she is nothing like what her name and her ownership of a hospital gown suggest. Hugging her black trench coat around her, she waits for her moment and follows another visitor through the ER door.

Tellar and I are on her heels, following her down a corridor and slipping behind a curtain. Gia is lying in a bed, her lashes dark half-circles on her pale cheeks, unaware there are three people standing in her room. As Coco shrugs out of her coat and removes her shoes, I go to Gia. Tellar turns off the heart monitor so it won't buzz when I pull the leads off.

"Gia," I whisper softly.

Her lashes lift, eyes glassy. "Chad? You came."

It kills me to think she believed I'd leave her. "I never left. I found you. I brought you here, and now I'm going to take you someplace safe."

"And leave me?"

"No, but you're going to go with Tellar, the friend who helped save you, and he's going to get you to a doctor. I'll be there soon."

She glances at Tellar, who's leaning over the bed now, and then back at me. "Promise?"

"Yes, sweetheart, I promise. It's going to get scary, though."

She tries to smile. "You need me to make a bomb?"

"Yeah," I say, smiling back at her as I pull out her connections to the machine. "Yeah. To blow up Sheridan's house."

"That would be . . . fun."

How she manages that word despite the kind of pain I see etched in her face, I don't know, but my admiration for her grows every second I'm with her. "We need to take your medication with us," I explain as Tellar hands me two IV bags and I lay them on top of her. "You need to hold onto these tightly. No matter what, hold onto them."

"Yes. Okay. I don't . . . remember what happened."

"Remember me. And us." I lean down and whisper in Gia's ear. "Alone isn't better. You were right." I stand then and look at Tellar. "Let's do this."

He nods, scooping up Gia, and I turn and do the same with Coco, who pulls her coat over her head to hide her identity. I inhale and I exit the room in a rush, and a nurse comes after me. "What are you doing? She's not discharged."

"She is now," I say, pushing through the double doors and entering the lobby. It kills me to know I'm leaving Gia behind.

SEVENTEEN

I EXIT THE HOSPITAL to find the open door of the SUV waiting for me, and I huddle down to allow Coco to climb inside. She quickly scoots across the seat and gushes, "That was a rush," pulling her coat around to put it on, perhaps the only one of us enjoying this.

Joining her inside, I slam the door shut and shout, "Go, Liam!"

He accelerates and calls over his shoulder, "Any trouble?"

"Not on our end."

"Is she out?" Amy asks, twisting around in the seat. "Is she okay?"

"I don't know," I say, already punching in Tellar's number. "Coco and I were the distraction. We couldn't tell what was happening with Tellar and Gia."

Coco pulls some flat shoes out of her coat pocket. "The staff was disorganized," she observes, "and Tellar's good at what he does. I have no doubt they got out. The real question is if they got away from whoever they're trying to escape."

"Voice mail," I announce at the sound of the beep I don't want to hear, already hitting Redial.

"He won't answer when he's on the alert," Coco says. "That's how he's trained."

"How did Gia seem?" Amy asks. "Could she talk?"

"She was weak," I say, "but more coherent than the last time I saw her." I punch Redial again.

Coco covers my hand. "You don't want him to answer to comfort you when he should be focused on protecting your woman."

My woman. I barely have time to process the rightness of those words, when my phone rings and I answer with, "Tell me she's okay."

"We forgot to warn her that the doc isn't working for Sheridan."

"Oh, shit."

"Yeah. She freaked out, and proved she has a whole lot of fight in her, but it took a lot out of her. She's hurting. Badly."

Pain. That's what being 'my woman' does for her. "Can the doctor give her something to help?"

"She has, and we're waiting for it to kick in."

"You have a black sedan in your lefthand mirror," Coco warns Liam softly. "I assume that's what you want—to be followed so the others aren't."

"I heard that," Tellar says over the phone, "and while that was the idea, it's become a problem."

"Why?"

"Apparently Gia's nervous system is reacting to the arsenic at a higher level than expected from her test. Dr. Murphy recommends the blood transfusion she was hoping wasn't necessary, and she wants to do it now, not later at the safe house. Any of us here would do it, but she's A positive and hard to match. Liam's O negative, the universal donor."

I lower the phone. "Gia needs a blood transfusion."

"I'll do it," Liam says, before I can even ask.

"I heard again," Tellar says. "The van we're in is large enough to do it on the road, but that means we need you here with us."

I curse, and think a moment, then lean forward between

the seats to tell Liam, "We're going in the front door of the JW Marriott Essex House near Central Park and out the back, but try to lose the tail before we do."

"Got it," he says, cutting hard to the right, forcing Amy and me to hold on to steady ourselves.

"That's five blocks from us," Tellar says, still listening in. "We're dropping Derek at the corner to grab a cab and get out of this, and then we'll head straight there. I'll text when we arrive."

He ends the call and Liam continues a wicked cycle of lane changes, dodging pedestrians and turns, that has Coco laughing with approval. "A few more radical moves like that one and no one will keep up."

Digging my phone out of my pocket, I offer it to Coco. "I believe they're using this to track us. When we get to the hotel, I'll carry you in to keep up the show that you're Gia. Once we're inside, you need to get a nice room. Order food and a movie, whatever floats your boat." I pull cash from my pocket and hand it to her. "That should allow you to go shopping afterwards."

She grins. "I do enjoy it when Tellar calls. What do you want me to do if the phone rings?"

"Ignore it."

"And when I leave?"

"Destroy it. They'll call Liam if they want me."

The phone buzzes with a text and she glances down at it. "Tellar's at the hotel."

"And so are we in about sixty seconds," Liam calls out, turning onto the street. "I'm going around to get Amy. Make sure Tellar knows Coco's the first one exiting on the other side."

As Liam stops at the hotel door two doormen greet us almost instantly, and I murmur an explanation about my sick wife who I need to carry inside, drawing out the conversation long enough to let Liam get to Amy. The instant he has her out of the vehicle, I scoop up Coco and dash for the door another attendant holds open for me.

"We owe you, Coco," I say, setting her down. Then I'm on the heels of Liam and Amy, traveling the long expanse of the hotel past shops and elevators, my hand under my jacket, resting on my weapon. Tellar appears in the exit doorway and Liam hands Amy off to him, quickly following behind them. At the exit I hesitate an instant, scanning for trouble I don't see, and then in several long strides I enter the silver van behind Tellar.

Tellar dashes for the driver's seat and Liam, who's sitting in the front row seat with Amy, motions me forward. "I have the door," Liam says as the van launches into motion. "You go to Gia."

Quickly moving past the empty second row, I find Dr.

Murphy squatting beside Gia, who lies across the long back seat with blankets piled on top of her, trembling, her eyes closed. "How is she?" I whisper, kneeling beside her.

"The arsenic continues to attack her nervous system. She's fine for a while, and then in pain."

"And you think the blood transfusion will solve that?"

"It's going to help push the toxins out of her body."

"Won't it push the medication out of her system, too?"

"Yes, but Tellar grabbed another bag of meds before he left. Don't ask me how he managed it. I'm just glad he did."

"Why is she shivering?"

"Nerves, shock, and the IV fluids can do that to some people." She turns on her heels. "I'm going to get Liam's part of this done. Shout if she needs me."

"Thank you, doc, for everything—for taking care of Gia, and for what you've done for Amy."

She squeezes my arm and moves away, while I move closer to Gia, caressing her cold cheek. Her lashes flutter, then lift, and seeing the awareness in those blue eyes is heaven. "Hey," I say softly, covering her hand with mine.

"Hey."

"How are you?"

She wets her dry lips. "Cold."

"I know, sweetheart," I say, stroking her hair. "Liam's giving blood for you now. The transfusion will help you feel

Lisa Renee Jones

better, and by the time it's over we'll be in the Hamptons, where you'll be able to rest more comfortably."

"Do you still hate him?"

"He's not making that easy. He keeps helping and doing all the right things."

"Such an asshole," she murmurs weakly.

"Exactly," I say, wondering how she can possibly joke in this condition. "Do you remember anything about what happened?"

"You. Saving me. Jared? He's missing?"

"Yes. He left me a message and said you were with him in the subway, running from someone."

Her lashes lower and she shakes her head. "No . . . that doesn't feel right."

She stirs something that's been bugging me for a while now. How did Gia get from a subway back to that coffee shop? I frown, thinking about the SUV. Where was Jared's laptop? I could have missed it in the chaos, but it had been in the front seat.

"Why are you making that face?" she asks.

I blink and refocus on Gia. "What's the last thing you re-member?"

"You," she repeats. "Just you." She squeezes her eyes shut and I watch the pain flicker over her delicate features, wish-ing I could make it end. "Hurts. It hurts."

"What hurts?"

"Everything."

I start to move, to get help and she says, "No. Don't go."

"Dr. Murphy—"

"Can't help. Just . . . need to close my eyes."

I ease back down, stroking her hair, caressing her shoulders until she relaxes into steady breathing. Sleeping, I think, until I lower my head to the seat beside her, and somehow, as weak as she is, she manages to rest her hand on my head. Like she needs to know I'm here. I am here, in every sense of the word, in a way I haven't been in a very long time.

I'm not sure how long we stay like that before Dr. Murphy breaks us up, claiming my spot beside Gia to start the transfusion. Gia's alert, watching the blood flowing into her arm, as she murmurs, "Maybe this will make me a brilliant architect."

Liam's low rumble of laughter reaches us, mingling with Amy's, while Dr. Murphy gives a conspiratorial whisper of, "Let's hope it doesn't make you as arrogant."

"I heard that," Liam calls out.

Amy laughs and joins us, introducing herself to Gia, and I leave the women to chat, going to the front of the van to conference with Tellar. "Any word from Coco?" I ask.

"Apparently the hotel makes killer chocolate chip cookies. Other than that, nothing."

"Killer cookies. She's a piece of work, that one. "

"We have enough history for me to assure you that is true."

"I won't ask," I laugh, noting the dimming horizon. "How much longer?"

"A little under an hour."

I nod and turn to find Liam sitting forward, elbows on his knees, and I join him. "The famous Liam Stone in a simple van, no jacket, sleeves rolled up. Who'd have thunk it?"

"I'm much more of a simple man than you might think."

"Prodigy. Protégé. Billionaire. You are not a simple man."

"Humble beginnings," Liam states, "and a father in jail for drunk driving. Simpler than you think."

"I read that about you. I have to admit I didn't expect you to share it quite so easily."

"We are the sum of everything we've been and will be," he says.

"Life as a math equation. Spoken like a true architect."

"Spoken like a man who's watched the woman he loves coming apart at the seams, after years of suppressing her past to survive it."

"I know she's hurt. I hurt *for* her, and now Gia's become part of the same circle of lies. Thank you for what you did for her today."

"I don't need your thanks," Liam says. "I need your trust."

"Trust," I repeat, the word playing on my tongue, unfamiliar but getting more familiar by the minute, it seems. "Amy told you about the cylinder?"

"Yes. And I told Tellar. I trust him."

There is that word again.

"I know you spent time in Egypt, studying the pyramids."

"Yes," he confirms. "I did."

"Did you know some believe the secrets of the Great City of Atlantis are buried somewhere beneath one of those pyramids?"

"I do, actually."

"And do you know why? It's said that they could harness the power of the universe, and such power corrupted those who used it and they self-destructed. The secrets to that power are said to be protected so that it can't happen again. The moral of the story being that power corrupts. I believe you are honorable right now. I can't know that won't change."

His lips curve. "No. But if it does, and it won't, you could always just choke me to death, like you promised before."

I give him a deadpan stare and then, to my surprise, I laugh. "Yes, I could. And I would."

"I have no doubt that that's a good thing. You could, but you won't unless you have to, as proven by the fact that you could have killed every one of those consortium members after your parents' death."

"I thought about it. I've thought about it often, but each of them has connections outside that group, and I have no idea how many of them know about me. So instead, I gathered resources and prepared for a conclusion, and I planned to follow with revenge. At this point, I just want the conclusion."

"Which is what?"

"If I knew that, we'd already have one."

"I might have some ideas on that."

"You don't even know what I have. And what were you thinking, making a special appearance at an event you *knew* a consortium member would be at?"

"We were going to set a trap. Given all that's happened, they'll be ready for us now, so we'll have to think of something else. And as of about fifteen minutes ago, I do know exactly what you have."

Stunned, I turn to look at him. "How?"

"Dr. Murphy managed to install a bug in Sheridan's office during her last visit. Derek, who I trust implicitly, is monitoring the feed while Tellar has been occupied. Apparently things just got more complicated. We aren't in this alone anymore. Derek just overheard Sheridan making a deal with the Chinese, after someone told him Rollin is alive. He didn't know that before. And I don't think I have to tell you how big a problem the Chinese suddenly being involved is."

"Does Amy know?"

He gives a sharp shake of his head. "Not yet. She's been through hell lately, and I'm not looking forward to the fear this is going to create in her. But we have to tell her. And maybe knowing will stop her damned blackouts. What does Gia know?"

"Everything but where the cylinder is." I take a risk, testing him by adding, "No one knows that but me."

And he passes the test with a vehement "Keep it that way," followed by "What we don't know, we can't tell willingly or unwillingly. You can't give up the cylinder. It's a nuclear bomb. Industries would crash. Jobs gone. We're talking complete economic and world collapse. If one man controlled that cylinder he could re-create everything under his power."

"That's right. But I can't destroy it, because one day the world might need it. And they'd never believe I destroyed it, anyway." My brow furrows as a plan, that damn plan I've been looking for forever, comes to me. "But what if we make them all believe someone *else* has it?"

"Rollin?" Liam supplies.

"He's the perfect fall guy. He's faked his death. He's crossed his father."

"Agreed," Liam says. "But we have to find him to use him, and that's going to be a race against his father. Sheridan was furious about the betrayal. He's on the hunt for Rollin, with someone feeding him information. That means they'll either be preoccupied fighting each other, or coming after us from all sides."

"Sheridan's the one who grabbed me. Rollin must have someone inside his father's operation. How else could he promise the cylinder to anyone? We need to know who."

"I spent time in China for work. I have contacts, people that I trust within certain cautious boundaries—but I can't make those calls until we get to the safe house and I have privacy."

Gia's voice carries in the air, stronger now it seems, with Amy's laughter on its tail. "Safe house," I repeat. "It's not safe. *They* aren't safe."

"No," he agrees. "They aren't."

I look at him. "Then this is war."

"Yes," he agrees. "This is war."

Then Dr. Murphy appears and motions me to the back. "Gia is asking for you."

I exchange a look with Liam—two men united, fighting for their women—then I head to the back.

Amy smiles at me. "We're debating the merits of locking Sheridan in one of Dad's dig sites versus poisoning him with arsenic. Or both."

"Remind me not to piss you two off."

"We will," Amy promises, scooting forward to kiss me on the cheek, whispering in my ear, "I adore her." Then she leaves to join Dr. Murphy and Liam up front.

I reclaim my spot by Gia.

"I love her," Gia says. "She's not an asshole like you, at all."

I smile. "I love it when you talk dirty to me."

She laughs and then flinches, her lashes lowering as she whispers, "You haven't seen anything yet."

I lean down and kiss her cheek, wishing like hell I could keep her out of this. She knows my sins, and she isn't afraid. But this is *war*—a war I have to win, no matter how vicious, illegal, or bloody I have to be. And she's going to see who I really am.

EIGHTEEN

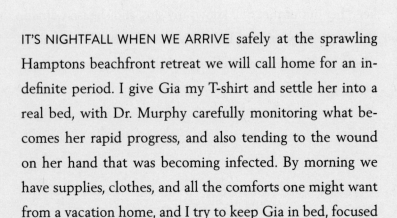

IT'S NIGHTFALL WHEN WE ARRIVE safely at the sprawling Hamptons beachfront retreat we will call home for an indefinite period. I give Gia my T-shirt and settle her into a real bed, with Dr. Murphy carefully monitoring what becomes her rapid progress, and also tending to the wound on her hand that was becoming infected. By morning we have supplies, clothes, and all the comforts one might want from a vacation home, and I try to keep Gia in bed, focused on recovering, not on the unknowns outside these walls.

Not an easy task, considering she wants to get up and join the roundtable in the kitchen Liam has labeled "the War Room."

Both my sister and I rise to the challenge of occupying Gia in her bedroom "prison" as she calls it, relieved when she agrees to a *Matrix* movie marathon while I'm present, reverting back to *Sex in the City* while I spend time chasing leads on Rollin with Liam and Tellar.

I also get a lot of one-on-one time with Amy. We talked for hours on end, and still I hold back information to protect her. I have to protect her. It's all bittersweet. She's angry with me and happy to see me. And I'm angry with me, and happy to see her.

Days pass and each morning I wake from nightmares of the fire. And each day I get hungrier for this to end. Day four is the breaking point for me. I jerk upward from the bed, and I am still half-living my sleep-induced fantasy of slamming Rollin's head into the window as I'd wanted to the last time I'd seen him. If I'd killed him, my parents would be alive.

"Chad. Chad."

Gia's voice breaks into the haze of my half-sleep. "Are you okay?" Her hand comes down on my arm, a soft caress over my skin that sends a chill down my spine, but I do not pull her to me or kiss her as I normally would. I am too on edge, too out of myself, and in need of a release that she can't give me right now.

"Nightmare," I murmur, throwing off the blankets and walking to the shower, turning on the hot water and climbing inside before it even warms up, shivering in the cold, savoring the heat. The water pours over me, and I do not fight what I feel. I revel in the hatred inside of me, no matter how toxic it might be. I buried it for years. I need to feel it and deal with it now.

The curtain moves and Gia climbs inside, naked and too thin, wrapping her arms around me. "Do you want to talk about it?"

"You should be in bed."

"I'm feeling better. But you aren't. Talk to me. Please."

I could shelter her. I should shelter her, but I do not. "Remember when I told you I strangled the man who set the house fire?"

"Yes. I remember."

"Liam uncovered some details about Rollin. He was disinherited right before the fire. I gave him money that day. I think he set the fire and then disappeared."

"That explains so much. It answers questions you needed answered."

"Knowing who and why only makes me angrier. But

father or son almost killed you, too. If I get the chance, I *will* kill them, Gia. The bruises from my beatings might be fading now, but I'm still broken. I'm trying not to be that man for you and for my sister, but you need to know that the part of me that wants them dead—he's still a part of me."

"I know who you are. I know what you are. And I know what you feel more than you realize, I think."

I study her, this woman who does seem to see me for all that I am, and I don't know what to make of it. "I am not a scientist or a doctor. Or a billionaire architect. I'm a treasure hunter, a man who walks lines I shouldn't walk. A thrill seeker. An adrenaline junkie."

"A man who knows when the payday isn't all that matters." She smiles. "And a man who really, really loves the word *fuck*."

And just like that, I'm laughing. I'm fucking laughing and pushing her against the wall and kissing her. Gia does that for me. She's changing me. In this moment, I feel it. I feel her. And us. And I feel something I haven't dared in a lifetime, it seems. A reason to live that isn't hate and revenge. But the hate and revenge still feel pretty damn good.

Lisa Renee Jones

AN HOUR LATER, I leave Gia and Amy for a final checkup with Dr. Murphy before Coco is to pick the doctor up to escort her on an extended vacation meant to ensure her safety. I, in turn, claim a spot at the kitchen table opposite Liam, with Tellar on my left, and join their work to turn Rollin into our endgame. And I do not miss Liam's intense scowls, or the ridiculous fact that his black T-shirt is perfectly pressed. He knows we don't have control over this situation, and he's overcompensating. Nor do I miss the irony of my opposite approach, with my fantasies of banging Rollin's head into a windshield. Tellar, it seems, is somewhere in the middle of the two of us, and I can only hope that gives us balance.

I've barely guzzled the thick syrup Amy calls coffee when I glance up to find Gia standing in the doorway, having traded in her pajamas for faded jeans, a pink T-shirt, and sneakers.

"Gia," I say, standing, fully intent on insisting she go back to bed, but she is already moving toward the table, planting herself in a chair.

"I'm staying. Amy is with Dr. Murphy, and she says I'm fine to move around a bit." I arch a disbelieving brow, and she says, "Ask her. She's still here." She grabs my coffee cup and sips, then crinkles her nose. "That's horrible."

"Hey now," Amy scolds, entering the room. "I made that."

"I'll make the next pot," Gia volunteers.

"Thank you," Tellar says. "Amy seems to want to please Chad more than the rest of us, and apparently my last pot wasn't much better."

"Welcome back, Ms. Hudson," Liam says. "Have you been feeling the tingles of architectural creations?"

"No, I have not, Mr. Stone. It appears I will not become a brilliant architect but will remain a humble chemist, damn you."

"A rather brilliant chemist in your own right, from what I understand," he replies. "You were on Sheridan's top secret team."

"I was," she confirms. "And it felt like an honor. I really thought he wanted to save the world."

"How do you think Napoleon and Hitler managed to get so many followers?" Liam replies. "We're just glad he didn't brainwash you, or Chad might not be here right now."

"Right," she says, twisting her fingers together on top of the table a moment before she looks at me. "Still no idea how Sheridan found you?"

"None," I confirm.

Her teeth worry her bottom lip a moment before she says, "And no one has contacted us to demand or threaten us to get the cylinder that I don't know about, right?"

"No," Liam replies. "We're on radio silence."

"We're certain Sheridan is waiting us out," Tellar says. "Expecting one of us to surface. We just aren't sure how long that will last before they get impatient, especially since the Chinese are putting pressure on him."

"Yes," she murmurs, her gaze going to me. "They know you're with Amy and Liam now, so I'm sure they'll call Liam."

I arch a brow. "That wasn't a question, so why does it feels like one?"

"Did you tell Jared where the cylinder is, and that's the reason we aren't being contacted? Could he have told Rollin, and Rollin is negotiating a sale?"

My gut twists with what she isn't saying, but it's in her eyes, and lingering in the room. "Jared didn't turn on us. He had six years to give me up to Sheridan, and he didn't. He escaped and went underground, or he's dead." She doesn't reply, but the room seems to wait in irritating unison for my confirmation. "No, I did not tell him where it is. No one knows where the cylinder is but me."

Collectively, they all seem to sigh. "As it should be," Liam says. "You have to be the only one who knows."

"It can't stay that way," Amy argues. "There has to be a way the world gets it if it's ever needed."

"I don't disagree," Liam says, "nor do I believe Chad would, but now is not that time, and the first order of business is making sure it's forgotten, assumed lost. Rollin remains our best fall guy, but we have to find him." Liam motions to the piles of paperwork on the table. "Rollin has to be hiding somewhere in this pile of paperwork."

I grab a file. "Then I say we all have to look again at everything we've already looked at." I glance around the table and everyone nods in unison and grabs a file.

HOURS LATER, COCO has entertained us and whisked Dr. Murphy away to safety, and we are all exhausted, the sun settled low on the horizon. I glance up and realize that Gia and Amy have disappeared. Concerned that I've been too absorbed in the file I'm reading to realize Gia is sick, I push myself to my feet and go in search of her. As I pass through the living area, the drapes flutter, the door opens to the heated porch, and Amy's voice stops me in my tracks.

"What if I'm pregnant again?" Amy asks, touching on the one subject she hasn't spoken to me about.

"Getting sick once does not make you pregnant," Gia assures her. "We're all under a lot of stress and it wasn't that long ago that you miscarried. Your body is exhausted."

"Losing my baby was the worst moment of my life aside

from the fire," Amy says, her pain slicing through me, reminding me that knowledge is helping her cope, but the heartache is far from gone. "It was like I'd been given another chance at a family," she continues, "only to have it ripped away."

"I know," Gia says softly. "That's how I felt, too. I lost my dad. Then I lost the baby and . . . then . . . I lost the chance to try it again with someone who matters."

Stunned, I grab the couch. Gia lost a baby?

"He really didn't care that you lost the baby?" Amy asks.

"He was relieved."

"While you were destroyed," Amy supplies, her voice heavy with understanding.

"Yes," Gia replies, her tone raspy, affected. "And alone, but you aren't. Not anymore. You have Liam."

"Gia," Amy says. "You aren't alone. You have me and Liam and Tellar. We're family now. And most of all, you have Chad."

"Do I?"

"How can you question that?"

"It's . . . complicated."

Complicated? What the *fuck* does she mean by that? I run a hand through my hair, trying to understand what I've done wrong in the past few days to make her feel like I'm not here for her. That I don't want to be with her.

Liam's voice comes from the kitchen doorway, and Amy

and Gia lower their voices, having an exchange I can't make out, before Amy's footsteps sound, fading into the closing of the door. It's then that it hits me that I've eavesdropped, like a total dickhead. But I'm here, and she's spoken that damn word *complicated* and I intend to know why.

Stepping forward into the line of the curtain, I find her at the railing, under a heater, her dark hair fluttering with the wind off the nearby ocean. "How much did you hear?" she asks without turning.

I step onto the porch and cross the wooden floor to stand next to her, resting my hands on the railing, looking out at the waves crashing on the sand. "All of it."

"What do you want to know?" she asks, tilting her head to look at me.

"Everything now, but pretend I just said only when you're ready."

She doesn't laugh, inhaling instead, still not looking at me, seeming to stare at the skyline that is nothing but black speckled with dots of light. "When my father died, I was lost. Jason was my college professor. I guess I needed a father figure, because I thought I loved him." She laughs without humor. "God. I was so adolescent, giddy in every way. I don't know how I got pregnant. We used protection, but when it happened it seemed like a gift. I wanted that child. Oh, how I wanted that child." Her wishful, sad tone turns hard as she adds, "But he didn't. He told me to get an abortion. I was devastated. I refused."

I wait, expecting her to go on, finally pressing with a gentle "Gia?"

She lifts her hands and rambles almost matter-of-factly. "My appendix ruptured and I miscarried. A freak thing. I almost died and then they told me that there was damage. You know the rest. I . . . choose the wrong men."

I grab her, wrapping her in my arms, brushing hair from her face to find pure anguish in her eyes, but I am hurt by her implication that I too am the wrong man. "What did that mean?"

"It means we're complicated, just like I said to Amy."

"You think I'll leave."

"Of course you'll leave."

"I know what I said—"

"Over and over, you said it. I told you alone wasn't better. I did. I meant it, but we don't know each other."

"What? We do. I want to know more."

"No. No, I don't. I don't want to feel what you make me feel."

"What am I making you feel?"

"Confused."

I back her against the railing, my legs framing hers,

hands cupping her face. "You aren't pushing me away. I don't know why you're trying."

"Amy needed you and you stayed away from her."

"To protect her, Gia," I argue, hearing the accusation in her voice. "Is that what this is about? You think I'll leave. I'm not leaving you."

"Chad."

I squeeze my eyes shut at the sound of Tellar's voice. "Now isn't a good time."

"Make it a good time." The hardness in his voice has me releasing Gia, who immediately retreats, hugging herself.

Frustrated, I turn to face Tellar, finding his spine erect, his expression pure stone. My brow furrows, and I don't have to ask if there's a problem to know that there is, nor do I miss the irony of having sworn I would end this, sparing Gia and me nothing in the worst of moments.

I look at her, willing her to look at me, but she doesn't. Amy exits the side door again, a well-timed companion to Gia, and for reasons I can't explain, it feels almost too well-timed. But as I step toward the living area with Tellar, and Amy moves toward Gia, I frown when she doesn't look at me. What the hell is going on?

Following Teller to the kitchen, I find Liam sitting at the same spot that he's occupied for days, but his eyes are not on his computer screen. They're on me. Silently, he motions to the seat beside him, giving me the impression he wants me closer than in the past, the conversation tighter. I join him, and Tellar claims the seat across from us. They share a look, and unease has me snapping, "What the hell is going on?"

Liam's lips press together a moment before he asks, "How much do you know about Gia?"

Just the question punches me in the chest with dread. "Why?"

Tellar answers: "Because looking at the files again made me realize we didn't have one on Gia."

"I had it on my computer that disappeared from the SUV," I reply. "Jared pulled it for me when we were in the city."

"So you reviewed Jared's file?" Liam asks.

"Yes. Completely." I narrow my gaze on him. "Whatever you aren't saying, just get to it."

"Does the name Madison Cook mean anything to you?" Tellar asks.

"That's the man who created the cylinder," I reply.

"That's Gia's father," he says.

"No," I say, rejecting that bomb. "That's impossible. Her last name is Hudson, not Cook, and she told me that her father was a chemist at the university. Cook was a scientist at NASA, who worked on the cylinder there until funding was cut and Sheridan offered him private support."

"And the files that Jared gave you confirmed that Gia's father worked at the university?"

"No," I say, a knot forming in my stomach. "He gave me her employee record from Sheridan's company records."

Tellar slides an iPad in front of me, showing me Gia's birth certificate. "Gia Hudson. Mother: Gia Marie Hudson. Father: Madison Cook."

Barely believing what I'm seeing, I run my hand over my face. "Her parents were never married," Tellar says, pointing out the obvious. "And Jared seems too good to miss what I've found this easily. Did he know her before you did?"

"No," I say, praying that answer is right. "She doesn't trust Jared."

"Or she was afraid that he'd tell her secrets," Tellar offers.

"I don't trust Jared," Liam says. "I never did, but right now, Gia's the one we need to focus on. We don't know what she wants done with her father's cylinder. If it's the same as us, we don't have a problem on that end. We need to know for sure, though, and I'm not sure how we make that happen."

"She wants the same as us," I say. "I'm sure of it."

"You didn't know her history," Liam argues. "You can't know her motivations."

I scrub my neck. "I was an asshole to her. I played up

being a treasure hunter when I thought she was working for Sheridan. I told her that I would do anything for money, including selling her back to Sheridan, to scare her into helping me."

"Since she kept her mouth shut about her past," Tellar says, "I'd say you were convincing, which leads to another problem."

"What problem?"

"Records show that her father died in a car accident a month before your house burned down," Tellar explains. "I did some digging and someone was sloppy. Her father was in Alaska the day he was supposed to have been killed in a car accident in Texas."

My anger rises swiftly, barely contained. "Be careful where you're going with this, Tellar."

He holds up his hands. "Hey man, I don't believe it was you. I'm simply stating facts here. You told her you'd do anything for money and she knows you got the cylinder from somewhere and her father was obviously murdered."

Liam's gaze jerks to the right and I follow it to find Gia and Amy standing there. "Gia," I say, rising to my feet, but she has already taken off.

NINETEEN

"STAY BACK," I shout as I dart around the table and follow Gia, exiting the kitchen into the living area just in time to catch a glimpse of her disappearing behind the curtains and onto the porch. Running after her, I exit to find her already down the stairs to the right and fading into the darkness of the beach.

"Gia!" I shout, going over the top of the railing and landing hard on the ground, my body jolting with the impact, but I don't pause, afraid of losing her in the darkness. "Gia, wait!" But she keeps moving and I launch into a run, aware

Gia is wearing nothing more than I am; her jeans and T-shirt are no match for this cold even if she wasn't still weak from being poisoned.

I watch her turn left, stumbling on the sand, and it's all I need to catch her. She tries to catch herself and before she recovers, I shackle her wrist, pulling her around to face me.

"Yes," she hisses. "I'm his daughter. You said you'd do anything for money. You said—"

"I didn't kill him." She jerks against me and I pull her to me, shackling her leg with mine, holding her wrists between us. "I swear it on everything I love or have ever loved that I didn't do it. My family. My sister. You, Gia. I'm falling in love with you. I didn't kill your father."

"No. No, don't say that word. Did you know he was murdered?"

"Yes, but I didn't get the cylinder from your father."

"Liar!" She jerks and twists and trips us both. She falls backward and I end up on top of her as she squirms wildly.

Pinning her hands by her head, I straddle her. "Stop, Gia. Stop and listen to me. I got the cylinder from Rex Lenard, your father's former college professor. He retired in Alaska." She pants several times, breathing deeply, but she isn't fighting me anymore and I use that opportunity to explain. "I don't know what made your father feel he had to hide the cylinder, but he was too obvious. I followed him to Alaska."

"So you were there when he was there."

"Only to see Rex, and I got to Rex too late. Someone in a ski mask, who I can't help but think was Rollin, was there when I got there. I fought him, but he'd stabbed Rex and Rex was bleeding out. Rex told me where he had hidden the cylinder and why it had to be protected. With his last breath he begged me to protect it, and I promised I would."

"What happened to my father?"

"I don't know, sweetheart. I knew he'd been killed. I knew it was probably murder, and I wanted the hell out to protect my family."

Her face crumples and she bursts into tears. I release her arms and hold her, burying my face in her hair. "I'm sorry, Gia. If I'd known who you were, I would have told you sooner."

Her arms wrap around my neck, and relief at the acceptance in the act washes over me. "I didn't really believe you did. But you kept talking about regret, and how bad you are, and it's my father, and I was tormented and scared because—"

I lean back, trying to see her face in the darkness. "Because?"

"Because I was afraid I was blinded by what I feel for you."

"Which is what?"

"Too much. Too much."

"Not enough," I say, lifting myself off of her and scooping her up. She curls into me, shivering in my arms. I quickly cover the stretch of beach, walking up the steps to the empty porch. Eager to warm her up, I track through the living area and down the long hallway. I enter our bedroom, kicking the door shut, the moon finally peeking from behind the clouds, illuminating the dark room through the sheer blinds.

Bypassing the bed, knowing we need to talk and figure out where this has led us, I settle Gia on a chaise near the double doors leading to our private patio, grabbing the blanket on the back and covering her. She curls her knees to her chest, and it's torture, but I do not touch her. Even so, the enormity of the situation is starting to hit me.

"Were you plotting revenge against me?"

"Oh, God. No, Chad! I didn't even know my father was murdered. I didn't know Sheridan was a bad man until the day I helped you escape. He was—this is so hard to even say now—Sheridan . . . is my godfather."

"He is *what?*"

"Yes. He and my father were friends, I thought. When my father died, I was in Austin, in college. Sheridan was in Austin, of course, because of his company, so it was logical that he came to me to deliver the news and comfort me. He told me my father had asked him to look out for me. He paid for my education, and on the day I graduated, he gave me a special gift: my father's journal with partial equations and notes about his dream for a universal clean energy solution. Sheridan knew I'd spent a lot of time in a lab with my father, and he encouraged me to take those notes no one else could decipher and use them to continue my father's work and finish it."

"I'm guessing you have the legal rights to your father's work."

She nods. "Yes. All intellectual property. I'm not sure how or when that would have come into play, but that has to be why he hired me and kept me close."

"I'm guessing you signed legal paperwork that somehow signed away your rights, and you didn't know. And I assume he thought you might know more about your father's work than you said you did or even realized you knew, thus making you a good investment all around. You did say you were onto something."

"I told you that because I didn't want you to figure out who I really was. You didn't trust me. I was sure you'd think being my father's daughter would make me look worse to you, or make me a bigger treasure to a treasure hunter."

"And I threatened to sell you to the highest bidder! I wish you would have told me sooner."

"There was never a right time, and then Jared came into the picture. I was sure he'd figure out the truth, and was relieved when he didn't because I didn't trust him. But the fact that he didn't made me wonder if he knew and didn't tell you."

"You were right to distrust Jared," I say, hating the truth, hating it so fucking bad. "He's too good not to have known. Where's that journal now?"

"I have a copy, and I'm sure Sheridan does as well, but the original was in the lab the day I overhead Sheridan's conversation and helped you escape. And—it hurt, but I burned it."

My hand comes down on her leg. "Why burn it, if you knew he had a copy?"

"Because not long before that day, I'd found a key sewn inside the journal cover and ripped it open. I didn't want him to see I'd torn it open."

"And the key goes to what? Do you know?"

"I knew immediately it was to a jewelry box that once belong to my mother."

"And?"

"And inside, I found a piece of paper with an equation scribbled on it. It had my name on it and it said *For your eyes only*. I played with it being a part of the formula to create the cylinder, but it didn't even make sense."

"But you never gave it to Sheridan?"

She shakes her head. "No. It said for my eyes only, and I kept it that way."

"Where is that piece of paper?"

"I burned it as well, but I kept the equation. She turns and lifts her hair, showing me the tattoo on her neck.

"Holy fuck, Gia!" I grab her arms. "That could be the answer everyone is looking for. We're getting it removed."

"It's all I have left of him, Chad. I can't lose it, and you didn't even notice it. I have a lot of hair."

"I should have noticed it. It has to go. We'll find a place to keep it safe, carve it into a mountainside somewhere or whatever, but you can't have it on your body. And no one but you and I can know. Not even Amy. For their protection, and yours."

"Yes. Okay. But that really sucks, Chad."

"I know, sweetheart. Believe me, I know, but it has to be this way."

"Yes. Okay." She squeezes her eyes shut a moment and then looks at me. "That day, at the car lot. Do you remember you told me your family died six years ago?"

"Yes. I remember."

"That was when it hit me that my father was murdered, and the man I'd known as my godfather had done it. That's why I went into the bathroom. I melted down. I tried not to, but it doubled me over."

I pull her to me, holding her close. "I'm sorry. I was an ass to you that day."

"Yeah. You were. A *really* big ass." She inhales and lets it out. "Do you think . . . could my father be alive? Maybe they have him in a lab somewhere?"

I don't know what to say to her. They killed my family. I know they killed her father. She shakes her head. "Never mind. I know he's dead. Sheridan wouldn't need me if he wasn't." She buries her face in her hands and murmurs, "I just don't want him to be."

I cup her face, forcing her gaze to mine, and I dare to say what I have not even allowed myself to think. "I know, Gia. I want my family to be alive, too. But we have each other, now. I know I pushed you away. I told you not to trust me. But it was only because I wanted you too much. And because I was, and am, falling in love with you."

"I am too," she whispers. "I'm falling—"

I kiss her, deep and slow, and when I finish, I murmur, "Don't tell me you feel the same as I do. I don't deserve that yet, but I swear to you, Gia, I will." I try to kiss her again and she presses her fingers to my mouth.

"Don't try to be what you aren't. That never works for people. They wake up and realize they can't do it, and they leave."

They leave. It hits me then why she'd thrown my leaving

Amy in my face earlier. She's lost everyone in her life. Her mother and father, her unborn child and even the godparent she thought she'd had. And all I've done is tell her I'm leaving her, over and over and over again. "I'm not leaving."

"Until you do."

"Gia, I know you see how I left Amy. I know you heard how many times I said that *we* didn't exist. I realize now that I've spent six years of my life aspiring to be a man worthy of the blame I felt I deserved for my parents' deaths, filling the holes inside of me with everything wrong, not knowing everything right was out there. And I know what's right is you." I roll her to her back and she tangles fingers in my hair. "I can't breathe when I think about losing you."

Her fingers curl on my jaw. "Then don't talk yourself into leaving."

"I'm not going to take that fear from you with words. I'm just going to stay." My lips quirk. "No matter how many times you call me an asshole, or how irritated I make you. We'll fight and we'll make up. And it'll be good."

"You could just not be an asshole," she suggests.

"I'm still me, sweetheart—so maybe I should just practice apologizing." I brush my lips over hers. "By doing what I'm going to do, and what I should have already done. Make love to you for all the right reasons, instead of fucking you for the wrong ones."

"Chad," she whispers, and I swallow my name on her lips, kissing her passionately, intensely—licking into her mouth, tasting her, and then slowly undressing her, reveling in each new spot my tongue can travel. She moans, delicate, sweet moans that thicken my cock and soften my heart.

By the time I toss the last piece of her clothing away and settle between her legs, finding her clit, lapping at it, then sucking, she is already coming unglued. *This* is power. The only kind I need. I lift her legs over my shoulders, dip my fingers inside her, take her to the edge and back, and do it again. And finally, when I am hard and hot, and in need of her body wrapped snuggly around mine, I carry her to the bed, spreading her legs again and settling between them. I watch the pleasure ripple over her face when I bury myself inside her. Brushing my cheek against hers, I roughly promise, "I am definitely not going anywhere. And neither are you," thrusting into her a moment later.

That's when the wildness starts, the frenzied hot need that has my hands under her hips, lifting her to drive deeper, to take more. Now we are fucking, and it's the best damn fucking of my life. Because she's the best damned thing in my life. The woman who has pulled me back from the edge of hell, where I wasn't burning alive, but raising hell of my own. Now, I'm putting it to rest.

But when I finally pull Gia into my arms and she falls asleep, I stare at the ceiling, with Jared on my mind. And I keep thinking about Gia disappearing at the coffee shop, and how I never once questioned her. Never once did I think she'd left and betrayed me. But I have always held back with Jared, telling myself it was about protecting him. *He walked away from treasure hunting for honor. He was better than me.* It doesn't make sense. It just . . . doesn't.

And yet, while I could reason away many things, no one else knew where I was when Meg found me. No one else. It's then that I know we can't just wait anymore for something to happen, digging through paperwork, waiting for answers. Hell can't be put to rest until we shove Sheridan and Rollin Scott inside the hole.

"Gia, wake up."

She shifts and lifts her head and then jolts upright. "What's wrong?"

"Nothing. Just the opposite. Get dressed. We need to make plans."

"Plans?"

"Yes," I say, grabbing my jeans and pulling them on. "I said we were going to end this, and we are. Can you make a flawed but convincing prototype of the cylinder?"

"Maybe. I have the schematics."

"Where?"

"Several remote electronic storage accounts, and a lock-box in Texas."

"That might be all that we need." I motion her forward. "Hurry. Get dressed."

She scrambles to the end of the bed, rushing to the pile of her clothes by the chaise lounge. "What are you thinking, Chad?"

"I'll explain once we get everyone together. I'm still piecing it all together in my head."

Five minutes later, Gia and I enter the kitchen to find Amy, Liam, and Tellar at the table, with no signs of taking a break. When all eyes go to Gia, she holds up her hands. "Yes, my father created the cylinder. Sheridan killed him and be-friended me. I never knew the cylinder existed. I fully intend to protect my father's legacy by not allowing it to destroy the world. That's all for now." She motions to me and sits down.

I lean on the back of a chair. "And that about sums up the prelude to a realization that just hit me. That work for everyone?"

Tellar gives Gia a steely look. "Why didn't you tell us all of this before?"

Gia bristles slightly and then lets her self-confessed ner-vous habit of being a smartass rise to the challenge. "I was busy being poisoned with arsenic by the man who killed my father."

"Okaaaay then," Tellar says. "Works for me."

"I'm satisfied," Liam states.

"Good," I say, claiming my seat. "Let's talk about a new strategy. We set Rollin aside. We can deal with Sheridan first, and we do that by going straight to the Chinese."

Tellar leans forward, glaring at me. "What are you drinking? They're far more dangerous than Sheridan and Rollin, and we have nothing to offer them."

"Actually, we do," I reply. "Gia has her father's journal with notes and equations related to the cylinder, and a schematic for an early prototype."

"Both will keep the most brilliant of scientists swimming in circles," Gia adds. "My father coded it so it only meant something to him. It's a jumbled confusing mess to everyone else."

"Sheridan had the journal for six years, and no one he hired ever figured that out," I add, leaning forward. "The plan is, we offer them the journal and schematic in exchange for crushing Sheridan and his consortium, and Rollin along with them."

Liam shakes his head. "We don't know how much Sheridan has told the Chinese. There is no guarantee they'll settle for a journal and schematics. It's too risky."

"It would be if I were talking about going to Sheridan's

people," I agree. "But I'm talking about one of the many radical groups tired of government oppression."

Amy's eyes go wide. "Radicals? That sounds dangerous."

"We left dangerous for vicious six years ago, sis," I remind her. "It's time to get our lives back."

"All the more reason that I don't want you in added danger," she insists. "We can't be sure Sheridan's Chinese contacts don't know who you are. Why wouldn't they just come directly after you once Sheridan is out of the picture?"

"No way would Sheridan tell them who I am," I say, "or who Gia is, for that matter. If Sheridan disclosed his sources, the Chinese would bypass him, and his payday."

"I'd agree with that," Liam adds. "I have zero concern that Sheridan gave away his sources. The man is giving away power. He wants guaranteed cash, and that means the cylinder goes direct from him to them."

"I'm actually surprised he's giving up the power," Gia comments. "Knowing him, I was certain that's what he was after."

"Money *is* power," Liam says, "and at some point he had to realize that no matter how cautiously that cylinder might be released to the public, it will rock the economic world as we know it. We can't tell the Chinese the prototype works."

"No one but Chad has ever seen the cylinder," Gia replies, "including me. For all anyone knows, what we're giving them is all there is."

He gives a nod and glances in my direction. "It's a good plan. I have connections in China, people I trust that can connect you with the right people—but then what? We need a clear-cut plan."

"It goes through me," I say. "No one else. I offer them what we have in exchange for what they have."

"How do they get to Rollin if we can't?" he asks.

"Jared," I say tightly. "I believe he's working both sides. If I call Sheridan and tell him I have the cylinder, Rollin will find out and counteroffer. I'll let the Chinese know what I'm doing and coordinate the timelines."

Liam taps the table. "That only works if you're right about Jared."

"He's the only one who knew where I was in order to insert Meg into my life, and yet Sheridan is the one who kidnapped me."

"But he showed Amy a picture of Rollin with Meg," Tellar argues.

"To gain my trust," Amy says, her voice strained. "That picture and Chad's voice mail convinced me to trust Jared, and to share things Chad meant for my eyes only."

"He's a master manipulator," I say, a low growl of anger permeating my tone at just how deep and long his betrayal runs.

"Someone tried to grab me in Denver," Gia says. "Jared

knew I was there. He must have told Rollin, and Rollin thought I knew something that might help him win the race against his father."

"Exactly," I say. "And he left Jared with me, trying to get my secret."

"And if he couldn't," Gia says, finishing my thought, "he figured he'd trap you and Amy together and use her to make you talk."

Amy pales. "If we make this deal, do I dare believe this is over? That we'll be safe?"

My eyes meet Liam's and we share a look of torment. We both want to say yes, but neither of us is willing to build her up and risk tearing her down again.

"It means we have hope," Gia says, taking her hand, "and that's more than we had yesterday." She glances around the room. "Let's call China."

TWENTY

WE AGREE THAT I'M the only one to be identified to the Chinese, for everyone's safety. With this in mind, Liam makes phone calls to his contacts in China and cautiously puts out feelers with people he trusts, who he knows will limit his involvement. Once he's made the calls, though, we can do nothing but hole up in the safe house and wait. And wait, we do. For three long days we are all climbing the walls, but finally Liam's contacts pay off. We are given the contact information for a high-ranking, English-speaking leader in a powerful radical opposition group. Finally, it's time to put our plan into play, and the ball is in my court.

We gather in the War Room, with me at the head of the table, Liam at the opposite end, and Gia, Amy, and Tellar present as well. A piece of paper sits before me with the name and number of the contact we need, written in Liam's neat, controlled handwriting. Phone in hand, I hesitate and do not dial, but it's not about doubt or regret. Instead I simply inhale on a moment that is about these people around me, the tension in their faces, the nervous energy emanating from them. And what I feel—the unity, the support—is something I have not felt since I sat at a table with Amy and my parents. I *trust* these people. *Really* trust them, and it makes me realize that no matter how I craved having a confidant, a friend, in Jared, it was more about not being alone than it was about trust. Alone isn't better. I knew that even then.

Resolved to carry this through to the bittersweet moment of what some call justice, and what I call revenge, I punch in the number. There are three rings before a man with a heavy accent answers and I introduce myself.

"I've been expecting you, Chad," he says and laughs, quite amused, as he adds, "I am Chen, but I am sure you know this already. Explain what it is that makes you reach across the world."

I share our situation, explaining how Sheridan and Rol-

lin Scott are working on the cylinder with a Chinese diplo-
mat we already know from Liam's sources this man despises.
"I have the schematic for the most recent prototype, and the
notes from the scientist who created them."

"Where is this scientist?" Chen asks.

"Dead. Sheridan and Rollin didn't want to share the
profits."

"And you have these things how?"

"I'm in love with his daughter, who Sheridan and Rollin
just tried to kill as well."

"Why kill the daughter?"

"To convince me to hand over the information she did
not want released."

"But she is willing now?"

"She almost died. She wants this over."

He is silent a moment. "Why are you offering this to
me?"

"Revenge. Sheridan and Rollin Scott want this. They
can't have it, and neither can anyone supporting them."

He is silent a moment. "How much?"

"The complete destruction of Sheridan Scott, Rollin
Scott, and the consortium supporting Sheridan's operation."

"No money?"

"I have money."

"Hmmmm, yes. Revenge and blood, these are the riches

of many a man. Send me the items. If am pleased, I will give you your revenge."

"I'll give you half the journal and half the schematic up front. The rest after you deliver your part of the deal."

He pauses—one beat, two. "Transfer the documents to me electronically. If I am pleased we will make our deal." He gives me an e-mail address. "I'll be in contact if I am interested."

"Wait," I say when it's clear he's about to hang up. "Seventy-two hours, or I give it to someone else."

"Ninety-six hours."

"Fine," I agree.

The line goes dead and I set the phone down, wasting no time keying my computer to life, but feeling the expectant stares of everyone around me. "He wants the documents electronically transferred," I announce, glancing up. "He'll be in contact if he's interested."

I can almost hear everyone suck in air, as if leveled by the uncertainty I've delivered. Tellar stands and disappears beyond the counter dividing our War Room from the main kitchen. I watch my screen as the "sending" icon becomes "complete." "It's done," I say, leaning back to run my hands down my legs. "And now we wait."

Tellar returns, setting a bottle of tequila and five shot glasses on the table. "I'd say we all need this right about now."

Everyone at the table comes to life at his offering, cheering him as he fills our glasses, the mood steadily becoming more optimistic. Surprising me, Amy accepts her shot without hesitation, her actions confirming she is not pregnant after all. I am both relieved and sad for her, but this isn't the right time. Not yet. But soon, I hope.

Lifting the glass, Amy smells the tequila and crinkles her nose. "I have to warn everyone, I'm a lightweight and a giggler."

"I'll carry you, baby," Liam promises her, a gleam in his eye that would have made me want to punch him two weeks ago. Now, I'm just damn glad she has a man who protects her and loves her.

I glance at Gia to find her watching me. Winking, I lean in close to her, nuzzle her neck, and whisper, "I'll carry you, too."

She gives me a playful scowl. "Oh, Chad, you have much to learn. I'll drink you under the table."

I lean back and arch a brow. "Really?"

"No," she snickers. "But it sounded good."

I wrap my arm around her and Tellar lifts his glass, while we all follow. "To fucking up our enemies," he declares.

"To fucking up our enemies," I agree, and everyone laughs, clinks glasses, and downs their shots, Gia and I laughing at each other as we do. We all stand, and I throw Gia over my shoulder and carry her to the bedroom.

EVERY NIGHT FOR three nights, I wake in a sweat, reliving the fire in my nightmares. Each time, Gia is there for me, kissing me, fucking me, bringing me back to this world, and finally making love to me. And I am not alone, no different from everyone else. On day three, we are all sitting in the War Room when Amy has another blackout, her first in weeks, and scares the shit out of all of us.

It sets Liam into control mode, insisting we need a backup plan. He dials China again and intentionally puts a buzz out through his contacts that we are looking for a backup buyer. Bedtime arrives and we've still heard nothing.

On the eve of the deadline, when Gia and I finally enter our bedroom, she starts pacing, as if my habit has now become hers. I try talking to her. She paces more, and I take her to bed, where we don't make love. We do a whole lot of fucking. And then we do some more. And finally we curl up together and sleep. Despite that, I wake from a nightmare in the throes of flames and fire, and find Gia is not in bed, a cold draft alerting me to the open door leading to the deck off our bedroom.

I grab my jeans and pull them on, and I have no idea why, but a sudden shooting fear for her safety overwhelms me, and I dart for the door, shoving back the curtain. Gia stands at the railing in only my T-shirt, shivering in the cold wind blowing off the water, staring forward to where the sun has begun to break the horizon. Certain she knows I am here, I gently snag her wrist, and she jerks, yelping in surprise as I lead her inside and shut the door.

"Are you trying to freeze yourself?" I demand, grabbing her robe and wrapping it around her.

"*Yes*," she replies, shoving her arms into the robe, her teeth chattering. "I am. I just want to feel something other than fear and worry."

Understanding seeps through me, in a far too familiar way, and my hands go to her shoulders. "I get it, sweetheart, I do. Waiting sucks. It guts you. That's why I kept treasure hunting all these years. I could find a way aside from mass murder to save Amy, and the cylinder, and those hunts gave me the rush I needed and a lot of money if Amy and I needed it. If *we* need it, Gia."

"I don't want money, Chad. I want a real life. I want to work in a lab, the way Amy wanted to live at archeological dig sites. I want to take a walk with you and not fear being grabbed and poisoned with arsenic."

"I know. Just have faith. We aren't doing nothing. This is going to work. I feel it. I know it." I lead her toward the bed. "Come try and rest a little while longer."

She shakes her head. "No. I can't. I think I'll take a run."

Then my phone rings by the bed. I've carried it with me everywhere for days, and it had been quiet. I launch myself at the nightstand, grabbing it. I sit on the bed, and Gia goes down on her knees in front of me. Our eyes meet, anticipation between us, and I draw a breath and hit Answer to hear: "We are satisfied with the terms, but Rollin is recorded as dead."

A crazy mix of relief and adrenaline rushes through me. "He was disinherited by his father. He's trying to steal what we have to sell out from under his father."

"Make the call to lure Rollin out now, then, and get me details. Preparations for the destruction of Sheridan and his consortium are already underway." The line goes dead.

"Well?" Gia asks, on her knees beside me now. "What happened?"

"They're in, sweetheart. We just have to set the trap for Rollin."

"Oh my God. Could this really happen? Could it be over?"

I grab her and bury my face in her neck, drawing in the sweet scent of woman, *my woman*, who I am not letting anyone else hurt. "Yeah, sweetheart. It's happening. This is going to work."

She leans back. "Now what?"

I glance at the clock, which reads six in the morning. "We wake Sheridan and set the bait for Rollin."

She settles back to listen in, staring at me as I listen to the line ring once, twice. Sheridan answers, his voice like sand in a wound, and I don't waste a good greeting on him. "It's Chad, you piece of shit. You win. Gia almost died. No one else gets hurt. I'll give you what you want."

"You do know how to wake a man to sunshine," he drawls, and I can almost see the gloat on his face. "When? Where?"

"Full circle. Texas. The same spot where I last met Rollin."

"When?"

"I'll be in touch." I end the call.

He autodials back, and I have not protected the number, on purpose—I want Jared to hack his phone records and show up. I'm looking for a standoff. I let the phone ring and stand up, pulling Gia to her feet. "Let's go share the news."

I lace my fingers with Gia's and we walk into the hallway, and I laugh as Gia shouts, "The Chinese called!"

I hear doors start opening around the house. "I guess that's a good way to wake them up." I motion her forward and we make it to the living area before we are faced with

Liam and Amy, both in robes, while Tellar arrives in just his boxers.

"They called?" Amy asks. "What happened?"

I relay the entire conversation. "Gia and I will leave for Texas tonight."

"I'll go with you," Tellar says.

I shake my head. "No. You protect my sister. Gia and I will hole up in a safe house I have in Texas until we're sure this is done."

"It's not done until we find a way to truly protect the cylinder and make it available to the world if it's needed," Liam points out.

"Then I plan to convince Gia to get the fuck out of Dodge with me for a few months."

Amy's eyes go wide. "You're leaving? No. You can't leave. I've only just found you again."

"Just for a little while, sis. We aren't disappearing. We'll be in touch." I wrap my arm around Gia. "I just need some time to convince Gia I'm not the asshole she's always calling me. I think I need some time to convince myself, too."

Gia turns in my arms, her hand on my chest, teasing me. "Don't totally stop being an asshole. I might not like you anymore."

I cup her head and kiss her and she refocuses on Liam, Amy, and Tellar, her laughter fading into a gravelly, emotional confession. "I love you all. I want justice for you. I want happiness for you. I want this to be as over as it ever can be for any of us."

Her words, drenched with the heartache that had her standing out in the cold, fill the room, expanding and sweeping over all of us. Amy makes a choked sound and wraps her arms around Gia. I step toward Liam, motioning him to walk with me, stopping a few feet away. "If anything happens to me—"

"Don't let it," he snaps. "Or I'll come yank you from the grave."

"While I appreciate the power of a command given by Liam Stone, I'm the only one who knows where the cylinder is. If I die, it's gone. If I don't come back, tell Amy to look for our father and Tombstone. And no, I'm not foolish enough to bury it in my father's grave."

"Amy will understand the clue?"

"It'll take her some time, but she'll figure it out if she has to."

My cell phone rings, and I dig it from my jeans pocket, glancing at the unknown number. "If this is Rollin, he's either listening in on his father, or Sheridan immediately called Jared." I hit the Answer button and hear "Hello, Chad."

The sound of Rollin's voice slithers down my spine, grating my nerves, and not just because I hate the bastard—also because, with this quick response, I've proven my theory about Jared and lost the last shred of hope of his innocence. "Dead man walking," I say. "How's the zombie apocalypse going for you?"

"Better than it has been for you lately. Sell to my father and I'll keep coming for you. Sell to me and I'll kill my father and go away."

I go along with his silly, worthless ploy. "I hate you, you bastard, but you do know how to make a deal appealing. How much?"

"Five hundred million. Enough for you to disappear for good."

"You don't have that much money."

"My buyers do," he assures me.

"Half up front, and half when your father's dead."

"When and where?"

"You know where. You were obviously listening in on your father's phone call. Same time. Same day of the week." I end the call and redial my China connection, relaying to him my plan to trap Rollin. When I disconnect, I inhale and look around the room. "It's done. Two days from now—Thursday night at sunset—we deliver Rollin to the Chinese. Gia and I will arrange a flight and leave in the next few hours."

"Don't you dare get killed," Amy exclaims, throwing her arms around me. "Don't you dare."

"I love you too, sis," I say, and my gaze connects with Gia's over Amy's shoulder, and in her eyes I see understanding. She knows where my head is and what I intend. I didn't make a promise I can't be sure I can keep. I love Amy, and I love Gia. I will fight for them with my life, but I am still no hero. I set up this meeting with Rollin for a reason. I believe he set that fire in my house, and that he killed Gia's father. I plan to find out the truth. And if I'm right, I will be his Grim Reaper.

TWENTY-ONE

TWO DAYS LATER, and only two hours before my meeting with Rollin, Chen has rejected the meeting site I picked, saying it's too open and impossible for a sneak attack, but I've convinced him I have a plan. One I can't share with Gia without putting her in danger. In the meantime, I pull the new black Jag Gia helped me pick out the day before up to the door of the Jasmine Heights restaurant that had once been my house. Leaving my coat behind, my black short-sleeved T-shirt and jeans are my only protection from the near freezing temperature and light, cold drizzle. It doesn't stop me from rounding the hood of the car. But I am not seeking a way to hide from the heartache that is this place for me. I simply want to feel and remember every last second of this moment.

I open the door for Gia and she pulls the hood of her parka up as she stands and steps into the wet chill of a gloomy evening, frowning at the sign above the restaurant. "Red Heaven? What a strange name."

"Sheridan owns it. This is where my house burned down."

"Oh, God." Her hand comes down on my chest. "Chad. I'm sorry. The name. It's—"

"Fire and blood and death."

Her fingers curl in my now damp shirt. "*Why* are we here?"

"Back where it began, sweetheart. A place to say I'm sorry. To say good-bye."

"You want . . . to go inside and eat?"

"No. I don't." A black sedan pulls up beside us. "That's Coco. You're going to get in the car and stay with her until this is over."

"What? No. I deserve to see him die."

My hands go down on her arms. "You do. I know. But as I stand here, where my parents were burned alive, I am begging you to do this for me. Her expression crumbles. "How am I supposed to not worry and wonder what's happening? You could end up dead."

Coco walks toward us, dressed for battle in cargo pants and a black jacket, which I have no doubt hides a number of weapons. Good. I want her armed. I want Gia safe.

Gia follows my gaze and whirls on Coco. "I'm not going with you. I heard you helped save my life, and thank you, but not today."

Coco just looks at me and hands me a package. "That's a wire," she says. "We'll be able to hear everything going on."

"That's not good enough," Gia argues, turning to me, her parka hood falling down. "I want to be there."

My hands go to her face. "You're going to park a mile away from the meeting spot and wait for me on a private jet that's waiting to take us to Dallas. The pilot is a friend of Tellar's and Coco's. Coco is my backup. If she hears a problem, you'll stay with the pilot and you'll be on that plane."

"What about Dr. Murphy?" she demands as I lead her to the passenger side of the sedan.

"We got her a bodyguard," I assure her.

"You planned this and didn't tell me. You're such an asshole, Chad."

I wrap her in my arms, cupping her face. "An asshole who loves you, Gia. I need you to know that. I *love* you."

Tears pool in her blue eyes. "I love you, too. Asshole."

I smile and kiss her. "Now go. I want you out of here." I open the door to Coco's sedan and have to force her inside. She stares up at me, willing me to let her out. I hold the door shut while Coco joins her and quickly revs the engine, backing the car out of the parking spot.

I watch her until they're gone, and then return to the Jag to grab a black jacket, sliding it over my shoulders. My gaze lingers on the "Red Heaven" sign once more before I start walking. Entering the building, I stop at the hostess station, aware of the rows of booths and the long wooden bar with televisions overhead, but in my mind I see my home. I see walls and couches and the kitchen table where Amy and I talked on the night of the fire. I see stairs where there are none, and flames.

I walk to the bathroom and put on the wire, exiting to claim a booth. I go so far as to order a burger and fries, buying time for my presence here to be the bait for the enemy I'm seeking.

And just that easily, faster than expected, even, I hook my fish. Rollin sits down in front of me, thinking he's throwing me off my game, when this is my game.

He arches an arrogant dark brow. "Imagine meeting you here, like this."

"Imagine," I say, my tone sardonic, my fingers twitching to be around his throat. I want to kill him.

"Needed a walk down memory lane before the big meeting?" he asks, sounding amused, his voice a bit raspier now. His skin is more tanned. The wrinkles around his black, soulless eyes are deeper.

I mentally talk myself down, sticking to my plan when I walked in this door. "Nice suit, Rollin," I say, noting the expensive fabric. "Guess you aren't out of that money I gave you quite yet. You were disinherited, and needed the cash."

He smiles, and it's evil, a wicked twist of his thin lips. "It was a good gift you gave me that day. My father didn't even know about the meeting, but he would have kept coming at you. He would have figured out you gave me the cash."

"So you killed my family." Somehow my tone is flat, unemotional, but the knife on the place setting is far too near my hand considering how much I burn to kill him.

"I do what I must."

I want to kill him. I want to be that Grim Reaper. But Chen made it clear that if I act on my own, he pulls out. I inhale and let it out, asking, "And Gia's father? Was he on your 'must' list?"

"He was on my father's 'must' list, and killed too soon. My father thought Rex had what we wanted. Turned out you got there too quickly. So," he says, tapping the table, "we're here. It's warm inside. Let's just do the exchange. I have the cash in the car."

I lean forward. "I came here to say good-bye to my parents. I wasn't foolish enough to bring the cylinder. It's being delivered to the drop site."

"Well then, I guess we'll have to drive there together." One of his suited goons stops beside the table, shoving back his jacket to flash a gun. "Let's go, shall we?"

"Not yet. I haven't had my burger, and you aren't going to shoot me without that cylinder."

"Okay. You eat, and we'll shoot the next customer that walks in the door."

I throw my hands up. "Fine. But the cylinder won't be there until the set time." I push myself out of the seat and Rollin's goon shoves me toward the back door.

My lips twist at the predictability. This is what I want, what Chen wanted when we set this trap. I walk down the hallway, toward what I know is a deserted, graveled back lot, with little to no lighting. I step outside and into the headlights of a car, shoved and forced to right my footing. Straightening, I find three men forming a line in front of me, and when I see Jared is one of them, my blood boils.

His eyes meet mine, and he doesn't blink or look away. He is just here. With Rollin. Without remorse for his actions. "You fucking traitor," I spit.

"It was time for this to be over," Jared calls out.

"It's time for *you* to be over," I say, launching myself at him, only to have the two men beside him draw their guns.

"Careful," Rollin says, moving to stand in front of me. "We don't need to get bloody when we're playing nice."

"If he stays, there is no deal."

"Five hundred million says you can tolerate him," Rollin says, and he's barely spoken the words when engines roar in the near distance, and we are suddenly swarmed with motorcycles manned by men in ski masks. There is a crazy rush of activity, and then everyone in Rollin's group has a gun at his head and is being shoved into a car.

One of them grabs Jared, and I shout, "Wait!" crossing to stand in front of him.

"Why? Why did you do it?" I demand.

"I didn't want to, man. It was a bad hack, and I ended up in trouble."

"With Rollin?"

"No. It was a setup and they held me captive."

"You let them."

"I tried to set you free by just giving them what they wanted."

"You believe that, don't you?"

"I was protecting you."

"Oh, really? Well, I'm not protecting you." I wave to the

man holding him and turn away, walking toward another man waiting for me at the door.

"Documents," he says.

I reach in my jacket and hand them to him. "What's going to happen to them?"

"Whatever we want to happen to them."

I inhale and let it out, not sure why I care what happens to Jared. But I do. I open the door and walk inside Red Heaven.

Gia and Coco walk in, having been alerted by the Chinese when it was safe.

Gia rushes to me and hugs me, and I hug her back. "Is it over? Is it really over?"

My cell phone rings and I quickly answer it to hear Chen's voice. "Turn on the TV behind the bar." The line goes dead.

I grab Gia and motion Coco forward, grabbing the remote the bartender has left on the counter. Switching channels, I find an image of Sheridan being walked out of his offices in cuffs. The caption reads: "Oil mogul and associates arrested on suspicion of selling U.S. secrets to China."

I turn to Gia and my hands come down on her arms. "It's really over." I pull her to me and kiss her fast and hard, needing that connection with her, before I take her hand

and lead her toward the door. Stopping at the door, I take one last look at my past. It's gone, but it will never be forgotten. And as I face forward, leading us into the night, it's with the hope that Gia, the woman who has made me whole again, is my future.

GIA AND I talk to Liam and Amy on the way to the airport, relief and some uncertainty in all of us. It's midnight by the time we arrive in Dallas and make our way to a hotel for the night, planning to go to the property I own the next day when we can stock the kitchen and make it home for a few months. Still being cautious, I check us in with fake IDs, not ready to call this over until we have a few months behind us and a long-term plan to deal with the cylinder in place.

Once in the room, we order room service and Gia strips to her T-shirt and panties while I go down to my boxers. We've just finished eating when the news reports that Rollin has been captured after an anonymous tip regarding his location was received, along with proof to connect him to his father's illegal activities.

"Oh, thank God," Gia sighs. "I thought they were going

to kill him, and I really didn't want blood on our hands." Her brow furrows. "But no word on Jared. You're sure the Chinese took him?"

"Yes," I say grimly. "They took him, but unfortunately he wasn't a part of the deal we made with the Chinese. He's a smart manipulator, and I wouldn't put it past him to negotiate his life for his services."

"How bad is that for us?"

"We can't know, and I don't like loose ends. Even Meg's disappearance bothers me, though I'm of the opinion she outlived her use and Rollin got rid of her."

"Rollin's proven he places no value on human life."

"Greed is dangerous, and it changes people. Case in point: Jared."

"No," Gia says, her hand sliding to my leg. "Jared just showed his true character, the same way you did when you made the choice to protect the cylinder rather than take the money and run. I hope this lets you see that you aren't the monster you believe yourself to be."

"I believed *he* was the good one out of the two of us. Some part of me wants to believe there is more to Jared's story, like there was to mine."

"Maybe—"

"No." I shake my head. "I saw the look in his eyes. He's not the man I thought he was, and we need to protect the cylinder once and for all. I think I have a solution." I show her the hotel notepad I've been doodling on.

She glances at it and gives me a curious look. "Circles inside circles? You were drawing those on the plane, too."

"A perfect circle," I explain, "unbroken by being protected by many layers."

She shakes her head. "I don't understand."

"The loose ends make the urgency to protect the cylinder greater. My idea is to create a circle of people all over the world, a diverse group from all walks of life. Each has one piece of the puzzle, and passes that piece down through generations."

"How would we pick the people?"

"Good question. Obviously, we need to think through criteria and a vetting process. And we need to do it sooner than later. We bought time with what happened today, but the circle will take time to develop, and we need to be aggressive about making it happen."

"Agreed, but in the meantime, I was thinking on the plane—you *are* the only one who knows where the cylinder is."

"If anything happens to me, I made sure Liam knows what to say to Amy. She'll find it."

"Which is better than no clue at all, but anything that's linked to Amy is dangerous for her. And Amy and Liam are always together. What if something happens to him? What if we place the clue in a sealed envelope, and pay an attorney to mail it to certain people in a certain order if we're out of touch for more than a certain amount of time? So maybe Liam, then Amy, and if neither of them are alive, Tellar?"

I give her a slow nod. "That's a good plan. Yes. It needs some logistical thought, but it works. We'll pick some random attorney in Kansas or some crazy location no one will think we'd even consider, and set it up."

"Good. That makes me feel more secure until we set up the Circle of Trust." She gives me a tentative look. "Chad. I want to know where the cylinder is. It's my father's work. I just . . . I want to know."

"What you don't know, you can't tell."

"Don't do that to me. Please. I'm begging you. If anyone suspects the cylinder exists, they'll come after me anyway. And if they make me talk, you've given me a clue that leads to Amy. Amy is safer if I know. Nothing should lead back to anyone but you and me. No one else can be allowed to get hurt by this. We're a team now, Chad. You and me. We battle this. We take the risks."

She is brave, selfless, and I swear I fall more in love with her in this moment than in the moment before. Everything inside me wants to protect her, but she's right. When I gave her that clue, I already took her to a new place in this story.

I pull my computer from my suitcase and clear the table to power it up, pulling up images of a small cemetery in Glenwood Springs, Colorado.

"A cemetery," Gia murmurs.

"Yes," I say. "This cemetery is in a small town; it literally sits in the middle of a cluster of houses in a middle-class residential neighborhood." I enlarge a specific gravesite. "I buried it there."

She blinks and reads the tombstone. "Doc Holliday?" She gives me an incredulous look. "You buried it with Doc Holliday?"

"My father and I loved the movie *Tombstone*, and we went to the gravesite during a road trip years ago."

She shakes her head and then starts laughing. "You're crazy. I'm with a crazy man. No one else would think of this."

I lie her down on the bed and rest my arms by her head. "I have a lot of Doc Holliday in me, sweetheart, and he's a wild card."

"I guess I'm in love with a wild card, then."

"Well, then, as Doc Holliday, or rather, Val Kilmer, said in *Tombstone*, 'I'm your Huckleberry, baby.'" And I fully intend to turn the laughter that is her response into a sigh.

The End—but stay tuned!

Liam and Amy return to complete the Circle of Trust
while they fight for a final happy ending. There will
be challenges, tears, torment, and of course passion—and
you know Liam Stone will be fighting for his woman!

Look for

Unbroken

Coming September 2015 from Gallery Books